ELIZABETH EULBERG
TAKE A CHANCE ON ME

SCHOLASTIC INC.

If you purchased this book without a cover, you should be aware that this book is stolen property. It was reported as "unsold and destroyed" to the publisher, and neither the author nor the publisher has received any payment for this "stripped book."

Copyright © 2025 by Elizabeth Eulberg, Inc.

All rights reserved. Published by Scholastic Inc., *Publishers since 1920.* SCHOLASTIC and associated logos are trademarks and/or registered trademarks of Scholastic Inc.

The publisher does not have any control over and does not assume any responsibility for author or third-party websites or their content.

No part of this publication may be reproduced, stored in a retrieval system, or transmitted in any form or by any means, electronic, mechanical, photocopying, recording, or otherwise, or used to train any artificial intelligence technologies, without written permission of the publisher. For information regarding permission, write to Scholastic Inc., Attention: Permissions Department, 557 Broadway, New York, NY 10012.

This book is a work of fiction. Names, characters, places, and incidents are either the product of the author's imagination or are used fictitiously, and any resemblance to actual persons, living or dead, business establishments, events, or locales is entirely coincidental.

ISBN 978-1-5461-2927-1

10 9 8 7 6 5 4 3 2 1   25 26 27 28 29

Printed in the U.S.A.   40

First printing 2025

Book design by Stephanie Yang

FOR DARREN AND BAS:
Who knew "hey, if you ever want to visit London . . ."
would lead to this new life of mine?
Thanks for letting me take over your place, mates.
My parents, however, might want to have a word with you.

Also by Elizabeth Eulberg

The Lonely Hearts Club
Prom & Prejudice
Take a Bow
Revenge of the Girl with the Great Personality
Better Off Friends
We Can Work It Out
Just Another Girl

AUTHOR'S NOTE

This story features a character who struggles with control issues, including disordered eating. There are discussions of body image, overexercising, and calories. As someone who still struggles with accepting her glorious self, I did my best to treat these issues and characters with sensitivity and kindness.

To anybody out there who battles with themselves, please know that you're enough and also can never be too much.

1

"Why *am* I here?

"That's an excellent question. I've spent the last eight hours flying over the Atlantic asking myself that very thing. Along with *What are you thinking, Evie? What's the plan? Have you even a shred of common sense?*

"So here's the truth: I have no idea. A week ago, I thought I'd be spending my summer like always: working and hanging out. It's the summer before my senior year. It's supposed to be filled with being fun and carefree. And then . . . well, everything just fell apart. I won't bore you with the details of all the drama, but let me assure you, there was a lot of drama. *A lot*."

I pause for a moment to rub my tired eyes since I can never sleep on planes.

"So yeah. Don't get me wrong, I'm thrilled to be here. I'm sure I'll get no sympathy for spending my summer abroad, but it does come with its own issues. I seem to be running away from one problem just to land in the next. I won't even get into it, but trust me, this was the last place I thought I'd be. When I really think about it, most people would just get a pint of ice cream to drown their sorrows, but *noooo*, *I* had to flee the United States. So, as you can tell, things are going great for me right now. Just swell.

"But I'm going to try to be positive. I mean, what other choice do I have, right? At least, I can't think of any. Especially because I haven't slept in—" I try to do the math, but my brain isn't cooperating. "A while. So yeah. I've got a lot of work to do: on myself, on my relationships, on what on earth I'm going to do with myself for an entire summer—but I'm not technically here for work, so I guess to answer your question, I'm here for vacation. Except the first thing I'm going to do when I get settled is sleep. But not too long—don't want to get jet lag. Although it's not like—"

The customs agent interrupts me by stamping my passport and motioning for the next person in line.

"Oh," I say as he hands my passport back.

He gives me a curt nod. "Welcome to London."

2

Keep moving, keep moving . . .

I drag my feet over the white-and-red-painted Chelsea Bridge a few hours after landing. My only plan right now is to defeat jet lag. It's way better than having to deal with the questions that keep flooding my head. Then once I'm adjusted, I can figure out what else to do. I was in such a rush to leave my home back in Winnetka, Illinois, I hadn't thought any of this through.

As I approach Battersea Park, a large Victorian park on the River Thames, I decide to focus on the positive. I get to spend the entire summer in London. I never get sick of seeing all the touristy sites or walking around a museum or park. And I love an afternoon tea with the fire of a thousand burning suns.

While my mind wills me to keep moving along the waterfront promenade, my body has other ideas. I take a deserved break on a bench and study the redbrick residences across the river.

Okay, here's the thing: I know what I should be doing. When I think about it, the only way to move forward is to start erasing the past. I take out my phone and study the newest messages from my former friends: *I'm so sorry. Talk to me. I swear I didn't know.* Blah, blah, blah. Well, that's enough of that. With each tap of the delete and block buttons, an unpleasant scene from last week flashes in my head. If only a button could block memories so easily.

All that remains are messages from two people: my mom and my roommate for the summer.

His messages began the second I connected to the Wi-Fi in his shiny, super-posh flat.

HIM: Please alert me when you arrive and take a car.

ME: Already in the flat. Took the tube.

HIM: Why didn't you take a car? And switch your phone to roaming. I'll pay for it.

See, there's a benefit for having a cheap cell plan: international roaming is super expensive. The last thing I need right now is to be connected to every moment of life back home.

ME: There's Wi-Fi everywhere here.

HIM: Don't start.

ME: I'm not starting anything, simply stating facts.

Pretty much every coffee shop, store, pub, restaurant, you name it in London has free Wi-Fi. I'm just a press of a button away from seeing the backstabbers back home celebrating their summer without me.

Isn't technology delightful?

One could think his motivation for having me available to him 24/7 would be because he's simply concerned about my well-being.

Absolutely not. For him, it's about having control over me. That's always his endgame.

Saying *always* isn't really fair. There was a time when he was human. When he was caring and wonderful.

That person disappeared years ago. It was a different time. He was someone else completely, and I guess so was I.

HIM: Evie.

ME: But yes, I got in safely. Thanks for your concern, Dad.

I feel my eyes get heavy, and I stand up from the bench to keep walking.

There's a possibility that perhaps attempting to figure out my life on little sleep isn't the best idea. But what else do I have to do today? Tomorrow? The rest of the summer?

The sound of an acoustic guitar cuts through the quiet. It's followed by someone singing. I glance around the nearly empty park. Usually, buskers hit up the more touristy places: the London Eye, Piccadilly Circus, Tower Bridge, Covent Garden, Hyde Park. I walk toward the music and see a tall, lanky guy around my age, playing his guitar with his eyes closed, not a soul around.

He sways back and forth as he strums with more force. The wooden body of the guitar has been worn down from his playing. His messy black curly hair moves in the wind. He's wearing a white T-shirt with several holes in it, faded gray jeans, and a black-and-white plaid scarf around his neck.

When he opens his mouth again, it's more of a wail that comes out. "*I am the wreckage of your void, haunted by the emptiness without you.*"

His voice breaks at the end.

He continues to repeat "without you," each time with more anguish.

You have got *to be kidding me.*

I came to London to get away from the pain, not to be confronted head-on mere hours after landing.

The busker suddenly stops singing and opens his eyes. He's looking directly at me. Sadness is washed over his face.

I feel my pockets for change, but I don't have any. And I certainly don't want to get in a conversation. Sure, Old Evie would've wanted to talk to him since he's, like, cute or whatever, but New Evie has learned from her mistakes. Or at least I hope to God I have.

Besides, what would I even talk to him about except our mutual heartbreak: *Oh, hi, you're also miserable? Isn't it just the worst?*

Once again: no, thank you.

So I turn on my heels and walk away.

I've got enough problems of my own.

3

"Oh my God, it's so great to finally meet you!"

I'm attacked by a blond twiglike beast the second I return to Dad's big, fancy flat. Her grip is tight and she smells of lilacs and desperation.

While I don't personally know this woman, I know her kind. She's one of Dad's numerous interchangeable girlfriends.

They're all the same, starting with their names. It's either (a) they're spelled with an unnecessary *X* (see past gems Xtina and Dextiny), (b) they're named after an herb or flower (I'm not kidding, I've met a Sage and an Arugula), or (c) they go by their social media handles, like his classy girlfriend last Christmas who introduced herself as "at gymbabe69." He's met them at either (a) the gym, (b) London's hottest new restaurant/bar/club, or (c) a pressed juicery or organic grocer. They're all in their midtwenties and stay around for about two months, *if* they know how to play Dad's game.

"Hello," I reply coolly, looking around to see if my father is home. Of course he would forget to mention he has a new girlfriend—or even be here to welcome his only child—but she is no doubt under the impression that he's talked about her like a normal single father would to his daughter.

"You must be exhausted," she states. I take her in. She's petite, with ginormous breasts, bleached blond hair, fake eyelashes, and a tight black dress so short I pray she's wearing underwear for hygiene's sake.

She is one-thousand-percent Dad's type.

"Your dad is running a wee bit late," she says with an eye roll. "But he wanted to make sure you're ready for dinner. We're going to Sketch!" She claps like she's been given some ridiculously expensive bobble of jewelry.

I'm too exhausted to survive a long dinner with this *girl* and my father. Although I could've gotten forty hours of sleep on a cloud, being swaddled by puppies and fanned by angels, and I'd still be too tired for this crap.

"Let's look at your clothes!" She grabs my hand to drag me to my room, but I stop her.

I know exactly what's going on here. Dad has employed his newest plaything to pick out clothes for me and do my hair and makeup so I can be "acceptable" at the swanky London restaurant he wants to parade us around.

No surprise, this girl is strong—probably from spending hours at the gym every day. "I'm good," I reply as I attempt to hold my ground.

The door to the flat opens and Dad strolls in. He throws his keys in the Waterford crystal bowl next to the door. Even though he's coming off a ten-hour workday, he's as put together and handsome as always in his still-crisp tailored suit. Every strand of his short brown hair—which matches mine only in color, not tidiness—is perfectly styled. He doesn't sport a millimeter of stubble—thanks to the barber who comes to his office every morning to give him a fresh shave. He's tan, he's fit, he's half the man he used to be.

"Evie." He nods before coming over to give me a hug. "It's lovely to see you."

No matter how long he's been this version of himself, I'll never get used to his hugs now. They're cold. They're formal. They absolutely suck.

"Hey, Dad."

"Awww," the girl coos.

"How was your flight?" he asks.

"Good."

"Good."

"Yep."

The girlfriend keeps looking back and forth between us, probably wondering when we'll start acting more like father and daughter and less like two strangers stuck in an elevator talking about the weather. While we have similar features—same button nose, oval face, and dark brown eyes—our personalities are completely opposite. I'm a fun, warmhearted person and he's a robotic jerk. But hey, that's just my opinion.

"Ah, so . . ." He starts but doesn't finish.

We used to never be like this, but now we're both so aware of how self-conscious we are around each other, and we both know that we're aware and it makes us even more stilted and awkward and it's just a vicious cycle.

He gives my shoulder a squeeze. "Well, let me get a good look at you."

Oh great, things just got worse. Fun.

Every flaw on my face is currently being scrutinized. His eyes linger on the pimple that developed on my chin somewhere over the Atlantic. They then drift up to my eyebrows.

"Poppy, darling, you should take Evie to your salon, or show her how to use tweezers," Dad says to his girlfriend, who *is* named after a flower, thank you very much.

Unlike Poppy, who has had every inch of her skin plucked, exfoliated, tanned, and shined, I've decided to let my eyebrows be natural. They're full, but I've been known to pluck a stray hair here or there.

"Maybe do something about this hair as well," he comments as he picks up a strand of my naturally brown, slightly wavy collarbone-length hair. You know, the hair I got from him.

The concept of natural is very foreign to my father.

But the awkwardness is just beginning as Dad looks down at my body, currently clad in baggy jeans, a striped T-shirt, and flip-flops. *Awesome.*

Now, I don't like to put emphasis on someone's weight. A well-adjusted person looking at me would see a fairly average teenage girl. I'm not skinny, nor would I be considered the loaded f-word. I've got my mom's smaller bone structure, but with some curves from Dad's side. Since my father—the opposite of well-adjusted—believes you can never be too rich or too thin, I instantly tense up at his gaze.

"You should join us at spin tomorrow. Poppy's an excellent instructor." He gives her a wink and she responds by giggling.

"Thanks, but I'm going to sleep in." I pull myself away from his judgmental gaze and reach into my worn backpack. I take out a bag of cheddar-and-onion crisps. To my father's abject horror, I open it up and pop a crisp into my mouth.

It's one of my favorite things to do in front of him. Every day, I'll go to a grocer and scour the selection of potato chips (known as crisps in England), then proceed to eat them in front of him. I could bring a different guy home every night and Dad wouldn't be as offended as he is right now. Honestly, sometimes it's the only way to get an emotion out of him. And hey, if that requires me to eat some delicious crisps, win-win.

"Those are disgusting," he says with a curl of his lip.

"I think you mean *delicious*." I put three more in my mouth.

The only sound in his pristine, bright white marble kitchen is of the crunch of the crisps.

I hold out the bag to Poppy. "You want one?" I ask with an intentionally full mouth.

She looks at me as if I were trying to hand her a rattlesnake instead of complex carbs.

"Evie, please don't start," he says as a look of disappointment flashes on his face. It's a look I've become quite used to.

Don't start. It's the same thing he texted me this morning. Basically, he wants me to just shut up and behave. In fairness to my dad—which is a concession I don't give lightly—I would never act this way with my mother.

But the difference between the two is that my mom actually parents me. She cares about me, the person, and isn't so fixated on the outside. And oh yeah, she didn't up and leave me.

I bat my uncurled and mascara-free eyelashes at him. "My sincerest apologies, Father."

Then I shove a few more crisps into my mouth.

"Please get ready for dinner. Your current attire is entirely unacceptable," Dad replies evenly. It's clear that his patience is already running thin.

At least we have that one thing in common.

"I'm going to stay in," I admit, then throw in a yawn for good measure. Part of an uneaten crisp falls out of my mouth.

He sighs. "Evie, it's your first night here. I haven't seen you in months. I went out of my way to make these dinner plans for you. It's not easy to get a booking."

"Yes, but you didn't ask me what I wanted to do on my first night."

You never ask, I want to add. That's why he likes these young girls. They're simply content to go along with his plans, especially since that means an expensive meal and—*if* they behave—a nice trinket or two.

His daughter, however, can't be bribed.

"Fine," he replies with a huff. "I was looking forward to spending some time with my daughter, but have it your way. Poppy and I are going out to enjoy a lovely meal."

"Have a wonderful evening," I reply, not even hiding the bitterness.

Dad shakes his head. "Honestly, Evie, if this is how you're going to be the entire time you're here, it's going to be a long summer."

No kidding.

4

The benefit of being in a jet lag–induced sleep coma is that I missed seeing Dad when he got home from dinner *and* when he left in the morning. The only items on the kitchen counter were two crisp twenty-pound bills with no note. I left the cash behind. He should know better by now. It's a point of pride that I don't take any of the money he tries to throw at me. *I* am not for sale. Although it's tempting. A week in London costs months of my coffee shop earnings. I'm not sure how I'll be able to afford a whole summer with my meager savings, even if I can get a job. No point stressing, since I don't even know how long I'll actually end up staying here.

After a shower to feel human again, I head to the Sloane Square tube station to decide where I'll spend the day, and I end up at the Tower of London, the medieval stone castle that has kept the modern office buildings from completely taking over. I weave between the tourists as I walk the perimeter of the castle, letting the history soak in before walking across Tower Bridge. I notice a couple trying to fit the Tower of London in their selfie.

"Do you want me to take your picture?" I offer.

"Yes, please," the guy replies with an accent as he hands me his phone.

"Where are you from?" I line up their smiling faces and try to not have a twinge of sadness as they wrap their arms around each other.

"Germany," he answers.

"Oh, where?"

"You know Germany?"

"Uh, not really. I'd like to visit someday. I know it's a super-quick flight. I need to take advantage of the fact that London is so close to Europe."

They reply by posing for me.

Oh, right. The photo. That I'm supposed to be taking.

I snap a few pics, then check to make sure they came out okay. "You both look fabulous."

The couple smiles as they study the photos. "Thank you."

"No problem. I can do more. Or if you want I can—"

"It is okay. Thanks." He gives me a small nod as they walk away hand in hand.

While I stand there like an idiot.

So this is your summer. Aimlessly walking around while you avoid dealing with your problems, and stalking tourists. Well done, Evie. Well done.

I put my earbuds in to block out the completely reasonable—yet inconvenient in the fact I'm still in denial—thoughts in my head. As a kid, Dad made me a UK bands playlist I still listen to today.

I put it on shuffle, wondering who is going to accompany my walk: the Beatles, the Rolling Stones, Queen, the Smiths, Joy Division, Oasis, the Kinks, Radiohead, Blur . . . The list goes on and on. He may be a jerk, but my dad has great taste in music.

Had. Because now he likes to go to clubs and listen to electronic dance music and pretend that he's not a forty-five-year-old man whose midlife crisis has been going on for ten years.

I push down my anger as I walk along the other side of the Thames. Maybe I'll walk all the way down to the London Eye. I can cross over the river again to visit Westminster Abbey. And Buckingham Palace.

I have all day.

I have all summer.

Then why do I feel like I have nothing?

There are a couple of tourists gathered around a guy playing a guitar. He seems familiar, then it hits me.

No way. Just no way. What are the odds?

It's the same busker from yesterday. We're both miles away from where we were. I slowly approach, but there he is. In the same gray jeans, but this time with a black T-shirt. His plaid scarf is tied around a belt loop in his jeans. His eyes are closed again.

I pause Queen, who is telling me to find someone to love. No offense to Freddie Mercury, but there's something about this guy's voice that causes my entire body to erupt in goose bumps.

"*There's nothing left inside of me,*" he bellows as he taps a beat with his worn black Converse sneaker.

Seriously? Can this guy read my mind? Or is this the universe forcing me to come to terms with what happened instead of running away?

As I study his face, I wonder whether my heartbreak is as visible. His radiates like a scorching heat. Whoever broke his heart did a proper job stomping all over it.

I honestly thought that kind of passionate love existed only in books and movies. Certainly not an emotion a teenage boy could possess. At least none of the ones I know.

The feeling of loneliness I've been trying to shove down comes up again. My summer had been mapped out. They Who Will Not Be Named and I had a Summer Shenanigans list of things we were going to do, both big (Six Flags, boating on Lake Michigan) and small (Pizza Wednesdays, Pool Sundays). While they'll be gathered around the big corner table ("our table") at Mario's tonight, I'll probably be eating a packet of crisps by myself in Dad's empty flat.

Am I really going to randomly walk around alone for the entire summer? Maybe I should just go to my grandparents' house in the country. There's less to do there, but I could at least . . . I don't know.

That right there is the problem. *I don't know.* I'm stuck.

There's a smattering of applause as the guy finishes. A couple of people drop some coins in the open guitar case by his feet. Since I finally have change, I reach into my pocket for a few pounds, and freeze as I see him look up. There's a flash of recognition on his face.

"Are you following me?" he asks with a tiny curve of a smile.

"No, I—I—" I stutter, not prepared to have an actual conversation with him. Up close, I see he has these bright green eyes.

"London can be a surprisingly small place," he says with a laugh. His face seems to have relaxed since he stopped singing.

He looks less like a tortured soul and more like a regular teenage dude.

I think about how I turned my back on him yesterday. He doesn't seem put off by it, even though he does remember me. I have an itch to talk to somebody. There's no way I can keep quiet the entire summer. Honestly, the last forty-eight hours have been hard enough. I'm a talker. It used to be one of my friends' favorite things about me, until I said a few things they didn't want to hear.

It's going to be a long and lonely summer if something doesn't change.

I open my mouth, think better of it, and close it.

Of all the people to strike up a conversation with, it shouldn't be some random heartbroken boy. I should just go online and see if there's some expat teen group I could join and just—

"Do you want to get a coffee?"

Whoa. Hold on, Evie. Did that just come out of your mouth?

Sure did.

His eyes open wide. "You're American?"

I nod.

"I've heard you lot can be quite forward."

Oh my God. I can't believe I did that.

I can.

But then again, this guy is probably used to girls being "quite forward" with him. He plays all these heartbreak songs on a guitar. If that isn't teenage girl catnip, I don't know what is.

"Oh no, I'm not," I start. *Wow, you're making such a great first impression.* "Look, I just . . ." I take a deep breath. "I'm on my way to Borough Market, so I thought if you were taking a break, I'd buy you a coffee because I've heard you play a couple times and you're really good. You don't have to come, that's totally cool. Unless you do want some coffee, and then that's also cool. Whatever. No big deal. And I guess I should make it clear that I'm not interested in anything romantic, like at all. Especially with a guy. No offense, but I'm just not going there. Lesson learned, if you know what I mean."

Stop talking, Evie.

It's like I haven't been able to have a real conversation with anybody in days, so a bizarre stream of consciousness has come vomiting out. It's the customs officer all over again, which by the way, I could've used the automatic gates with my British passport, but *no*, I *chose* to stand in line to talk to someone, because that's how desperate I've become. I did the same with the cashier at Tesco's yesterday. And the porter at Dad's building this morning.

"I understand," he replies as he puts his guitar away. "My friend Fiona is a lesbian."

"No, I'm not . . . I'm just saying that I'm taking a break from dating. So I'm not asking you out. Just for coffee. As a wow-you're-really-good-at-playing-guitar coffee, not because you're hot." *Sweet baby Jesus.* "I didn't mean that. I mean, you're fine looking and all, I'm just saying it's coffee."

Evie, you need to scrounge up the tiniest thread of dignity you have left and turn around and walk away without blabbing another word. Keep walking until you hit Scotland because dear Lord girl, you're a mess.

A ruddiness spreads over his cheeks. "Well, with an invitation like that . . ."

So *of course* I keep talking. "Ha! Yeah, right. I mean, no worries. It's cool if you don't want to go. It's cool if you do. Just whatever is cool," I blubber, realizing I've used the word *cool* about fourteen thousand times. *Cool, cool, cool.* "Simply a girl wanting to drink some coffee because she's done with dating because men are the worst."

For the twelve billionth time this week I ask myself, *What are you thinking, Evie?* Who on earth would want to hang out with me after that pathetic display?

He picks up his guitar case. "Can't say I blame you for that." He begins to walk, then turns around. "Shall we?"

What? *Seriously?*

I'm both in shock and incredibly grateful. I begin to walk next to him before he can change his mind. Maybe hurt recognizes hurt.

"I'm Aiden, by the way."

"Evie."

"Hey," he says with a nod.

"Hey."

5

Well, this is completely awkward.

To be fair, I've recently become the queen of horrifically embarrassing human encounters. So much so that I flew across the Atlantic because of it. Pity it's now an international phenomenon. I should be given a crown or something to warn people of my inability to behave in public. It is a rather dubious talent to be able to turn something from normal to uncomfortable to *oh-my-God-make-her-stop* in record time.

Aiden and I walk in silence for a few minutes. My mind is busy trying to figure out what I can say to erase his first impression of me.

I honestly don't remember the last time I had to make a new friend. All of my (former) friends and I had grown up near one another. When you're little, you're bunched together in classrooms. It's not that I have trouble talking, *obviously*. I can have an animated conversation with an inanimate object. But the last few days my mind has been so scattered that I have trouble focusing on anything, mostly because it'll be too devastating when I do.

Besides, it's not like we're going to become friends. It's just coffee and somebody to talk to. A somebody who lives thousands of miles away, so said embarrassing encounter will be my secret.

Unless something happens and I go viral. *Again*.

"So," he begins. "Where in the States are you from?"

"Near Chicago," I answer, realizing it's best to be short, succinct, less . . . me.

"Ah."

More silence. He's asking about me so I should get to know him.

"Where are you from?" I ask.

"London."

Of course he is.

"What brings you to London?" he inquires.

I debate how much to tell him. He's already gotten an earful.

"My dad is from here. Well, he was born in Devon, but now lives in London. So I come every summer."

"The whole summer?"

"Uh, maybe?" I hadn't really planned out farther ahead than *get out of town immediately*.

He glances at me. "You don't seem that thrilled about it."

"Oh, well. I'm excited to be in London. I love it. It's the greatest city in the whole world!"

He laughs a bit, causing the corners of his eyes to crinkle. "Really?"

"Yes!" I wave around the Thames and point to the Tower of

London across the river. "You're surrounded by history. The Tower of London is a thousand years old. *A thousand!* Here, there's this intense beauty that has a rich history, well, except . . ." I glare at the cranes that clog the gray skyline. London is one of those places where you stumble upon a cathedral hundreds of years old next to some modern glass eyesore. It shouldn't be a shock that I'm on the side of the past. Unlike my father, I don't believe newer is always better. "And don't even get me started on my love of your baked goods: crumpets, scones, and oh my God, clotted cream. And the things you Brits do with a potato: mash, chips, crisps, gratins." My stomach growls, since I haven't eaten since breakfast.

I was hungry when I first woke, but Dad only has green juice in his refrigerator, so I went to a coffee shop nearby to grab tea and a scone. I'll have to hit up M&S on my way home to buy some real food, which I'll no doubt have to hide. Like I should be shamed in wanting to round out my diet to include protein, dairy, and Dad's mortal enemy (aka carbs).

Aiden studies me for a moment. "I guess you don't really appreciate where you come from as much as people from other places do."

"Yeah."

"So what's the bad part of being in London for you?" he asks.

"It's complicated."

"Ah, complicated," he says with an understanding nod. "Yeah. Many things are."

"My dad and I don't really get along," I admit. "We used to, and then everything changed a few years ago and now I can barely stand the sight of him."

I figure it's best to leave it as vague as possible. And also omit the parts that make me want to curl up into a ball and have a good cry.

"That has to be rough," Aiden replies.

"Yeah."

We make our way to Borough Market, one of my favorite spots to eat in London. There are stalls that serve delicious meat pies, fish and chips, Scotch eggs, pastries, and pretty much anything else you'd want to eat. Then you enter the market where you can get fruits, vegetables, meats, cheeses, bread, olives—everything your stomach desires.

"I avoid this place on the weekend," Aiden says. I love how British people pronounce *weekend*. There's an odd emphasis on the latter half: week*end*. "It's rammed."

"Yeah, I once forgot it was Saturday and came here for lunch." It's late afternoon on a Wednesday, so it's fairly busy, but not packed.

"A Saturday? And you lived to tell the tale?" he exclaims and we both laugh. Aiden points to the corner. "That stall has the best coffee."

We walk over, but I can't help staring at all the food. I know I said coffee, but I'm starting to feel a little lightheaded. As we wait in line, I steal a glimpse of Aiden. We've been walking side by side and I haven't been able to get a good look close-up. He has a square jaw, with just a hint of stubble, and he's a few inches taller than me.

Tall, dark, and handsome.

If that's your type.

We both order—iced chai for me, black coffee for him. When I reach into my pocket to pay, Aiden waves it off. "I've got it. It's your welcome-to-London beverage."

"No," I protest as Aiden pulls out a leather wallet and pays. "Well, then let me get us snacks. I haven't eaten in a while."

"I'm good, but you go ahead."

I don't need to be told twice.

As we walk around the stalls, I debate between a meat pie, since when in London and all, and a vat of macaroni and cheese that's calling my name. And no matter where one is in the world, mac and cheese is a must. I try to not slobber on the glass partition as I watch my mac and cheese being dished out.

"I don't think I've ever seen a human being so in awe," Aiden remarks as I'm handed a steaming pile of pesto mac.

"Oh, I really like food," I reply just as my stomach growls.

We go over to a section of seats and sit down. I take a bite and close my eyes as the gooey cheese melts in my mouth. "Delicious," I reply, as I inhale another spoonful. "So, how long have you been busking?"

"Not very long. Just a few months." He leans his guitar on a railing.

"You're really good."

"Thanks." He blushes slightly at my compliment. "I picked up the guitar a few years ago. Began plucking it. Played all the songs people play on the guitar—mostly Beatles and Oasis, being a proper Brit and all that. I never took lessons, just played around. Then I sort of got serious with it."

"Isn't it required for all guitar players to learn 'Wonderwall'?" I ask, thinking about how my (now ex) friend Theo became obsessed with that old Oasis song when he started taking guitar lessons last year.

"It was 'Blackbird' for me. That was the standard."

"What about those songs I heard you play? Did you write them? Or are they famous in the UK but Americans have never heard of them?"

"Oh, you've never heard those songs before?"

"No."

I had assumed he wrote them. First, buskers don't usually play super-depressing songs. And second, Aiden looked absolutely heartbroken while he was singing. So maybe he didn't write them, but I get the sense that he's definitely going through something.

Unless he's a brilliant actor and playing up the sympathy card for tips.

"Yeah, my mum is always talking about how she can't believe her friend in the States doesn't know Robbie Williams, since she's been in love with him since she was a teen."

"Who?"

"Exactly." He takes a sip of his coffee and keeps his eyes straight ahead.

"So that was a Robbie Williams song?" I make a note to look him up later.

"Oh no, but there are loads of UK bands I can recommend for you." He plays with the lid of his coffee.

"Cool, thanks."

"And is it true that you Americans don't worship the legend that is David Beckham?" He shakes his head at me.

"Please, my father is British, so I know all about—and I quote—*proper football*."

"Thank goodness you've been educated," Aiden says as he does an exaggerated sigh of relief. "So the rest of your family is back in America?"

"Yes, my mom, stepdad, and my brother, Josh." I feel a twinge of guilt for leaving them behind. "Do you—" I start but Aiden cuts me off.

"How old is your brother?"

"He's four and a handful, but he's also at the age where he believes anything I say. Like that I flew the plane here and I'm best friends with Santa Claus. That keeps him in line during the holidays. Don't mess with me or I'm calling the big guy."

Aiden looks over at me. "*You* know Santa Claus?"

"*Totally.* I've got connections and can get you a hookup, but it all depends: have you been naughty or nice?" I cock my eyebrow at him.

Wait, are you flirting?

No, this is just coffee and getting to know some random dude.

Sure, sure, sure.

Aiden puts his hand over his heart. "Nice, I'm always nice."

"Uh-huh." I shake my head at him.

Where have I heard that before? Oh, right, from the "nice guy" that ended up stomping all over my heart.

No way am I going there again.

"So, I just went through a breakup," I admit with a sting, but I figure it's best to once again remind Aiden that this is purely a coffee chat.

Now it's Aiden's turn to cock his eyebrow at me. "I reckoned from your earlier soliloquy about the male species," he says with an amused smile.

"No fair, I have jet lag!" I defend myself even though there's truly no defense for whatever it was that I did back there. Nervous breakdown? Verbal diarrhea? Experimental theater?

"Ah, yes, the well-known side effect of jet lag: dumping on the opposite sex."

"Not that your kind doesn't deserve it," I fire back, because let's be honest, boys are *the worst*. Then I take a giant spoonful of pesto mac to shut myself up.

"You got me there," Aiden says with a tiny nudge. It's the first time we've touched. I ignore the spark I feel. It's probably static cling. I wasn't lying to Aiden when I said I'm over dating.

I scrape the bottom of my container and resist the urge to lick the last remnants of cheese.

Before I even realize it, it just sort of slips out. "My dad is super weird about food, so I have to eat while I have a chance."

"Oh really?" Aiden leans in, really listening to me.

"Yeah, he used to enjoy a nice meal, then he just . . . changed. So now it's all wheatgrass shots and judgment with him."

"I'm sorry," he says, and I believe he genuinely means it.

"It's okay."

He tilts his head. "Is it, though?"

I'm taken aback. I usually dismiss Dad's behavior with a shrug, as there's not much I can do about it. I feel a prick behind my eyes when I'm reminded about my first visit with Dad to Borough Market when I was six. We laughed as I ran from stall to stall. There's no laughter between us now. No shared meals with a smile. I usually try to avoid him at mealtimes altogether.

"Oh well," I say with a shrug.

As I've already established, I'm a talker, but there's a part of myself I do hold back. I've been burned so many times by trusting the wrong person. Maybe that's why I don't mind blabbing to strangers. I let it all out and then move on. Even still, I don't want someone as temporary as Aiden to know about the real damage my father has left in me.

There's a buzzing coming from Aiden, and he reaches into his back jeans pocket for his phone.

"Hi, Mum," he says into his flip phone.

That's right, he has a flip phone.

"Of course, just having a bite with a friend," he says.

There's a flicker of relief that he's referred to me as a friend and not a deranged foreigner.

"See you soon," he says before hanging up his phone. He sees me staring at it. "Go ahead."

"Go ahead with what?"

He grimaces as he holds up his phone.

"Oh, *that*." I smile at him. I'm going to relish the chance to tease him for a change. "Was that recently unearthed after an excavation of a medieval site?"

"Ha-ha."

"Did you have to take a class on hieroglyphics to be able to use it?"

Aiden looks at me unamused, until the corners of his lips tip up. "You're not saying anything my friends haven't already ribbed me for."

"Your friends sound delightful."

"Oh, they'd love you."

"Who wouldn't?" Except for, you know, my entire high school.

Although, it is sort of nice to have fallen into a comfortable rhythm with this stranger.

"Listen, I've got to go," Aiden says as he straps his guitar on his back.

"Oh, of course." I try to hide the disappointment in my voice. "Well, hey, Aiden, nice to meet you and thanks for the chat." I stand up, unsure what to do next.

It was nice to have someone to talk to, even for a little while. It also helps that Aiden doesn't know me enough to see all the cracks in my façade.

"And, ah, good luck to you, sir, in all your future endeavors." I give him a little bow.

Good God, there is something really wrong with you.

"Oh." He looks down at the ground. "Have you been to South Bank?"

"Of course. It's one of my favorite places to walk around. I love the different views you get from the Golden Jubilee Bridges." On one, you get the London Eye, Big Ben, and Parliament. You move to the other and see St. Paul's and the Shard, the tallest building in London.

"Well," Aiden begins as he kicks the pavement. "I'll be playing there tomorrow after school."

Wait a second. "School?"

He shakes his head. "Yes, unlike Americans, we Brits do not get the luxurious months off school. I still have three weeks left in term."

I wouldn't classify what happened to me as lucky. But I guess if I had to have a public meltdown, I am lucky it was the last day of school. No way I could have survived going back for a single day, let alone three more weeks.

Aiden continues, "I usually busk after. So I'll be in that area. I'll leave it a mystery to exactly where so you can make it seem like a total coincidence to run into me again."

"Or I could avoid you entirely," I tease.

"I'm afraid that's the option some people would take."

I doubt that. But then again, what do I know? About anything, but especially about guys. My track record with them is not the best. Which is exactly why I need to make a swift exit.

"Yeah, maybe. Well, see ya around," I say as I turn my back on Aiden.

It was nice to talk to someone and all, but I need to learn from my mistakes.

6

"Tell me the truth, Evie."

"Everything's fine," I assure Mom over FaceTime an hour later. "I mean, Dad is still a jerk, but I went out today—"

A high-pitched scream cuts me off as my half brother, Josh, comes roaring onto the scene.

"Hi, Evie!" He puts his face right in the camera so I get a close-up of his not-at-all-clean nostril.

"Hey, Joshy!" I call out with a laugh. "How are you fee—"

"I got a new truck."

This is, indeed, major Josh news.

"You did? What kind of truck?"

A wheel of a red fire truck comes into view. "This one!"

"Is that a garbage truck?" I tease.

"No!" Josh shouts. "It's a fire truck."

"It is? Are you *sure* fire trucks are red?"

"Evie, be serious," Josh says with the hilarious righteous indignation of a four-year-old.

"Okay, serious question: how much do you miss me, Joshy?"

Josh starts making a fire truck noise as he walks out of the shot.

I'd be offended if that wasn't how pretty much every conversation with him goes, even when we're in the same room.

"So he seems to be feeling better."

Mom laughs. "I hadn't realized what a handful he was until you left."

"Sorry." I don't hide my cringe.

I knew leaving meant Mom and Stuart wouldn't have their go-to babysitter available. Take today. Josh had a fever, so he couldn't go to daycare, which meant Mom had to work from home. If I was there, I would've been able to take care of him. Just like I do during the school year. I'd pick him up after school, unless I had a shift at the coffee shop or practice. I usually started dinner or at least made Josh dinner. Poor kid exists on chicken nuggets and fish sticks half the time. I may appreciate good food, but I am not at all competent in the kitchen. I can microwave like nobody's business, though.

"Are you sure you're okay I'm gone?"

"Of course. I know things have been difficult for you, even if you won't talk to me about it," Mom says as she rubs her tired eyes.

"I needed a break," I state.

There's no way I could tell her that the break was also from her new family. I love Josh and adore being his big sister, but there are times when Mom, Stuart, and Josh are in the living room watching some cartoon or putting a puzzle together that I feel like I'm crashing their nice little unit. My presence looms over our family photos, because I got my height from Dad. So often people get confused about the tall brunette standing next to the nice couple and their young son.

"I know, honey."

We're both quiet for a minute. I never talk about Dad to Mom anymore. It's a topic we avoid, because he burned us both. I'm sure she'd like to erase him entirely from her memory if it wasn't for the fact that I share half of his DNA.

"How weird is this: I saw this busker yesterday," I begin as I've been itching to tell someone about Aiden.

"Uh-huh," Mom replies, but her attention is off to the side. "Josh, go get your shoes. Sorry, Evie, I need to run a few errands before my one o'clock meeting. I'm listening." She stands up from the table to clear some dishes.

"Yeah, so I was in this quiet park yesterday, and saw—"

"Joshua, what did I say? Get your shoes, *now*."

Mom's back is to me while she places some dishes in the sink. It wouldn't matter if I was on FaceTime or not, this often happens. Josh needs more attention than I do, but still.

"Go ahead, Evie," Mom says over her shoulder.

"Never mind, I'll talk to you later."

"Huh?" Mom snaps her fingers. "Bring the shoes here."

I hear Josh moan before he stomps next to Mom and then disappears, presumably because he's on the floor.

"So, I guess I'll go," I shout into the void.

No response. Mom's head is barely visible while she puts on

Josh's shoes. I wait for a minute to see whether she'll turn back to me. Then another minute passes.

"Okay, well," I say loudly. "I'll talk to you later. Bye."

Nothing. I hang up and stare at the blank screen. "Nice talk," I reply to an empty flat.

I collapse on the floor feeling even worse, and here I thought that couldn't be possible. I don't have anybody to talk to: Mom's too busy, Dad is Dad, and my friends, well . . .

Instead of spiraling further, I tackle another inevitable task: unpacking. Usually when I visit Dad, I live out of my suitcase. But I have to constantly remind myself: *you're here all summer.*

I dump out my clothes that were quickly thrown into the suitcase when I decided that I had to get out of the US ASAP. Something falls and rattles on the hardwood flooring. I kneel down to find Josh's favorite Hot Wheels fire truck. He must've slipped it into my suitcase before I left.

I stare at the small metal truck, knowing how much he loves it.

My bottom lip trembles. This small gesture means so much. That there's someone out there to whom I matter.

I hold on to Josh's truck as I walk around Dad's flat. He was one of the first people to swoop in when the Chelsea Barracks was announced. His shiny, brand-new complex sits on what was once a former army barracks. Now it houses the extremely wealthy.

His three-bedroom flat is like the other places he's lived. All in increasingly posher neighborhoods. Everything is slick and new, mostly in hues of gray with an occasional deep-blue accent.

Entering it, you'd think it was a model apartment. There isn't an ounce of personality or any relics that indicate an actual human being lives here. No photos. No trinkets. Only the most expensive items from luxury stores.

"Always buy the best," Dad once told me during a visit. "If you have the best, people will treat you the way you should be treated."

He gave this advice to his daughter, who was wearing clothing from Target. The only luxury items I have are from him: Tiffany jewelry for my birthdays, which remain in their blue bags. Mom puts his child support in a college savings account, even though he said he'd pay for my college. I don't want to need anything from him. In fact, I *don't* need him.

Says the girl who is currently staying in his flat for the summer.

I realize I should be grateful that I'm able to jet off to London. Dad does pay for the plane tickets—it's part of the divorce agreement. I know it's an incredible privilege. It's just at the current moment in time I don't feel very lucky to be here. It's a constant reminder of why I had to go away.

I begin to unpack my suitcase, but exhaustion takes over me. I lie down on the plush bed in the guest room. I close my eyes and try not to think about all the people I've left behind.

♪♪

"Evie!"

I'm jolted awake and let out a yelp upon seeing Dad standing over me.

"Have you spent all day sleeping?"

"No." I sit up and look at the clock. It's nearly eight at night. "I went for a long walk, talked to Mom, started to unpack."

"Maybe you could finish," he says as he takes in the piles of clothes I left around the room.

"Yeah, sorry," I say, knowing how much he likes things to be clean and orderly.

"It's okay," he replies. He gives me a smile. "This is an improvement over your room when you were little. You needed to see all your clothes when you got dressed. No need for drawers, just leave it on the floor."

"I've always been more of a visual person," I reply with a shrug.

"Okay, then, can you"—he sweeps his hand out at the mess I've left—"do *something* with all of this?" And at that he gestures his hand up and down like I just randomly threw everything out of my suitcase without any care for where it landed.

Which is exactly what I did.

And then something unexpected happens: I let out a laugh.

At something my father's done.

His eyes get wide in surprise. "So I take that as a yes?"

I give him a thumbs-up.

"I see we're finally getting somewhere." He gives me a wink, a playful aren't-we-having-fun wink. It's something I haven't seen from him in so long.

He holds out a bag from Waterstones bookshop. "I picked up something for you on my way home." It's a guidebook: *London's*

Hidden Walks. "I know your favorite thing is to wander around, so I thought this might give you an idea of other places to visit . . . since you're here for a while."

"This is nice, Dad. Thank you." And I mean it.

He's trying, I tell myself. So maybe I could try as well.

I start flipping through the book to see where I'll go. It would be nice to have some kind of purpose when I wake up each day.

"So," he begins as he sits on the bed next to me. Like we're going to have a little chat. We haven't had any kind of chats in a long time. "Where did you explore today?"

"Tower of London."

"Classic Evie. Do you remember that diorama you did back when you were little on the Tower?"

"I do." I smile at my father.

"Your teacher was none too happy you used red marker to denote blood."

"Like I'm supposed to just ignore the decapitations. Hashtag justice for Anne Boleyn!"

We both share a laugh. I repeat: *my father and I share a laugh.*

"Did you go inside? Try to steal the Crown Jewels?" Dad's eyes are actually sparkling.

"I admit nothing!" I say and find my shoulders start relaxing around him.

He, in turn, loosens his tie. "Then where'd you go?"

"Borough Market."

His eyebrows shoot up. "And what did you eat?"

And there it is. Why did I bother to get my hopes up? We were both melting a bit, but then he had to bring up food.

Yes, when one has been to a food market, it is reasonable to inquire about what that person ate, but with Dad it's a loaded question.

"Probably more saturated fat than the recommended daily allowance," I answer honestly.

"Evie, you have to start taking care of yourself," he replies with a tsk.

Here's the thing: of course, any parent would want their child to take care of themselves. *However*, my dad's main concern isn't about my health. That's the shield he uses. Everything with him boils down to appearances.

The joke I make that my dad's half the man he used to be is true. Around his thirty-fifth birthday, he had a premature midlife crisis. He decided he was going to start working out and watching what he ate. We started going on family walks and cut out fast food, bread, pasta, and soda.

After a few months, Dad declared Mom and I were slowing him down. He started going on jogs, which led to runs, which then prompted him to join a running club so he could compete in the Chicago Marathon. The pounds melted off his sturdy frame. My dad had been a bigger guy, but it suited him. As his size shrunk, his temper began to rise. He scolded Mom for taking me to McDonald's. He stormed out of the house when we welcomed him home from his first half-marathon with a homemade cake.

Soon being "thin" wasn't enough. Dad started upgrading everything. He left his job at a small real estate investment firm for the biggest in Chicago. He went from shopping for clothes at Macy's to ordering suits from some swanky tailor on Michigan Avenue. He traded in his Jeep Grand Cherokee for a Cadillac Escalade.

It was out with the old, in with the new, the shiny, the perfect. He didn't want any reminders of his past. He took down the pictures around the house from my parents' wedding and the first seven years of my life. He was ashamed of who he used to be.

It shouldn't come as a surprise that Mom and I were next.

So now when the topic of food or exercise comes up between us, it turns into a whole thing. A reminder of not being enough for my own father. Although by how much I annoy him, I may be just too much.

He sighs as he gets up from my bed. "I had a long business lunch, so I'm going to another spin class. Put on your workout kit and come with me."

"Pass," I reply. There is no way I'm going to an exercise class with my dad. He'll judge me for either sweating too much or not enough.

Here's a dirty little secret I've never told my dad: I'm on the track team at school. I like running and often run along the Thames when I visit. It helps clear my mind. I like making my heart race. But if I tell him, he'll ruin it. He'll turn the running I do as a type of meditation into numbers: how many miles I clock, the calories burned. The fact that I would do any act of exercise without wearing a monitor to break down every step would be incomprehensible to him.

"So you're going to spend all summer sitting around, eating crisps?"

"Oh, that does sound heavenly," I reply with a fake smile.

He takes a deep breath. "Okay, then. I'll be off." But he pauses at the door and looks back at me. "I've made a booking for us to have afternoon tea at the Ritz on Friday, like when you were little."

And just like that, I soften again. Dad rarely acknowledges the past. Whenever we'd visit London, we'd go to high tea, just him and me. There's a part of me that's touched that he would remember. That he would do this for us. Mostly I'm shocked he'd be willing to have refined sugar for me.

"That sounds really nice, Dad," I admit.

Huh. Maybe, just maybe, we can use this summer to start rebuilding all that we have lost. When I'm in London, there are all these reminders of how we once were. I can only hope that my old dad—the caring, funny, sweet dad—has to be somewhere inside this robotic creature.

Maybe this summer won't be so lonely after all.

7

There was a time when I didn't mind being lonely.

I figured it was better being alone than opening yourself to someone who could end up hurting you.

I think the most messed-up part is that I had this thought when I was nine years old.

Nine.

If it weren't already obvious, it was a rough childhood. Just ask my therapist.

I did eventually let in a couple of friends. I met Meredith and Lindsay in middle school. We'd have sleepovers. We'd sing along to boy bands and Disney musicals. I didn't mind when we'd get giddy and talk about boys when they were limited to fictional ones. That was harmless. A cartoon character couldn't break your heart.

As we got older, I would uncharacteristically keep my mouth shut when they'd start talking about boys in our school. Real ones that could take you on real dates with real kisses and real consequences. I'd simply smile along and pretend to be *so excited* when their crush messaged. But for me, I stayed away.

Until Sean came along.

"Do you know who likes you?" Meredith cooed at lunch in the middle of sophomore year.

My enthusiastic response was to shrug. I wasn't boy-obsessed like Meredith. Although, she rarely had the guts to do anything about it. More often than not, Meredith would join me as we watched Lindsay get ready for a date with a guy or—toward the end of freshman year when she came out as bi—girl.

"It's a good one," Meredith said as she wiggled her eyebrows. "As in part of the dynamic duo."

"Oh God." It was worse than I thought. "What a surprise, Theo Evans wants to date someone."

Theo was one of the most popular guys in school. Everybody loved him. The guys wanted to be like him—confident, cool, smart, personable, athletic—and the girls wanted to date him.

"Aww, Theo was one of my favs," Lindsay said as she fluffed her massive curls.

Of course Theo and Lindsay dated. And the weird thing was they got along better after they broke up.

"No, not Theo," Meredith continued. She looked like she was about to burst. "Sean Harwell!"

I groaned and let my head fall to the table. It wasn't like Sean Harwell was any better. He and Theo were practically inseparable and could always be found strutting down the hallway. The only exceptions were when it came to extracurricular activities. Theo was the jock with broad shoulders and light-brown skin that got darker during the summer, while Sean was tall, pale, with a thin frame, and was more into the drama department and indoor activities.

"Pass," I replied.

"For what it's worth, Sean is a sweetheart," Lindsay added. "After Theo and I broke up, he wanted to make sure I was okay."

The bitter person I had become couldn't stop myself for thinking that Sean was probably looking for sloppy seconds.

"Don't roll your eyes at me, Evie!" Lindsay wagged her finger. "All I'm saying is that he's a sweet guy. He's thoughtful. There could be worse guys."

There will always be worse guys, I thought. *That's not necessarily a compliment.*

"Oh!" Lindsay ducked down. "He's totally looking over here right now." She then popped up and waved to Sean.

"Are you two being serious right now?" I slouched in my seat.

"Sean!" Lindsay called out.

I swear if looks could really kill, Lindsay would've collapsed right there and then.

Meredith fully turned into a giggling heap while I tried to regain my composure. "He's coming over!" Meredith said in a not-even-attempting-to-be-quiet bellow.

"Hey guys," Sean greeted us. There was a slight tremor in his voice that I'd never detected before.

"Hi, Sean." Lindsay stood up. "Oh, that reminds me, I forgot something at my locker. Don't you also need to get something, Meredith?"

"Yes!" Meredith was near hysterics now. And she was supposed to be the lead in our upcoming musical?

They were both too busy falling over themselves to leave that they ignored my pleading stare.

Then it was just Sean and me.

"Hey, Evie."

"Hey."

"So . . . What do you think of the book Mr. Bradley assigned us for class? It's different, huh?" he asked.

"*Flowers for Algernon?* While it would be nice for Mr. Bradley to update his reading list from last century, or at least from the 1970s to include female authors and authors of color, I have to admit that I like it. I'm a fan of epistolary works."

Sean nodded along. "Yeah, totally." He paused a moment. "What's epistolary?"

"It's a novel written as a series of documents. Like how *Flowers for Algernon* is a series of Charlie's progress reports so we as the readers can see his intelligence grow from the surgery. And then, well . . . I won't give anything away depending on how far you've read. It's just something different. I also like oral histories, too. There's something about people talking about their personal experiences that always resonates with me. That's why I prefer books written in first person over third."

Sean smiled at me. He probably thought my mini monologue meant that I was flirting or something. I wasn't. That was just me. Ask me a question, I'll blab on and on.

"Anyway, I should go. Catch you later." I got up and walked away without giving Sean a second look or thought.

Until he showed up at my locker the next day.

"Hey, have you read this?" He handed me a copy of *The Color Purple*. "It's an epistolary novel written by a woman of color. Maybe after you read it we can watch the movie. There's also a musical. My mom said it's one of her favorites."

"Oh." I was stunned that he had listened to me yesterday. And then did research. Usually Meredith or Lindsay (or my family) blank out on minute twelve of an Evie tangent. "Thanks."

A couple of days later he brought me a bag of potato chips. "Hey, I saw these the other day and thought of you. I always see you eating them at lunch, but you call them something else."

"Oh, crisps. It's a British thing."

"Yeah, your dad's British, right?"

"Right."

"Cool, see you later!" He waved goodbye while I was stuck staring at the bag of potato chips.

Books and carbs: was there a quicker way to any girl's heart?

But I still couldn't figure out what his endgame was. So I kept up my wall.

The next week he followed me out of history class. "Hey, that was amazing what you did in there."

What I did was get in a debate with Ms. Diffin over the lasting implications of Brexit, when the United Kingdom left the European Union.

"Oh, thanks. You were probably the only one who thought so." Even while I was talking, I could see side-eyes and the "there she goes again" looks from my classmates.

"Is there some book or documentary you could recommend so I can learn more about it?"

That stopped me in my tracks. "Uh, sure."

Then I looked at him. He had a nice warm smile. He was trying. He was cute.

There was a little flutter in my heart that I tried to ignore.

"What's the harm in one date?" Lindsay said to me later that week. "He's a nice guy. He basically worships the ground you walk on and is willing to read nonfiction books on British history for you. What more could you want!"

Meredith squealed when she saw the corners of my mouth turn up.

So that was how I went on a first date with Sean Harwell.

He had quizzed Lindsay about my favorite foods and found a place nearby that specializes in macaroni and cheese (although who doesn't love mac and cheese? Masochists, that's who.). He had me pick out the movie. I found my hand tingling as his got closer during the night.

When our fingers touched, I felt a jolt. And I liked it.

With every sweet gesture—giving me a random rose on a Tuesday, bringing a truck for Josh, moving his work schedule to cheer me on during a track meet—I felt the ice that had built around my heart melting.

After a few months, my day didn't seem to start until he texted me good morning. I couldn't sleep until he sent me my good-night text: the kissy face with heart emoji.

It had taken me so long to get to the point where I could think of anybody in that way, that once Sean broke the barrier, he was all I could think about.

Sean and Theo began joining us for lunch and on the weekends. My small crew of two close friends blossomed into three friends and one sweet boyfriend.

Once I let go, it was easy to fall hard for Sean. He said and did all the right things.

The mere thought of him warmed my heart. I was a walking epitome of a sappy love song, and I couldn't have been happier.

For over a year it was wonderful.

I took a chance on love.

And then it all fell apart.

What's the harm? Lindsay had asked me.

A lot, it seemed.

8

I spent the next morning applying for jobs at various cafés across Chelsea and Kensington. Once they'd see the posh Chelsea Barracks address, the eyebrow raising would begin. If I was lucky enough to score an interview after that, the question about how long I'd be in London and my stuttering response would put the nail in the barista coffin.

On my walk through St. James's Park, I come up with a new plan. I'll put up flyers around Chelsea Barracks to see if anybody needs a babysitter. That doesn't require paperwork. And anybody who lives in that swanky estate would probably pay a lot for an evening out—if they don't already have a full-time nanny.

If all goes well, I'll be able to spend a summer in London without taking a single cent of my father's money.

It will annoy him to no end.

If not, well . . . I guess I'll become an expert at staring at walls and drowning out memories.

I turn the corner and my heart always does a little flutter upon seeing this particular big, beautiful boy: Ben.

There's always a surge of excitement I get whenever I see the major icons in London. It's this moment of: *you're really here!* And Big Ben is about as iconic as it gets. I've always considered the ornate golden clock tower as my personal welcome wagon.

However, if we're to get technical, Big Ben is the name of the largest bell. The tower is technically called the Elizabeth Tower. So henceforth, in the name of smashing the patriarchy, I shall only refer to it as Elizabeth Tower. She is my welcome wagon.

Well, mine and the hundreds of tourists swarming around the Houses of Parliament. I weave among the crowds gathered to take pictures as I cross Westminster Bridge with the London Eye slowly rotating ahead.

The tower starts chiming, alerting me that it's somehow already four in the afternoon. As I walk past the London Eye toward the Golden Jubilee Bridges, I freeze.

There's a busker up ahead.

Oh my God. It's after school and I'm in South Bank.

Aiden said he was going to be in South Bank after school.

I can't believe I forgot.

Or . . . *et tu, subconscious?*

I cautiously approach the busker but immediately see it's not Aiden. This busker has a sound system and dozens of people surrounding him as he plays "Wonderwall." I'm brought back to Theo sitting us down in his basement, a serious look on his face, as he played it for us the first time. Even though that song is like a gazillion years old, we found ourselves singing along with him.

All of that is gone. Those friendships are now collecting dust along with Theo's guitar, which he stopped playing only a few weeks later.

I don't need those friends. I don't need anybody.

But then why are you still walking along South Bank where you could run into Aiden?

You know what, I'm going to go to the Tate Modern, and if I happen to run into Aiden along the way, I'll simply say hello. Nothing wrong with that.

My mantra for this summer will be *Keep it causal. Keep it simple.*

As I pass the National Theatre, I notice someone in the distance with a guitar. I curse that my initial reaction is hope.

Hope that I won't be so alone.

As I get closer, the pit in my stomach drops as I realize it *is* Aiden. He's midsong with his eyes closed. There are only a couple of people passing him; nobody is stopping to listen. Maybe it's because he's not playing some old rock cover. Or the fact that pain radiates off him when he sings.

"*I am diminished, I am nothing, without you . . .*" he sings, his voice raspy.

When Aiden sings, I can't help but feel like I'm understood. That feeling of loss. Not just of a relationship, but of something more.

I feel like I lost myself when everything came apart back home.

Aiden plays one more chord, the black-and-white scarf now wrapped around his wrist.

When Aiden opens his eyes, he's not surprised to find nobody in front of him. He scans the area, then sees me off to the side.

His face lights up. "Hey! I wasn't sure if you were going to come, my one fan."

"Well, I don't know if I'm a *fan*," I joke as I approach him.

He stretches his arms above his head. "I'm chuffed you came."

You probably shouldn't be here, Evie.

Just say hi and then leave.

Hi and then leave.

Hi and then—

"Do you want me to do anything to help?" I offer because I apparently don't understand the meaning of *simple* and *casual*. "When I'm in downtown Chicago, usually someone shouts 'It's showtime' to get a crowd to gather. I have no problem being loud and drawing attention to myself."

Aiden looks thoughtful for a second. "Now, that's an offer that's hard to resist. I reckon if you start breakdancing it'll get us loads of gawkers."

"Hard pass."

See, this is the perfect time to just politely move on.

"Would you want to go for a walk?" He gives me an expectant smile as he begins to pack up his guitar. He puts the few coins in a plastic bag and pops it into the side zipper of his case.

No, you were just going to say hi. Tell him you're on your way to the Tate.

"Sure!"

Come on, Evie!

"I mean, walking is my favorite London-based activity," I continue because of course I can't shut up.

That's it, I'm out. You're on your own.

Aiden shakes his head. "We need to get you out more. Let's go this way. I have a place in mind I think you'd like."

We head back toward the London Eye.

"Hey, so I looked up that Robbie Williams guy and then went down a Take That wormhole," I admit. "They had some good songs. I really like 'Back for Good.' You should add that to your repertoire."

"You sound like my mum."

"Is that so? Well, she sounds like a delightful and intelligent woman with excellent taste. In fact, you should maybe think about starting a boy band. The UK needs one since it's been forever since One D broke up."

"Oh my God, you call them One D."

"Um, *yes*, young Evie was a loud and proud Directioner. I have a soft spot for British boy bands."

"Good to know," Aiden says with a playful smirk. "Which member of, and I quote, 'One D' do you think I'd be? Am I a Harry?"

"You wish you were a Harry," I fire back. Even though Aiden probably is a bit of a Harry: flirty and charming. He's also got a mop of curls. "I was more of a Niall girl myself."

Still am. What can I say, I'm a sucker for a guy who can sing and play guitar.

Oh God, I really am a sucker.

"Well, I don't think I'm a boy-band type. I can't really dance," Aiden admits.

"I'll be the judge of that." I motion in front of us. "Let's see some of your moves."

"Ladies first."

I continue walking even though I've been known to dance around my room and could probably still do the routine from the end of the "Best Song Ever" video.

Aiden's cheeks get red as he gestures with his chin. "Well, I figure you might be up for a snog."

This gets me to stop dead in my tracks. *Snog* is British slang for *kiss*.

"Oh, no, I meant . . ." Aiden stammers as he points to a hot-pink double-decker bus with the sign SNOG. "It's frozen yogurt."

"Yeah, I know!" (I did not know.)

Things Evie doesn't need in her life at this moment in time: boys and snogging.

Things Evie definitely needs: frozen yogurt and something to distract any thoughts involving snogging and this particular boy.

I take out my wallet. "This is on me, I insist."

Aiden puts his hands up. "Okay, I know better than to try to argue with an American."

"Especially *this* American," I reply.

We take our dishes of frozen yogurt as we retrace our steps along the Thames, away from the tourists.

"I really think if you start playing some One D and Take That songs you'd rake in the cash. Besides, it's really bringing up some not-awesome feelings for me. It's like PTSD listening to you."

Aiden looks down at his mango frozen yogurt. "Yeah, sorry about that. I promise to play something more upbeat next time."

Next time.

He also threw out the "we" earlier. *We* need to get you out more.

Alarm bells are ringing in my head. I know all too well what can happen when a guy starts to make promises.

"So, do you want to talk about what happened with your relationship?" Aiden asks.

"Ah, I think you got quite an earful from me yesterday."

He pauses for a moment. "Yes, but you didn't really say anything."

Um, I'm pretty sure I went on and on *and on* about my feelings toward the male species and how my dad's a jerk.

Aiden laughs at my confused expression. "Yes, you said a great many things. So, *so* many things. But only that you just went through a breakup. You didn't give any details."

"Oh, well, what more is there to say?" I reply lightly. "It's the basic story of girl meets boy, boy woos girl, then boy shoves a giant knife in said girl's back. It's a classic trope."

Aiden nods. "Can I be honest with you for a second?"

Yikes, that's never good. I mean, honesty is a nice concept and all, but usually that means he's going to say something I don't want to hear.

"Okay," I reply cautiously.

"Not to be forward or anything," he starts.

"Because that's really more of an American thing to do," I add. "I do believe 'twas I who bombarded you yesterday with a scandalous offer of coffee two-point-five seconds after meeting you."

Aiden is quiet for a second. I don't think he's going to continue until he takes a deep breath. "Listen, it's probably none of my business, but I think you're really hurt. You wouldn't have come all the way to London if you weren't. And maybe you're the type of person who likes to downplay their feelings. Hey, I'm British, so I understand about not being open, but I get this sense that you *do* want to talk about what happened. If you don't, that's okay. But maybe you should. And not make a joke of it, because it doesn't seem like something to laugh at."

My heart starts to beat faster and I find myself walking at a quicker pace, as if I can get more distance from what happened. I find it easier to make light of my situation than really dig deep. It's probably because I won't like what I find when I go there.

It's been easier for me to react with anger and bitterness than to admit the truth.

That I'm hurt.

My heart hurts.

I don't know Aiden. If I trust him, I guess it won't really matter. I can tell him the truth and not worry about being vulnerable because we live an ocean apart. He'll soon be a footnote in my history.

"Okay," I relent. Even that one word loosens the tension I've been holding in my shoulders. Just get it all out. I'll feel better and then I can walk away from Aiden and try to move on with my summer. "His name is Sean . . ."

Aiden listens as I tell him everything. About the books, the crisps, the trust that was building.

With each confession, I feel a weight lift off me.

We've nearly reached the Tate Modern by the time I come to the hard part.

We stop walking, and I lean against the railing. I clear my throat and study the blue dome of St. Paul's Cathedral across the Thames. "I guess I was so enamored that it took me a while to realize that Sean had been acting differently. I came up with excuses—he had the spring musical, we had exams, blah, blah, blah. I kept going over and over everything in my head, looking for something I had done to deserve his distant behavior. I even tried to talk to Meredith about it. But she was also busy and not returning my messages. Lindsay told me I was reading into nothing."

I can see Aiden studying me out of the corner of my eye. I can't help but wonder where I'd be right now if everything had been a figment of my imagination. But it wasn't. And here I am. In London with a boy I don't even know.

There's no turning back now.

I take a deep breath. "So last Friday at lunch, our final day of school, Sean sat on the other side of the table, as far away from me as possible and next to Meredith. They were laughing and having a great time. I dropped my spoon, and when I bent down to pick it up, I noticed Sean was rubbing Meredith's leg under the table."

"So yeah." I give an exaggerated shrug of my shoulders. "That was that."

We're silent for a moment. It's as if Aiden can sense there's more to this story. But it's not as if I want to share what is arguably not my finest moment.

"I'm so sorry. You must've been gutted," Aiden says to fill the silence. "The two people you thought you could rely on."

Exactly.

I finally turn to him and force a smile. "So there it is. I'd apologize that you had to listen to all of that, but you did ask for it—literally. We must all accept the consequences of our actions."

Aiden studies me for a second. "Why do I have a feeling that you didn't simply get up and walk away?"

He's known me for twenty-four hours and so has me pegged.

"*Of course* I said something."

Aiden laughs at my response. "I have to admit, I'd be a bit disappointed if you didn't."

"Yeah, I didn't handle it well."

I felt so hurt, betrayed, and like a complete idiot that I didn't see what was happening right in front of me. So I got up and started screaming at them. I don't remember everything that spewed from my mouth, but I do remember their faces. The deer-caught-in-headlights look with a major side of guilt. They didn't deny a single thing. Lindsay and Theo looked down at their lunches, while my world began to crumble apart.

"There was a bit of a scene." I close my eyes, humiliated at how much I ranted and raved in front of the entire school. *The entire school.* Apparently, a teacher tried to get me to calm down at one point, but I waved him off. One online report—because of course people were live streaming—stated that I held up my hand and said, "Back off, Mr. Gallagher, now is not the time!" to the PE teacher.

That was nothing compared to the finale.

"So yeah, after I ranted, I finished it all off with me throwing my Cherry Coke in Sean's face and saying 'You're a fake and a phony and I wish I never laid eyes on you' before I exited the cafeteria to the laughter of my classmates."

I take a deep breath and then I do something I never thought I'd do looking back on what happened: I start laughing.

"Oh my God!" I cover my face with my hand. "Even as I was going off on them, the voice in my head that tries to reason with me was all, *Stop talking, just stop.* But of course I didn't. To be honest, I'm proud that I stood up for myself."

Aiden smiles at me. "It does sound pretty wicked. But I'm sorry you had to go through that." He pauses and tilts his head. "Do I know that line from somewhere? What you said after you threw soda in his face."

Dear God, I'd hoped he wouldn't have noticed. "Yeah. It's from *Grease.*"

Aiden's face lights up. "*Grease?* As in the musical *Grease?*"

Embarrassment, thy name is Evie Taylor.

"Sure is." I had watched it the night before because Meredith was auditioning for the role of Rizzo at the local community playhouse the next weekend. I told her I'd help her rehearse. My attempt at being a good friend meant the movie was fresh in my head and the line simply slipped out.

Aiden fiddles with his empty cup of yogurt. "What happened after?"

Any remnants of laughter instantly vanish. The sting is still fresh. I'll never forget how the hallways parted when I walked by. As soon as I entered a room, people would whisper and stare at me.

But when I think about which part of last week hurts the most, it's this.

"Unfortunately, the backstabbing didn't end with Sean and Meredith. I found out that Lindsay and Theo had had their suspicions and didn't say anything to me for weeks. *Weeks.* Then after the whole cafeteria incident, they met up with Sean and Meredith to hear them out. So yeah, it's pretty clear whose side they took."

I don't blame Theo, he was Sean's best friend. But Lindsay. The one who told me that there was no harm in going on a date. Yeah, maybe one date isn't a big deal, but what if that leads to something more?

My throat hurts due to a sob that's trying to escape. Everything I've been pushing back is forcing itself out.

"I was so angry and hurt. I knew I couldn't spend all summer being surrounded by the memories, so I . . . just left."

There'd been something scratching at the back of my mind for the last few days. Saying everything aloud to Aiden has made me realize what it is.

Sean replaced me with Meredith.

Mom replaced me with Josh.

It's fairly obvious what my dad replaced me with.

What is it about me that people feel they can just shove aside? Am I that insignificant? Or is it just that I'm too much?

Tears are now streaming down my face, and I do my best to wipe them away.

Aiden unzips part of his guitar bag and hands me a tissue.

"Thanks," I say with a sniffle. "And sorry."

Aiden hesitantly reaches out and touches my shoulder. "Do not apologize for your feelings, Evie. They are valid. You didn't deserve that. And I hope you don't need me to be the one to tell you that you did nothing wrong."

I nod as I wipe away the tears. "So yeah, I suffered humiliation, lost my boyfriend and closest friends, and decided to fly across the Atlantic Ocean. As you can tell, things are going really great for me right now. I'm the very definition of living my best life. Aren't you glad you told me where you'd be busking today?"

Aiden looks at me with such concern it almost completely breaks me.

"Please make a joke right now," I beg. I feel as if I'm on the edge of drowning in memories and need Aiden to get me out of the thoughts that are weighing me down. "I'll help you out: I'm going to blame this on jet lag."

He opens his mouth as if he's going to say something else about how it's okay for me to be sad. I know it is, it's just I don't want to be sad. Or angry. I came to London to get away from the hurt. Instead, he takes my barely touched frozen yogurt cup, now mostly liquid. "Yeah, I'm going to hold on to this for now. Don't want you throwing it in my face."

I give him a grateful smile. "To be clear: you have to be, and I *quote*, a fake and a phony, *unquote*, in order for me to do that."

"I can verify that I've never been a fake or a phony," he says as he cautiously gives me back my yogurt but tucks a napkin into his shirt. "Just in case you get the urge."

He then places another napkin on top of his head.

I take a spoonful of the now not-frozen salted caramel. "So yeah, I just kind of needed a break from everything."

"That I totally get," Aiden says.

I also, right at this moment, need a break from my problems.

"Okay, enough about me. Your turn. Spill! Girlfriend?"

Aiden shakes his head.

"Boyfriend?"

"Not for me, although I'm a proud ally."

"Girlfriends—plural?"

He tilts his head at me like he can't believe I'd ask him that question.

"Well, what about the person you're singing all those songs about?" I ask. "Was it a bad breakup?"

"Huh?" He genuinely looks confused for a moment. "Oh. I mean, when you really think about it, are breakups ever good?"

"I think I handled Sean's and mine quite well. Very ladylike behavior."

Neither one of us can keep a straight face after that lie. We walk for a few minutes in silence. The tourists become thicker as we approach the Globe Theatre.

"You know, we're walking in the direction of Borough Market," Aiden finally comments.

"There are worse places to end up," I add. Dad has a work meeting until late, so maybe I'll pick up some dinner for tonight. Then I'll have to decide whether I want to hide any evidence of food he wouldn't approve of to avoid a confrontation or go all-in and leave grease-stained wrappers on the counter.

I have to remind myself that he's having afternoon tea with me tomorrow. It's not much, but for us it's something. I'll take anything I can get at this point.

Aiden's phone rings in his pocket. "Hiya, Mum. Okay. No worries. See you soon."

It's pretty much the same conversation he had yesterday. It's sweet that he seems to have a good relationship with his mom.

"Listen, I got to go," Aiden says.

"Okay," I reply.

This time really has to be goodbye. Learn from your mistakes, Evie.

Aiden nods. "Right, I'm meeting up with some mates tomorrow after school at a coffee shop in Kensington if you want to join us."

I hesitate for a moment.

Or I could hang out with his friends.

"Sure." Even though this is probably just a pity invite. "I mean, I don't want to be a bother."

"Not at all." A mischievous smile spreads on his face. "They'll never believe I met someone like you. I need proof."

"Oh, so I'm simply to be trotted out to amuse your friends," I say with a raised eyebrow. "I see how it is."

"Here." Aiden takes my phone and types in his number and the name of a coffee place. "I'll see you at four, yeah?"

See, this is a sign. I already have plans with my dad tomorrow.

"Oh, I'm meeting my dad at two." But I start doing the math in my head. There's no way my dad's going to have time for a leisurely tea. "I should make it by then. But my phone only works on Wi-Fi, so if you change your mind or are running late, you won't be able to call me."

"You don't have to worry about that with me. I'll be there when I say I'll be there."

9

Classical music—performed by a pianist and three string players dressed in tuxedos—fills the atrium at the Ritz as I wait for Dad underneath a huge chandelier the following afternoon.

I'll begrudgingly admit I was excited as I got ready for tea. I put on my deep purple A-line dress that I got (on sale at Macy's) for Homecoming. I even curled my hair and put on some makeup. I used to be a daddy's girl who loved to dress up for my special afternoons with him. If he's making an effort to do this for me, I can put on some lipstick. Although the thought of sitting next to him for two hours makes me a little nervous. We haven't had a real conversation in years. Will he spend the time criticizing me, or will we be able to get a part of us back?

"Evie!"

I turn to see Poppy, teetering on red stilettos, charging toward me. She's wearing a tight red skirt and black half-shirt.

"Hi." I try to push down my disappointment that it won't be just Dad and me. Although Poppy might be a nice barrier. Dad always plays the good father part better in front of others.

"Oh, I love this!" Poppy exclaims at my dress as she beckons me to twirl around. I do, simply because the dress *does* fan out nicely. When I stop, her face falls. "Your dad is so sad." She juts out her bottom lip, just like Josh does. "He's stuck in a meeting, but he sent me in his place. Now we can get to know each other, like sisters!" She claps her hands excitedly, even though I don't have the heart to tell her that if things went well with Dad, she'd be a step*mom*. Granted, one only a few years older than her teenage stepdaughter.

I don't know why I'm so shocked Dad isn't here. Every time I get my hopes up that things might become better between us, they're shattered. It kills me that even after all this time, Dad's rejection still stings. My head knows better, but my heart, on the other hand . . .

"Evie, you ready?" Poppy asks my blank face.

I give her a little nod. Not as if I've been given a choice.

Poppy bounces up to the hostess stand and we're escorted by a woman in a black floor-length gown to our table for two. A menu is placed in front of us and my stomach growls in delight. I had only a banana and—wait for it—green juice this morning so I'd be ready for all of the delicious food.

A waiter, dressed in a red vest and black bow tie, puts two glasses of champagne in front of Poppy and me. "Compliments of Mr. Taylor, who sends his apologies."

"Oh," Poppy coos as she takes a sip.

I follow suit. The English are a lot less rigid about alcohol. The drinking age is eighteen, so nobody thinks twice about giving a seventeen-year-old a glass of champagne.

A silver three-tiered holder is placed in front of us. On the bottom is a plate with two servings of the different finger sandwiches: ham with grainy mustard, cheddar cheese with chutney, cucumber with cream cheese, chicken breast with parsley cream, Scottish smoked salmon, and egg mayonnaise. I don't wait for Poppy as I start to eat.

Poppy studies the sandwiches and picks up a cucumber one. She takes a small nibble with her eyes closed, and sinks into her seat. "So delicious."

"I know, right?" I take a bite of the Scottish salmon. The portion is just an inch-wide strip that I finish in two bites.

Poppy is apparently on the same wavelength as she devours the rest of her cucumber sandwich.

"So!" Poppy begins as she picks up another. "Your dad tells me you have a boyfriend. Dish!"

And just like that, the egg mayonnaise bite goes dry in my mouth.

"Oh no, did I say something wrong?" Poppy puts her hand to her heart.

"It's okay," I assure her. "It's just that we broke up."

"He didn't tell me!"

"I don't think he knows."

Dad used to know every mundane detail about my life. When he'd come home from work, he'd sit me down and ask me about my day. I'd fill him in on every single thing that happened. Every. Single. Detail. Who I played with at recess. Who was being good or bad. I honestly think those daily talks where I just went on and on are why I can be such a babbling mess now. Oh good, one more thing I can blame on dear old Dad.

"What happened?" Poppy asks. She pushes her plate aside and puts her elbows on the table as she leans in. Her attention is fully on me.

It's a nice, sweet gesture.

I find myself softening around her. I could probably talk to Poppy. She seems willing to listen. She appears to want to get to know me.

"Oh, well . . ." I start, but then I realize after yesterday with Aiden, I don't feel the need to rehash everything. It's almost as if I let it out of its cage.

Sure, I still have the occasional feeling of bobbing down below the surface, pulled deep by loneliness and anger, but for now—right in this very moment—I'm doing okay.

"You know, I actually don't want to talk about it."

"I'm so sorry," she says just as the waiter comes with our tea.

"It's okay, I appreciate you asking."

Which is true.

We both stay quiet as our tea is served. It's practically an art form in England. A silver kettle is placed in front of each of us, along with a teacup and saucer made of delicate china painted with blue flowers. The waiter lays a silver tea strainer on top of my cup and begins to pour the passion fruit tea I ordered. It's a beautiful pink color.

"Smells delicious," Poppy replies as another waiter pours her lemon verbena tea.

Yet another waiter comes along with a top plate of desserts. We both lean in as he describes them: lemon tart, coconut and raspberry macaron, chocolate tart, and a cream puff with hazelnut filling.

"Fresh-baked scones will be out shortly," he replies as my stomach tries to take it all in.

"I know we just met." Poppy leans toward me. "But I think it's very important—in terms of our bonding—for us to not get up from this table until we've eaten every last bite."

I nod with respect. "It would be rude of us not to."

"Exactly!" she says with a high-pitched laugh. "And we mustn't be rude."

Besides, Poppy is a spin instructor. The girl needs fuel to work out. She puts an entire macaron in her mouth.

Huh. There's a slight chance I might like this one.

"What else do you have lined up for the weekend?" Poppy asks as she licks jam off her finger.

I take this moment to glance at my watch. "Can I tell you something?"

She perks up. "Of course, I want us to be friends."

I would've snorted at this idea upon first meeting Poppy. I might've judged her too harshly in terms of dad's girlfriends, and having this tea between the two of us makes me think that maybe she could be a friend.

As long as she keeps her tweezers away and doesn't expect me to go spinning with her.

"I met this guy."

"Oh!" Poppy exclaims so loudly that the couple next to us turns around. "Tell me everything."

"It's not like that. It's just, I don't have any friends here, and well, I'm supposed to meet up with him and a few of his friends in an hour. At first, I wasn't sure if I should go."

"Why not?"

Exactly. Why not?

You know why.

"Well, I do want to go."

"You don't need to say a word more." She waves over to one of the nearby waiters. "We need to hurry up the scones. My friend has a date. Best to bring round the desserts trolley as well."

I look at the plate of desserts in front of us. "There's more?"

"Yes! They bring out a cart with two other desserts."

Oh dear Lord, I love London.

"Well, it's not a date with this guy," I clarify. "Just hanging out with his friends."

"That's how it always starts."

"Not with me. I'm kind of done with dating."

"Sure, sure," she says with a wink.

"And one more thing," I add. "Can you not mention this to my dad?"

"It'll be our little secret, as long as you don't tell him how much I ate." She then picks up the lemon tart from the top tier and shoves half of it into her mouth. "Can I tell *you* something?"

"Please do."

Poppy giggles. "I always eat a massive bowl of pasta before going out with your dad. He's so uptight about food."

"Right?" I say as I do a Poppy and shove an entire macaron in my mouth.

"Look, I know all the work it takes to look like this." Poppy gestures down at her toned body. "But if you're not going to loosen up and have fun once in a while, what's the point?"

"Imagine being his daughter."

Poppy sets down the remaining bite of her tart. "I'm sure he's hard on you, but Evie, let me tell you something. Do not let anybody, and I mean *anybody*, ever make you feel less than. Ever."

I'm taken aback. It's such a kind thing to say to me.

Sean made me feel less than. Dad, too. Instead of facing them, I ran away from one and tried to avoid the other. Maybe I should stop letting these guys push me around. Make them realize that I am *not* replaceable.

"Thanks, Poppy. Really."

She gives me a wink as she takes a sip of her tea.

While I give my dad crap for judging people on how they look, I did the same thing with Poppy. I held her looks and being with my dad against her. But she's lovely. And funny. And kind.

I guess there are some people worth giving a second chance to.

Look at me. Emotional growth and all that.

I celebrate my newfound maturity by putting an entire chocolate tart in my mouth, to which Poppy responds with a delightful giggle.

Yeah, I do like this one.

10

Okay, Evie, I know it's hard, but let's try to not make a fool out of yourself.

That is, any more than you already have.

This should be simple.

Do: listen, ask questions.

Don't: incessantly babble, especially about your many, *many* issues.

When I walk into the coffee shop at four on the dot, I'm not surprised that Aiden is already there, a mug of coffee in front of him.

"You made it," he states with a bashful smile. He's got on another black T-shirt, this time with faded blue jeans. That same scarf, which at this point seems like part of a uniform, is loosely wrapped around his neck.

"I'll be here when I say I'll be here." I paraphrase his line.

It's true that not having a cellphone that has reception 24/7 has forced me to be more reliable. It's like what my mom would tell me when I asked her what she did before cellphones, aka the Dark Ages: "You got to a place on time."

I find my cheeks warm as he takes in my too-fancy-for-coffee-with-mates outfit.

"You look nice. How was tea with your dad?"

"He never showed, but it's fine!" I clarify to his fallen face. "Really. I ended up hanging out with his girlfriend, who isn't, despite my initial suspicions, an idiot. We went to the Ritz."

"Oh, that's quite posh," a voice says from behind me. I turn around to see a tall guy with dark-brown skin and floppy black hair. "Hiya, I'm Dev."

"Hey, I'm Evie," I reply as I reach out my hand to shake his without realizing he's holding two coffee mugs.

"Yes! The famous American." Dev slides into the seat next to Aiden. "We've heard."

I sit across from Dev. "I don't even want to know what kind of defamation has been spread about me."

When Dev talks, his entire face lights up. "I believe jet lag was involved, if that helps."

Aiden lets out a laugh while I scowl at him.

"It's not like I'm making up the concept of jet lag," I defend myself. "So yes, I was tired from a very real condition, and I may have just been a little off. Last time I checked that wasn't a crime. I swear I'm emotionally stable. And not a stalker."

Which is precisely *what an emotionally unstable stalker would say.*

"Told you." Aiden leans back in his seat. "Evie gets adorably out of sorts very easily."

"I do not get out of sorts!" I insist, even though I do.

"I believe he said *adorably* out of sorts," Dev points out.

"Well, I—" Aiden clears his throat.

I attempt to kick Aiden under the table, but Dev gives off a yelp instead. "Sorry, Dev. That was meant for Aiden."

"Not a problem—I can help you out." Dev turns to sock Aiden in the arm.

"Thank you," I say as Aiden groans, rubbing his shoulder.

Dev nods at me. "Anytime, Evie. And I do mean any time." He then waves his fist at Aiden with a laugh.

"Did I miss that there's a dress code?"

I look up to see a petite girl standing over us. Her hair is bleached white with a blue streak on one side, and her bright red lip makes her porcelain skin even paler. She's wearing black Doc Marten boots with fishnet tights, cut-off jean shorts, and a black-and-white-striped long T-shirt that hangs off one shoulder to reveal a neon-blue bra strap.

"I got you an almond milk latte," Dev says as he holds up a mug.

"Thank God, I need caffeine stat." The girl plops down on the seat next to me.

"This is Fiona," Aiden says to me. "Fiona, Evie."

Fiona gives me the slightest nod of her chin.

"Hi, nice to meet you," I say, to which she replies by taking a sip of her latte and avoiding eye contact.

"Ah, can I get you something, Evie? Coffee? Tea?" Aiden asks.

"I'm fine, thanks. I'm still full from afternoon tea." My eyes glance around for a bathroom since I rushed out of the Ritz, not wanting to be late.

Fiona snorts. "Is that why you're dressed up? For *afternoon tea*. God, what tourists think of as British culture . . ."

"I have a question for Evie," Dev states as he leans in. I'm happy at least one of Aiden's friends seems to want to get to know me. "Is it true that you randomly ran into Aiden at Battersea and then near the Shard? What are the chances?"

I steal a glance at Aiden but have to immediately look away. He has this intense way of looking at people, and I can already sense my cheeks becoming warm.

Dev continues, "And you've heard the songs he's written?"

Whoa. Wait. What?

"You *wrote* those songs?" I ask, even though he said he hadn't when we were at Borough Market. At least I thought he did.

Aiden stares down at his coffee mug. "Guilty."

Dev looks between us. "You didn't realize those were Aiden's songs?"

"No."

See, I *knew* there was something Aiden was hiding. That anguish in his voice and face when he sang about heartbreak was too real.

And he lied to my face. Or at least he withheld information. I can't help but feel a bit betrayed over this tiny omission.

"I'm jealous; he doesn't let us hear him," Dev says.

"Yeah, he's super private about it with us, his *real* friends," Fiona says with a hint of bitterness and whole lot of pointing out that I shouldn't consider Aiden my friend.

"Oh." I realize I'm now only speaking in monosyllables, which is very unlike me.

"Yeah." Dev nods. "But the fact that you saw him in two random places, it's kind of like . . . fate."

Fate.

Yeah, maybe it was fate.

"I'm dealing with a breakup of the boyfriend and best friend variety, and hearing Aiden's songs made me feel a little less alone," I confess, while giving Aiden a grateful smile.

"That's nice," Dev says, before he shoots Fiona a look. She returns it with another look I can't quite place. I'm not sure what it all means, but there's some sort of unspoken conversation between the two. Dev's phone beeps and he picks it up excitedly. "New posting!"

Aiden and Fiona groan loudly.

"What?" I look around, trying to get in on the inside joke.

"Becs." Dev's entire face is glowing. "The most beautiful girl in the entire world."

Fiona pretends to gag. "You have the absolute worst taste."

Dev gestures at his friends. "That's rather obvious with you lot, innit?"

Dev holds out his phone and I see the profile of a pretty white girl with long black hair. By scrolling through the many, *many* pictures she's posted, I can see she's a fan of the selfie. There are thousands of them. With different filters and always perfect makeup. Her head is cocked just so or she's playing with her hair.

"Play the video," Dev instructs me.

I hit the icon and her face fills the screen. "I'm bored. Should I do a Q and A? Like, what do you all want to know? Ask me anything."

"Is she famous?" I ask, to which Aiden laughs while Fiona slams her head against the table. "What? Who are these people she's talking to?"

"Becs has delusions of grandeur," Fiona replies, her head still glued to the table. "She's one of those people convinced that social media will make her a star. Or at least get her a bit role on *Made in Chelsea* or as a future *Love Island* contestant."

"Stop it! How dare you say that about my future wife," Dev scolds Fiona as he takes his phone back from me. "She's extraordinary."

Fiona lifts her head from the table. There's a red mark on her forehead. She rolls her eyes dramatically. "Becs has spoken to you once and you're convinced it's love." She holds up her index finger. "Once, Dev."

"And it was magical," Dev replies with a look of pure bliss on his face.

Fiona recoils in disgust and then turns her glare to me. "You alright?"

"Sorry?"

"Your leg is shaking the entire table."

I look down and, sure enough, my leg is going a mile a minute. "Oh yeah, I kind of need the loo."

"The *loo*?" Fiona rolls her eyes again—it's a gesture I think I'll be seeing a lot from her. "The *toilet* is to the right of the counter."

I excuse myself and feel foolish. I always liked the British nickname for the bathroom. No one here calls it a restroom, it's usually toilet, but I've liked saying "the loo" since I was a little girl. I thought it was a hilarious nickname. Still do.

When I get back from *the loo*, Aiden's head is in his hands, while Fiona and Dev are in a standoff.

"Ah, what's going on?" I ask to slice through the tension.

Dev turns his screen to me. It's Becs. "Hey guys, so what should I wear to Gavin's party tonight?"

"No," Fiona says with a frown.

"Yes," Dev replies.

"No, no, no."

"Oh, yes, yes, yes."

I look at Aiden to explain, but he simply holds out his hands like he's at a loss for words.

"Hey, Evie," Dev says to me with his eyes sparkling. "Want to crash a party?"

11

If it wasn't obvious, I am in need of some serious assistance.

So I called in the big guns—aka someone who probably goes to parties and makes good first impressions.

After all, she's won me over.

"Oh, I think this would look lovely on you," Poppy says, holding up a black ruched top. "The neckline gives a wee hint but doesn't give the whole store away, if you know what I mean."

I guess Poppy's one of those people who doesn't take their own advice, as I've been trying to keep my eyes glued to her face instead of the ample amount of cleavage she's currently advertising. Or maybe she and I have a different definition of the word *wee*.

"Try it on. I insist!" She pushes me into the bathroom. "This is so much fun!"

I'll admit it—and not even begrudgingly—it *is* kind of fun.

Never would I have imagined that I'd call one of Dad's girlfriends for assistance. But when I asked Poppy if she could help me figure out what to wear to tonight's party, she came over straightaway. I'm not sure whether this is proof of how desperate I've become, or if it could be that I maybe, possibly, want to be friends with Poppy.

Yes, she's everything I can't stand about Dad's girlfriends. But when I really think about it, I can't blame these girls. They get sucked in by Nigel Taylor's charm and bank account. It's more of a reflection on my dad than them.

I throw Poppy's black shirt on and am surprised it fits. Sort of. I tug on the tight material near my stomach. I'm not used to fitted things around my stomach and hips.

"Let me see!" Poppy knocks on the door.

As soon as I open up, she does her excited clap. "It looks amazing on you. I have a necklace that would go perfectly." She begins to dig through the huge duffel bag she brought. She unearths a long dangling silver necklace and puts it around my neck.

"Thanks so much," I say as I examine myself in the mirror. "I really appreciate it."

"Are you kidding? I was so excited to hear from you. I adored our afternoon together." Poppy takes a step back to examine me in her top and necklace, with my dark skinny jeans. "You look fabulous. I need to do one more thing. May I?" She points to my top.

"Ah, sure."

Then Poppy gently guides my back so I'm bent over and reaches into my bra and lifts each one of my boobs, and wedges the underwire underneath. She adjusts the straps so they're a little bit tighter. "There we go!"

Uh, did you just go to second base with your dad's girlfriend?

I sure did.

While I am a little stunned, I have to admit the shirt does fit better.

"Now to my favorite: hair and makeup!" Poppy gestures at an entire Sephora's worth of makeup and hair products she has laid out on the counter.

As she starts putting lotion on my face, I think about how Dad would love this. I'm being molded into the kind of women he finds appropriate . . . as long as I don't open my mouth.

Poppy's phone chirps. "Aw, your dad canceled on me for tonight. He has to work late."

"Sorry, he has a tendency to do that."

See: afternoon tea.

Or the months he spent telling Mom and me that he had a late-night meeting, when it was something else entirely.

"That's okay. I get that he's busy." She shrugs like she's not that disappointed. "Now I can look forward to an evening in. Put on some joggers, watch telly, get in a good night's sleep. I have a class tomorrow morning at six."

I groan. That sounds awful.

She laughs at my response. "It's brilliant. I put on bangin' music and get paid to work out."

Point taken, but still. Six in the morning. On a Saturday? No way.

We hear Dad come in. "Evie?" he calls out.

Huh. I thought he had to work late. Wouldn't be the first time Dad lied to a woman, nor the last.

Or maybe, just maybe, he wants to check on me. Maybe see if I want to do something. I've hardly seen him since I've arrived. He usually doesn't make much of an effort when I'm here, but then again, neither do I.

"In here!" I reply.

"Listen, I've got a date, but I'm just here to change—" he begins, but he stops as he sees Poppy in the bathroom with me, curling my hair.

I don't know what disappoints me more: that he lied to Poppy or that he didn't care whether his daughter had any plans.

"Oh, hello! Look at the two of you!" He tries to play that he's thrilled seeing his daughter and girlfriend get along, but I notice his back tense. He's never been in this position before. I normally don't give any of them a chance. I maybe meet them once and then Dad moves on to another target. He clears his throat. "Yes, I have a work date on my schedule that I forgot about."

And the BAFTA for worst acting and cover-up goes to Nigel Taylor!

"Hello, Poppy, my darling." Dad gives her a kiss on the cheek, and a not-even-subtle grab of her ass.

My dad is the absolute worst.

To her credit, Poppy doesn't seem bothered by Dad's . . . dad-ish ways. She gives him a playful swat on his arm as she continues to work on my hair.

"Anyways, yes, I'm just changing before I head out to a work appointment," he says, though he won't make eye contact with either of us.

Sure, sure. Dad's wearing one of his bespoke suits—how would that not be appropriate for this mysterious Friday night work meeting?

"Aren't you going to compliment your stunning daughter, Nigel?" Poppy gives me a little wink.

While I know she means well, I instantly tense up as he studies me.

"Yes. You look lovely, Evie." And I hate the brief flinch of pride I feel upon his compliment. His face softens just a bit. "I'm sorry I've been so busy at work. Maybe we can make some time this weekend?"

I put my defenses back up and shrug in response. I don't want to get my hopes up just to have him cancel on me because something better comes up.

See: him right now.

"So!" he says brightly, probably trying to get the attention off his poor excuse. "Where are you off to?"

"A party," I reply in a robotic voice.

"With Poppy?"

"No," I say evenly as Poppy mimes zipping up her lips. I know my secret is safe with her.

"Then with whom exactly?" Dad presses. "You've always been such a friendly girl, so no surprise that you've already made some friends."

I weigh how much to tell him. I know how the truth will sound. *Yeah, I met this random dude busking so I'm going to a stranger's house with him and his friends. He said he drives an unmarked van, is that weird? Should I have not given him my Social Security number? He said he'd make me a star!*

Okay, so maybe the part that's actually true isn't *that* bad, but I don't want to give him a reason to say no. So I'll do what Dad does best: lie. "I met these other teens in the complex. They invited me over to one of their flats to hang. They're nice. We were leaving the gym at the same time."

That last part might have been a stretch, but it worked.

Now I just need Poppy to not let on that it's utter crap.

Dad's phone pings and he looks down to check it. He grins at the message, but then puts the phone in his pocket. He glances down at the floor.

"Well, that sounds lovely," he says with a nod. "I'm glad you're meeting the right kind of people." By that he means people with money. He reaches into his back pocket and takes out his wallet. "Pick up something to bring, on your dad." He holds out a fifty-pound note.

"I'm good," I state. He knows I'd never take money from him. It's all a show for Poppy.

"Well, okay." He gives me one more glance. "You know, Evie, you're really turning into an incredible woman."

I almost don't know what to say. He's never said anything like that. He's usually avoiding me. We both are.

He continues, "It's nice that you're finally putting some effort into your appearance. You'd be gorgeous if you worked at it more."

And just like that, I hate him even more. I look in the mirror and see me, but a heightened version. Poppy has used highlighter to bring out my cheekbones, and my eyes are smoky.

I want to wipe it all off now.

Leave it to him to turn my pre-party into a depressing spiral of daddy issues.

"Okay, then." He grimaces. "Well, I'm off. See you in class, Poppy."

Dad goes in to kiss her and I see Poppy turn her face so his kiss lands on her cheek instead of her lips. Maybe I'm not the only one in this bathroom who can see through Nigel Taylor's lies.

After he leaves, Poppy gives me a smile. "You know, makeup is fun and all, but it's the inner beauty that always shines through, and that, my dear Evie, is what you have in spades. Glitter's got nothing on you."

I want to give her a hug. I also want to tell Poppy that I've seen this before. Dad canceling at the last minute. Him having mysterious late-night plans. It means he's moving on.

I want to scream at her that she can do so much better.

But instead I stay quiet. I don't want to get into any of that. I don't want to watch Dad leave another person's happiness in ruins.

I don't want any of it.

Poor Poppy.

12

There are plenty of differences between London and Winnetka, besides the whole monarchy thing. Parties in both places have loud music blaring, people packed into rooms, a couple or two making out on couches or pressed tightly to each other against a wall. The difference is that parties in London have an insane amount of alcohol. Most people are entering the cramped flat with cans of beer or bottles, since the majority of people here are probably of legal drinking age.

While I brought crisps.

You can take the girl out of Illinois . . .

But no. London Evie dresses up to go to parties. London Evie is going to make new friends and keep her mouth shut and be a new, better version of herself.

"This is bangin', yeah?" Dev shouts over the loud music.

The four of us—Dev, Aiden, Fiona, and I—try to make our way inside the flat, but there's a jam at the front door.

"You good?" Aiden asks as he's pressed against me.

I simply nod in reply.

So, yeah, I may still be a little hurt that Aiden lied to me about the songs he writes. Add that on top of Dad's continuing lies, and I feel a bit bruised. This is exactly why I need to be at this party. Widen my London circle. Maybe see if Fiona wants to hang.

"What's everybody up to this weekend?" I call out as we're stuck waiting for people to exit the front room.

"Studying and working," Fiona replies, looking anywhere but at me.

"Same." Dev scans the party with a hopeful expression on his face.

"Oh." I don't try to hide my disappointment. "Where do you work?"

"Sainsbury's," Fiona answers with a scowl. I decide not to share that I like to go to the Sainsbury's near Dad's to get lunch. They have a special where I can get a sandwich, crisps, and beverage and not break the bank. I need to set a budget so I don't go broke before I leave—whenever that may be.

"I tutor," Dev replies. He turns to Aiden. "You have your thing, right?"

"Yeah," Aiden says as he shoves his hands in his jeans pockets.

"What thing?" I ask.

"Oh, I do this concert thing."

"Different from busking?"

He shakes his head. "It's this thing I do."

Wow. Oh, wow. Slow down with all that information you're throwing at us, Aiden.

Aiden remains silent and nobody else fills me in, so I guess that's the end of that.

The mystery of Aiden continues to grow.

Not that I'm interested in solving it. Light and breezy, London Evie–style.

"You going to be okay tonight, mate?" Dev asks Aiden.

"Yeah." Aiden nods, while Dev and Fiona exchange a pointed look at each other. "Seriously, I'm just going to have water, I'll be fine." Aiden then looks down at his right hand and flexes it for a moment.

Ah, okay? I'm not going to pry. I don't need to know every single thing about Aiden. Although, that is weird.

We finally make it to the living room, where there's a group of people swaying along to the loud music.

"There she is!" Dev points to a girl who I recognize as Becs. Upon seeing Becs, Fiona lets out a groan and walks away from the group. "Becs!" Dev calls out to her, but she ignores him. "I got some pressies for you!"

With that, Dev disappears into the crowd.

Leaving Aiden and me alone.

"You look really nice." Aiden plays with the scarf that's still wrapped around his neck.

"Thanks." I wave his compliment away like Poppy didn't spend an hour on me. It annoys me how much I enjoyed his double take when we met outside the tube station a few minutes ago. "So were Fiona and Becs friends at some point?" I ask, trying to not only get the attention off me but to make some sense of the tension between Fiona and Becs.

"Yeah. They were quite close in school ages ago, but then they grew apart. Fiona hates talking about Becs, so Dev's new crush has been rather inconvenient, to say the least. Luckily, Dev's crushes come and go, so I think we're waiting him out. It's honestly best to not get caught up in it all."

"Noted," I reply, knowing all too well how much drama a relationship can stir among friends.

"Do you want to get something to—" Aiden starts, but then a rush of people come through the door, causing me to lose my footing and basically land on Aiden. I'm smushed up against his chest. It's like a hug without the arms.

And I hate how much I like it. The feeling of being close to someone.

I push myself off a stunned Aiden. "Sorry about that."

Aiden only nods, a flush creeping on his cheeks.

"I'm going to go get a drink." And away from whatever this feeling is that's starting to gnaw at me.

As Aiden said, it's best to not get caught up. I don't turn around as Aiden calls after me, instead I just push my way through the kitchen until I find a bottle of cider.

"Cheers!" I say to a girl who is next to me before she wanders back to her friends.

As I look around, it pains me how much I want to fit in. To be like everybody else here. Surrounded by friends. Having fun.

There's a group of girls next to me in a heated conversation about people I don't know. Then I glance to see Aiden near the door, studying me. As we catch eyes, he raises a bottle of water, while I look away.

Before I can talk myself out of it, I insert myself into the group.

"Hiya!" I say a little too brightly. A little too loudly. A little too Evie. "I'm Evie," I continue, as the four girls just look around to see if anybody knows me. "So do you all go to school together?"

They reply by staring. So I do what I do, not necessarily best, but what I do.

"As you can tell by my accent, I'm not from around here. In London for the summer, so this is my first proper London party and wow, you all know how to do it up. You have to be twenty-one to drink in the States. I'm from the US, obviously. I know sometimes people can't tell if I'm Canadian or American, but I have to say, it's usually best to just assume a person is Canadian since they seem to get insulted by people thinking they're American. I actually don't mind—believe me, there are times I wish I wasn't American, like when we do school shooting drills, but my dad is British so I guess I'm technically half-British and half-American. Is there a word for that?" They're all just staring at me, which makes me keep going. "I mean, what isn't there a word for?"

Shut up, shut up, shut up.

"Maybe Brit-can? Or no! Amer-ish?"

"How about annoying?" one of the girls says, to the laughter of her friends.

Can't say I blame them.

"Oh, um . . ." I feel that familiar sting of rejection. But this is different, these are strangers. It should be easier to accept than people who know me, but still. "Sorry."

I turn my back and bristle when I hear their cackles of laughter.

Honestly, what did you expect?

I get out of the kitchen to see Aiden leaning against a wall, by himself. My heart flips at seeing him. Someone familiar-ish. Someone I could talk to.

But no. I can find someone else. I can make friends. I'm not *that* big of a disaster.

If you say so. The evidence, however . . .

"Hi!" I blurt to a guy walking by while carrying three cups. "Need help?"

He doesn't even acknowledge me.

I turn around and bump right into Aiden.

"Hey," he says with a small smile. "You alright?"

"Yeah, sure, um . . ." I look around the party, hoping to find Dev or even Fiona.

Aiden places a hesitant hand on my shoulder. "So, I reckon I owe you an apology."

"What?" I say in surprise. "Oh, right, right. For the fact that you lied to my face."

Aiden cringes. "Yeah. However, in my defense, I never said I *didn't* write those songs. I just kind of . . . changed the subject."

I let out a laugh. "Are you trying to get out of this on a technicality?"

"I don't know. Is it working?" He nudges me, and I can't help but crack a smile. Talking to Aiden is easy. I don't know why I'm ignoring him.

You know why.

Aiden invited me here. He introduced me to his friends. And what do I do? The mature thing of pretending like he doesn't exist and making a fool out of myself.

London Evie is kind of an idiot.

"I just don't understand why you wouldn't tell me the truth," I admit. "I've been basically vomiting out every messy thing about me, so I'm not one to judge."

"You're right."

"I mean obviously. That's something you should get used to."

"Noted." He gives me a smile, then looks down at my nearly empty cider. "Want another one?"

I look back at the kitchen. "Um, probably not. Mostly because I don't want to go back in there. I perhaps maybe made a scene."

Aiden laughs. "Oh really? I'm gutted I missed it."

"Stick with me, kid, it's bound to happen again."

"Can't wait."

London Evie also never learns her lessons.

Nope, starting now I'm going to not insert myself into situations. I'll be prim and proper like a duchess in the 1800s. Drink with my pinky finger out and everything. Classy and dignified all the way.

"So why are you only drinking water?" I ask Aiden.

He looks down at his right hand again. "Oh, well, if you can believe it, I once made a bit of a scene at a party myself."

"Oh, spill! I want details!"

(I swear I'll be classy after this.)

Aiden grimaces. "Um, yeah, I got a bit drunk and . . . I punched a wall."

"You did what?" My mouth is open. Aiden seems pretty chill, but then again, what do I know? About anything, apparently.

"Not my proudest moment. I couldn't play the guitar for weeks." He looks down at the floor, and there's this flash of sadness in his eyes that stops me from prying.

See, I can learn! Even though I so want to know what on earth happened to make Aiden punch a wall.

"Well, as you know, I have a lot of experience with proud moments," I start, to get the attention off whatever is causing Aiden's face to darken.

Luckily, Fiona rushes over. "We got a problem. Dev's had two pints." She rolls her eyes.

"Yikes," Aiden replies with a grimace. He turns to me and that darkness is somewhat gone. "Dev's a bit of a lightweight."

We follow Fiona to the living room, where we find Dev sitting cross-legged on the floor, staring up at Becs, who is oblivious to his existence. He looks love drunk—and also regular drunk.

"I'll try to persuade him to leave." Aiden walks toward Dev and sits down next to him. He puts his arm around a swaying Dev.

I look at my watch. We've been here for barely an hour.

Lightweight, indeed.

"Listen." Fiona moves so she's standing right in front of me. Even though I'm several inches taller than her, she's intimidating. "You're a nice distraction for Aiden, but don't you dare screw him over."

"I would never," I protest. "It's not like that between us. He knows that. We're just friends."

Fiona continues to stare me down.

"Fiona, when I first met Aiden, I made it pretty clear that I'm not looking for a relationship. Like, I seriously went on and on *and on* about how I'm done with dating and how men are evil. My last relationship was an epic disaster. Friends. That's it."

"And don't you dare bring her up. Aiden's been through enough, he doesn't need to relive all that with you."

So there *is* an ex. It makes sense with the songs he's written.

Oh wow, I wonder if he punched a wall because he was angry about *her*.

"I won't," I promise, since I don't even know what I'm not supposed to bring up, since he's said zero about *her*, since not everyone has to share every single thought in their head. Although in Fiona's defense, I'd like to think if I met a new person, someone would tell them not to bring up Sean. Or Meredith. Or my dad.

Wow, I come with some serious emotional baggage.

Fiona doesn't look convinced, but she stops scowling at me to direct her attention back to Dev. Aiden is helping him off the floor. As they get their footing, three guys walk into the room who look identical: rugby shirts, short crew cuts, the feeling of entitlement. One of them hits the other two and points at Dev.

"Oh, look, it's curry boy!" They all laugh and high-five.

"Thank you, come again," another says in the same voice as Apu from *The Simpsons*.

Fiona grunts as she goes over and gets Dev from the other side.

"And it's the lezo to the rescue."

"Shove it!" Fiona spits at them.

"Just tell me which hole, sweetheart," one of the guys replies as he grabs himself.

A fury starts to boil in my stomach. It seems bullies are the same here as they are in the US.

"Come on, Evie, let's go," Aiden calls to me as he and Fiona start to exit.

I go to follow them out, but one of the bros stands in my way. "And who do we have here?" he looks me up and down, just like Dad does when he sees a potential new girlfriend.

Another guy comes over and starts circling me like I'm prey. "Oh yeah. Fresh meat."

I know guys like this. The ones who feel big by trying to make someone else feel small. He wants me to cower. He wants me to give in.

But no, I'm not going to insert myself into something Dev and Fiona might want me to leave well enough alone.

I try to walk around him, but he steps in my way. I go to the other side and he follows. The other two start laughing.

"Excuse me," I say quietly as I try to leave the room, but they've got me blocked.

My adrenaline starts to kick in. Being surrounded by these pricks.

Aiden looks over his shoulder and sees me trapped. His face gets angry, his jaw clenches, his fists ball up tightly.

The Aiden I know—for all of two days—seems very chill, but I could see *this* version of Aiden punching something. I do not want to be the cause of another scene.

"Just let me go," I hiss under my breath, hoping this random jerk will show me some mercy. Instead, he just keeps getting in my way.

The other two goons laugh. Aiden takes a step forward, but I shake my head. I can get out of this.

I will not cause a scene. I will not cause a scene.

Well, no more than you already have.

"Yeah, you'll do," the one guy says.

"Lowering our standards, are we?" another one replies.

That does it.

I'm just so sick of it all.

Of feeling less than by my dad. Of feeling replaceable by my ex-boyfriend. Of not being heard by my mother.

But right in this moment, I've had it with dudes who think they can treat women however they want. That we're here solely for their amusement and then tossed aside when they get bored.

"I'll do for what, exactly?" I ask, as I look him dead in the eye.

"You're American?" Which causes the guy to leer even more.

"Congrats on identifying an accent," I say with a slow clap. "I believe you owe my friends an apology."

"An apology?" He laughs, like it's the funniest thing he's ever heard. As if the concept of performing an act of human decency is beyond his limited mental capacity.

"Yeah. *Sorry for being a racist and homophobe* would be a good start. Or are those words too big for your tiny mind? How about simply, *Sorry for being a colossal jerk*."

This causes the two other guys to laugh. I give a quick glance to Aiden, Fiona, and Dev, who thankfully aren't horrified by my behavior. They seem to be both shocked and proud.

"Should've known you'd be a big tease with an even bigger mouth." The guy scowls at me.

Aiden takes a step forward, but I shake my head. I've *so* got this.

"Oh well, when you put it that way, of course, I'd love to get to know you more. I clearly had you all wrong." I make sure to roll my eyes dramatically, as sarcasm may be lost on this loser. "But seriously? What exactly have I done for you to call me names? Is it simply that I'm not impressed by your Neanderthal ways? Because I'd really love to know exactly what you expect to happen here. That you bullying me would make me laugh along with your stupid comments? That I'll suddenly lower my expectations to rock bottom because you're *such a man*? That I'm going to suddenly be attracted to you? What exactly is your game plan here?"

The guy blinks in response.

"Yeah, you're not used to being talked back to, is that right? You can't fathom somebody standing up to you. Doesn't feel good, does it? To have someone in your face and make you confront the fact that you are a sad, little person who can feel good only by being an absolute jerk."

His face begins to get red, his breathing shallow. This guy towers over me, and if he decides to get violent, it won't be good. But I notice that look of uncertainty in his eyes. At the end of the day, nobody wants to be called out and taunted, especially in front of their friends.

"I'm so glad we got rid of America," he finally says.

His friends cheer in response, but really? *That's* the best burn that he could come up with. Never mind that he's wrong. It was America who left Great Britain. It was a little something called the American Revolution—Fourth of July and all that. But I'm sure something as inconsequential as facts wouldn't mean anything to this ignorant dude.

"Well, I guess we have that in common." I pat him on the shoulder as I take the beer out of his hand. "To independence!" I shout as I pour the beer over his head. He stands there in shock as the foam runs down his shoulders, soaking his shirt.

"Let's go," I say with a flip of my hair as we walk out of the party, which is now as quiet as can be.

Nobody says a word until we get outside.

"I'm really sorry if—" I begin to apologize, hoping I didn't overstep my boundaries.

Fiona cuts me off. "Oh my God! Why are you apologizing? I'm just gutted I didn't think of that." Her mouth is open, her eyes wide. "Please tell me it felt great pouring a beer over that loser's head."

"It did," I confirm happily.

There's also a part of me that's starting to feel a little bit more like myself. Not sad or depressed, just me.

Maybe I shouldn't be hiding Real Evie so much. And hey, if that means bullies are going to get what's coming to them, well, bonus.

Fiona gives me a nod of respect. "Thanks."

"Anytime. Those guys were such idiots." Plus, British people can be too polite, so leave it to the American to be rude. Well, not all British people are polite, like those dudes. They are, unfortunately, universal.

Fiona's smiling at me and it's nice.

When I first boarded the plane, I assumed I'd have gotten so sick of my dad at this point that I'd already be in the countryside with my grandparents. That I might need to spend most of my time there.

Nothing about this summer has gone as planned.

First, I thought it would be like last summer. Working at the coffee shop and hanging with my friends and boyfriend.

Then I assumed I'd be spending it suffering with Dad.

But along came Aiden. Who is hiding some story. Who is hurting more than I am. He's helped me by bringing me into his life; I only hope I can be a small part of good in his.

And now . . . I don't know what to expect from this summer. I'm almost scared to admit it, but I'm excited to see where it could lead.

"That was amazing!" Dev stumbles toward me, his arm over Aiden's shoulder. "Aiden, Evie's absolutely brilliant, isn't she?"

I find myself holding my breath as I wait for Aiden's reply. The slow smile that starts to creep on Aiden's lips causes a flip in my belly.

"Yeah, she is."

Welp, this summer is definitely full of surprises.

13

After what was, by all accounts—save for one beer-drenched loser—a successful Friday night, Saturday was possibly the longest day of my life.

I'd left my bedroom that morning feeling like my big mouth had finally done me a favor, but then Dad had to burst my happiness bubble by side-eying my breakfast choices, so I spent the rest of the day with my bedroom door shut, avoiding him.

Because I wasn't miserable enough, I even went online and looked at all my former friends and ex having a great time without me. They were all smiles and selfies.

I'm so easily erased.

Needless to say, I was beyond grateful when Dev messaged me: "Since Aiden has the oldest phone imaginable, it is my great honour to let you know that he has requested your presence at High Street Kensington Station. Tomorrow midday."

Sunday couldn't get here fast enough, and me out of the flat.

When I walk out of the tube station, I see Aiden leaning against a wall. He's got a blanket under one arm and a backpack on instead of a guitar.

"Hey."

"Hey," he replies with a smile. "I thought we'd do a picnic in Holland Park. Sound good?" He pushes off the wall.

"Sounds great." I start to follow him down the busy high street. "Although you could've, you know, emailed. I believe you were bragging the other night that you had a computer with the internet at home and everything. So cutting edge!"

"I wouldn't call it bragging," he said with a shake of his head.

"Good, because it's nothing to be proud of."

Aiden glances at his ancient phone. "So, one minute."

"One minute what?"

He shoots me a crooked smile. "One minute before you started teasing me."

I stop dead in my tracks. "Excuse me? Whom exactly has been teasing whom?"

"I believe it's *who* is teasing *who*."

"Exactly!" I say as I point at him. I look at the other people walking around us, hoping someone will take my side. "I believe out of the two of us, I'm the one who has been teased relentlessly."

"*Relentlessly* is a pretty strong word."

"*Relentlessly*," I say, as I throw my head back in full dramatic effect. "You tease me—"

"I mean, you kind of tease yourself—"

"*And,*" I add as I swat his arm. "I'm just this sweet, innocent—"

"Don't forget quiet and demure."

"*Quiet* and *demure* young lady from the United States in a foreign land, and I'll have you know, *sir*—"

"Oh, we've become formal now, have we, *milady?*"

"Quite right, we haveth becometh formal, Sir Aiden."

"I like the sound of that." He gives himself a satisfied nod. "Sir Aiden Hutchison."

"Just let me finish my thought." I speed up even though I have no idea whether I'm walking in the right direction. I don't want Aiden to see the smile that I'm trying to hide, but he annoyingly keeps up with me. And now I can't even remember what point I was trying to make. "Oh right, you're the one that teases me while I'm just a—I'm just—"

"Sweet, innocent, quiet, demure," Aiden fills in for me.

"Yes, all of that. *All of it!*"

He pinches his lips together.

"What?"

"If you say so." Then he lets out a laugh. A very loud laugh. He doubles over.

"Bit much?" I fold my arms together, even though Aiden's laughter is the kind that can't help but make the other person laugh along.

"Oh, come on, you have to admit it's pretty funny," Aiden says between actual guffaws.

I bite the inside of my cheeks to stop me from smiling.

And fail miserably at it.

"Ah!" Aiden points at my face.

"Fine, ha-ha, I'm a loud, obnoxious American. But you, *sir*, are the one who is choosing to spend the afternoon with me."

"I never claimed to make good life choices." He gives me a wink before we continue to walk.

"You're hopeless."

"Utterly."

Even though *I* am starting to feel a bit hopeless around Aiden. I like our little banter. How much I was looking forward to this. How glad I am that it seems to be just the two of us.

But there's that part of me that knows he's hiding something. That his heart is even more shattered than mine.

Because of *her*.

I've never been so jealous of a person I know absolutely nothing about.

We turned into a park filled with green trees blocking the sun, which has been fighting against the gray London clouds.

"Whoa," I say when we get to this Japanese garden with colorful trees and a mini waterfall. It's like a little meditative haven in the middle of London.

"It's the Kyoto Garden. I take it you've never been?" Aiden says as he closes his eyes and takes a deep breath.

"No, I didn't know it was here."

London has so many parks I have yet to explore. I usually stick to the big ones: Hyde and Regent's.

We stop at the edge of the pond as we take in the tranquil setting. "This is my favorite spot." Aiden looks out at the waterfall cascading over rocks. "I don't know, there's something about it that calms me. Whenever I'm having a bad day or I feel overwhelmed, I come here. It's hard to describe, but it really reminds me of who I am. Or at least who I once was."

I nod along. I miss the girl I used to be. The one who believed, if only for a year, in love. That trusting someone wasn't going to rip me in two.

Yet here I am, starting to get those familiar chills around a guy who lives thousands of miles away from me.

"Well!" Aiden says suddenly, his voice back to its normal tone. "I'm hungry—shall we?"

We both sit down while he takes out some sandwiches from his backpack. He hands me a juice box. "Just thought we should be safe," he says with a wink as he opens up a bottle of water for him.

I groan. "You're never going to let me live that down."

He laughs. "Of course not."

Aiden holds out two sandwiches: egg mayonnaise and coronation chicken. I choose the egg mayonnaise and take a bite of the soft bread.

"And since I remember you once or perhaps a thousand times mentioning your love of crisps . . ." Aiden tips his backpack over and a dozen bags of different crisps come tumbling out.

"Did you bring any for yourself?" I ask as I start looking at all the different flavors. There are some classics like cheese and onion, as well as salt and vinegar, and then ones that they'd never have back home: prawn cocktail, crispy duck and hoisin, chili and chocolate, and onion bhaji.

"I'll be sure to keep my hands to myself." Aiden scoots back a few inches while I continue to paw through the crisps.

"What's the fun in that?"

What the what, Evie! What did you just say? What words just came out of your mouth?

"I mean—"

Yeah, what exactly did you mean? What is wrong with you?

The last one will probably be one of the great unanswered questions of our time.

Aiden cocks his eyebrow at me. "So it's the crisps that did it. Good to know."

"I mean, it should be pretty obvious that the way to my heart is through my stomach."

Just. Stop. Talking.

"So afternoon tea next time? All the scones you can want!"

Even though I love a scone, instead of blurting out even more nonsense that could be considered flirting, I look around the park while I eat my lunch. Part of me can't believe I've been in London for less than a week. So much has happened. When I really think about it, I don't mind my new reality. I'm in London for the summer. I've got new friends who take me to parties and parks, and let's not forget buy me a bunch of crisps. London Evie isn't that bad.

A kid goes running by us, screaming.

"He reminds me of Josh." I point to the boy who is going around and around a tree. "That kid runs and runs. And here's the thing, I can run fast—I should be able to take Josh on when he's running toward something he shouldn't—like, *I know it's a garbage truck, Joshy, but let's not run into traffic*—but wow, they shouldn't have age restrictions on the Olympics, because I'm pretty sure Josh could run a marathon in a half hour if he had enough sugar in him and there was a giant truck at the finish line."

Aiden laughs. "He sounds like a firecracker—like brother, like sister..."

"Josh wishes he was as frantic as me."

"I mean, who wouldn't?" Aiden gives me a little wink. "You must miss home."

The thing is, I'm not sure I miss *home*.

I miss Joshy. Yes, he's a lot, but he also has the best giggle and thinks I'm *hilarious*. He likes to snuggle when we watch cartoons. And he doesn't mind that when I make him mac and cheese I end up eating most of the box.

But *home* is a different story. I haven't had a real conversation with Mom since I arrived. Whenever I've reached out the last few days, it's never a good time to talk. Josh needs attention or she's late for something.

I can't help but feel like I'm an inconvenience to my own mother.

"I think the thing I miss the most is the way things used to be," I confess.

He nods. "Yeah, I get it. Although for me, I have trouble letting things go."

"Maybe I should introduce you to my dad. That is something he's an expert on," I reply bitterly. But then something hits me. "Oh my God! Aiden whatever your middle name is Hutchison, did you just open up to me? Share something about your life? Your feelings? It's about time!"

And that outburst makes Aiden close his mouth and shake his head.

"Sorry, sorry!" I quickly correct myself. "Once again, that mouth of mine. Which, as we've already established, is delightful, but honestly, I don't know when to stop."

"I think we also established that I'd rather you do all the talking." Aiden looks down at this hands, while I literally bite my tongue to stop from talking. "But yeah, I'm absolute rubbish at letting things go. I sometimes get really wound up and let it take over. I get so mad at the world sometimes, but then I try to convince myself that we have to go through difficult things so we can come out stronger on the other side, you know?"

"I guess," I start, but the thing is, I don't agree. "I personally don't feel any stronger. And this is embarrassing to admit—but I guess add it to the list at this point—I never wanted to be in a relationship. So now that I've had those feelings, I wish I never did."

Especially since those feelings are starting to surface again.

"I get it." Aiden gives me a shy smile, and even from that small gesture, my heart starts beating faster. "It's the best when you see someone for the first time and there's this spark. When a person comes into your life who you didn't know existed and then they're all you can think about." Aiden's gaze settles on me. "You wake up in the morning thinking about them and how you're going to be able to see them again. When you want to know every single detail of their life."

I'm struggling to breathe. I . . . want to know every single detail of Aiden's life.

You can't go through this again, Evie. Be smart. He's holding back for a reason.

I shake myself from my daze. "Yeah, well, if only those feelings went away once a knife has been shoved in your back."

"But you have to take chances," he presses. "Right?"

I force myself to look away from him. "Or you can play it safe and not get hurt." I groan. "God, I sound exactly like my father. Yesterday, between his judgmental gaze for eating cottage cheese—*cottage cheese!*—he was all, 'Don't get attached to people, like Poppy.' Finally, he has a girlfriend that I like, and he's going to dump her. *Her!* The jerk."

"Rough day?" Aiden asks, to which I reply by shoving more crisps in my mouth. "Do you want to talk about it?"

I stare at the sandwich in my hand. I eat more in London than when I'm home. I think it's my way of protesting everything my dad stands for.

But I don't think I can tell Aiden *everything* about my dad.

My friends only knew the basics: my parents got divorced and my father ended up moving back to London. The only time food issues came up was when Meredith once said she shouldn't have a second piece of pizza because she'd get fat. I had simply told her that I get uncomfortable when people talk about food in a negative way. The only detail I gave her was that there were issues when I was younger. Even that was too much.

Sometimes you bury something down so deep you can convince yourself it never happened.

"You know, I am completely capable of having a conversation without having to bring up my issues."

"Oh, I'm sure. Would you rather we talk about Niall Horan?"

"Can we?" I fan myself with a bag of crisps.

"But I'd rather make sure you're okay."

"I am." Aren't I?

You're not.

"But you're thinking of something."

"God!" I cover my head. "Get out of my mind."

"Oh, I'm so in your mind right now and cannot believe you think that of me." He opens his mouth in mock horror. "Don't get me wrong, I'm flattered, even though I wrongly assumed you were a lady. Such language."

"Aiden!"

"It's *Sir* Aiden now."

"Sir Pain in My Bum."

"Oh, come on." He takes his foot and lightly taps it against mine.

His green eyes are blazing into me and I look away. For someone who wants to be seen, to matter, I certainly get uncomfortable when someone actually does it.

Luckily, I'm saved by the chirping of his ancient phone.

"It's Fiona," he says.

"Can you give me pointers with her? I'd like to be friends with Fiona and sometimes I get the feeling she doesn't like me." What with the eye rolls and glaring and the time she threatened me to not screw with Aiden. I may have slightly won her over with the bullies, but my mouth has a tendency to undo any positives.

"Fiona's just cautious when she meets people. She's been burned."

"Haven't we all."

"Yeah." Aiden plays with an empty crisp bag. "She's a little overprotective of me. I might not be as tough as her, but I'm getting by."

Getting by? Aiden writes these achingly brutal songs about not being able to live without someone. He's always wearing a scarf that at this point I suspect *she* gave him. He won't tell me a single thing about the relationship, so I can only assume it was bad.

If Aiden is "getting by," then I'm the healthiest, most well-adjusted person on earth.

And we all know what a load of crap that is.

14

This is it. I am going to die.

"Let's move it!" Poppy yells at the attendees of her Tuesday afternoon spin class.

Including me.

The impossible has happened.

This is what I get for being so bored while aimlessly walking around London yesterday that I texted Poppy to ask if she wanted to hang out. Even a spin class is a break from the monotony of hiding from Dad.

I turn up the resistance on the bike and I try to keep up with Poppy. Her skin is glowing, a maniacal focus in her eyes as her blond ponytail aggressively swishes to the beat of the loud music. Now I understand why they have a basket of earplugs by the slick registration desk. I'm going to lose my hearing from this class, along with the tiny bit of pride I have left.

I'm grateful the room is dark, illuminated only by the red neon lights around the walls and the monitors on each bike. Nobody can see how much sweat is currently running down my face. No matter how many times I wipe with the towel—which is now drenched—it doesn't help.

"Get ready to jump in three, two, LET'S GO!" Poppy says in her best cheerleader voice. I join the class in standing up and down at Poppy's command. "ARE YOU GOING TO TURN THE RESISTANCE UP—YES OR YES?" she barks.

Poppy may be petite and pretty, but whoa is she scary when you give her a microphone and put her in front of a class.

"Let's see how everybody is doing." She hits a button and the screens on either side of her light up. Everybody in class is ranked. I'm surprised I'm in the middle of the pack, number fifteen out of thirty-two. I scan to see where the woman next to me is. She was sure to give me a look of disgust when I climbed on the bike next to her. It seemed Ms. Lululemon was offended by my Champion by Target clothing and my lack of thigh gap.

She is only two spots above me.

Oh, she is so going down.

I put the resistance on higher and speed up.

"GO EVIE!" Poppy cheers me on as I move up one position on the leaderboard.

I ignore the cramp in my side as I go toe-to-toe with this woman. But also I can't believe people actually pay to be yelled at while we're all slowly dying of dehydration and fatigue.

"Last song!" Poppy says, and I feel grateful. I only have four minutes left. I pick it up and let the adrenaline take over as I push past Judgy McJudgerson, whose screen name is "Joe'sGirl" because heaven forbid this woman has an identity of her own.

She lets out an astonished gasp as my name goes above hers on the final results. While I may possibly vomit.

We finish class with a much-needed stretch and I wait while different students talk to Poppy. She knows most of them by name and gives them compliments. There are lots of hugs and selfies, and I wonder what it must be like to have that effect on people. To make people feel. It's like Aiden with his music. Although Aiden's is more of the aching-heart variety, while I'm pretty sure Poppy is just going to make my entire body ache.

"You did great!" Poppy comes over and gives me a hug, not flinching at my sweat-soaked body. "I'm so glad you came. Now, I promised it would be worth it. Let's shower, and I'll take you somewhere special."

She guides me to the posh ladies' room, with private showers and Molton Brown toiletries. I usually prefer my showers to be on the scalding side, but I turn on the cold water first to shock my system into cooling down.

It doesn't work. An hour after class, sweat is still beading down my back.

"I'm so glad you texted me," Poppy says as she links her arm with mine and we walk down Elizabeth Street in Belgravia. The street is lined with high-end stores, and Poppy blends in with her strapless pink gingham romper and wedge sandals. She's glowing while I'm a hot mess.

My hopes go up as I see us approaching a pink building on the corner with flowers bordering the entrance.

"Please tell me that's my reward," I say as I point to Peggy Porschen Cakes.

"You earned it."

Peggy Porschen is always on my list when I come visit. They have the best cupcakes in London.

I try not to groan from my protesting muscles as I sit down on one of the metal chairs at the only free table outside. We're surrounded by smartly dressed tourists, all taking pictures of their desserts.

Poppy takes a deep breath. "Ah, I love sitting outside. We're lucky to have such a nice day."

There's currently not a cloud in the sky. My overheated body wishes it were a tad cooler, but I've got my sweaty back to the window, so only the people inside can see how gross I am. *Bon appetit!*

"Are you getting tea?" Poppy asks as she scans the menu.

"I need something iced."

"Of course!" She reaches into her gym bag and hands me a big bottle of water. "Be sure to drink loads of water today. You got in a great workout. I hope you come again."

My only response is to laugh.

"Hey, it can be addicting," she says as she considers the various cupcakes. "Do you want to get a few and share?"

"That sounds great." As I study the menu, there are the classic cupcakes—vanilla sprinkles and chocolate heaven—but I also want to try strawberry and champagne, vanilla salted caramel, carrot and lemon. Basically everything. I want to eat everything.

A waiter dressed in a pink button-down shirt takes our order and then we lean back and watch all the people walking down Elizabeth Street.

"I want to hear all about your weekend!" Poppy exclaims before she takes a sip from her lemon-infused water bottle. "Your dad must be so chuffed to have you around."

Nothing could be further from the truth. Since Saturday, we've only run into each other once. He and I have exchanged a total of six words. I'm not exaggerating.

HIM: "Oh, you're here?"

ME: "Yep."

HIM: "Okay."

ME: "Okay."

That's it. Not like I'm complaining. We've both been avoiding each other. I hang around the flat in the morning, then leave early in the afternoon and don't come back until around ten, when I know he'll either be out or asleep because he has an ungodly six a.m. gym class.

"How are things with my dad?" I ask Poppy cautiously.

Her shoulders slump slightly. "I think we're on our last legs."

"I'm sorry," I say, although Poppy can do so much better.

"It's fine," she says with a smile. "Listen, I knew what I was getting myself into when he asked me out after one of my classes. I'm not the first person from the studio your father has dated. I'm sure

I won't be the last. The woman to your right in class, Fennel, dated him last year."

"I'm sorry, did you say that her name is Fennel?"

Poppy laughs. "I mean, he does have a type."

"Yet you agreed to date him!" I stick my tongue out. It's too much to think about my dad with any woman. I feel even prouder of myself for beating Fennel's score. I doubt her dirty look was because she knew who my dad was, but if it was, well, I wouldn't have blamed her. And I hope she's happy being "Joe's Girl." He's got to be better than Dad.

Our three cupcakes and slice of the Glorious Victoria cake arrive, along with Poppy's hot tea and my iced latte. We take a moment to soak in the beautiful sight before us and, of course, snap a few pictures.

"I make it a point to post my treats to remind my clients it's all about moderation," Poppy says before putting half a cupcake in her mouth.

Yeah, I really, *really* like this one.

"You're amazing, Poppy." I want her to know how much I appreciate her. "How did you get into spin? Do you see that as, like, a long-term thing?" God, I sound like an adult. That makes me think for a second. "How old are you?"

I brace myself as Poppy shakes her head. "I'm twenty-four."

"Dear God."

She raises her eyebrow. "Did you think I was older?"

"No! It's just my . . ." Ugh. I don't even want to go there.

"Well, to answer your questions, I studied as a dancer. At first, I did spin to supplement my income, but I really like to make working out fun."

I give her a look. "You and I have a different definition of the word *fun*."

"Evie!" Poppy playfully slaps my hand. "And, well, I'm saving up to become a certified nutritionist. But I want my focus to be on balance. Obviously." She takes a delighted bite of cake.

"You're my hero." And I'm not joking.

Poppy leans back in her chair and puts her hand on top of mine. "Listen, Evie, no matter what happens with your dad, I'm grateful I met you."

"Me, too." I think back to when I first met Poppy. I had my mind made up about her before we exchanged a single word. "I have to admit something: I just thought you were another one of dad's cookie-cutter girlfriends."

Poppy licks frosting from her finger. "As I said before, he does have a type."

We both laugh. "No, I'm really sorry. I'm just glad he bailed on afternoon tea so I got to know you. I'll still want to hang out with you, even if you're not with him. I mean, if I'm being honest, I'd want to hang out more if you weren't."

Poppy brushes her hands together. "I guess that settles it then, your dad and I are done and dusted." She gives me a wink as she pours herself another cup of tea.

"You don't have to—" I begin to protest.

"No, Evie. I know he's only waiting for the right time to end it. I'm fine."

I give her hand a squeeze. "Okay."

"And Evie, I hope you give people a chance and don't always assume the worst of girls like me. We're still human. Everybody has something they're fighting against—even your dad."

I feel a twinge of guilt. I was so dismissive of Fennel because of how she looked and her username—although she did glare at me first.

Everybody has something they're fighting against—even your dad echoes in my head.

If I really think about it, my father isn't a happy person. He may be hurting, but he's also hurt me. A lot.

"I know," I admit. "But it's hard. I've been hurt by so many people. The betrayal by my friends is still so fresh." I force myself to think about what they must be going through. "Although, I just went ahead and blocked them like they meant nothing to me." I told myself it was because I didn't want to hear from them, but there's also a part of me that worried they wouldn't even bother to reach out at all. This way I'm in control of—

Ugh. That's such a Dad thing: *control*.

"Listen, Evie, I know they hurt you, and it can be a difficult cycle to break. But someone has to be the bigger person," Poppy says with an encouraging smile.

"Easier said than done." I sigh, just like my father.

If I force myself to dig deep, I know I'll come to terms with how much I miss Lindsay. And even Theo. How I can't imagine going back home and not having them be part of my life. How much it would hurt to see them with Sean and Meredith. How they took their side.

But then again, I cut them off before I could hear them out.

There's self-preservation and there's being stubborn. Aiden isn't the only one who has trouble letting things go.

Maybe I need to forgive Lindsay and Theo before I punch a wall. Reaching out gives me a feeling of hope and dread. Hope of gaining some normalcy back. Dread that it might be too late.

"Maybe it's time to loosen your grip on what happened back home." Poppy pushes the remaining bit of cake toward me. "Or at least listen to your friends instead of blocking them out completely."

I know Poppy is right. That I need to do something about Lindsay and Theo.

Although I know what I need to do most of all is finally let go of all my anger at my dad—if not for him, for me.

But if I'm being honest, I think that's one thing I absolutely can't do.

15

Different country, same mistakes.

I'm starting to depend on someone. To trust again. And yeah, I'm becoming a bit desperate as I find myself waiting for Aiden to have time between school and studying to hang out. Like Poppy, he also calls me out when I try to deflect a difficult subject by doing a soliloquy like I'm a character in a Shakespeare play. It's really, *really* annoying.

I make my way through the small streets of Soho to a coffee shop the next afternoon. When I look at my watch, I realize I'm a few minutes late. That was never a big deal back home—time was more of a fluid concept for Meredith. But Aiden is always on time. I speed to the coffee shop and find myself confused when I scan the tiny place and don't see him.

I guess there's a first time for everything.

"Hey," a familiar voice says to me.

I turn around to see Fiona.

"Oh, hey!" I say and try to wipe the surprise of seeing her off my face.

"Yeah, so Aiden can't make it. Something's come up," Fiona states with a bored expression.

I try not to think about how much I really wanted to see Aiden. How much I was looking forward to spending more time with him. "Oh, is everything okay?"

"Yeah, just something he had to do."

"Okay."

We both stare at each other.

She sighs. "You should be grateful that Aiden's a good bloke, because he begged me to come here since Dev couldn't reach you on your phone."

I've spent the last couple of hours aimlessly walking around Mayfair, without connecting to Wi-Fi.

"That's really nice of you."

Fiona grimaces and holds out a ten-pound note. "He gave me this and said we should have a coffee on him."

"Oh."

There's silence between us. Did Aiden do this on purpose to get Fiona and me alone? I'm sort of hoping that's the case. Because it would really suck if the second I start showing trust in someone he bails.

Although that would be typical.

No, I am going to look at this as a good thing. I'm going to make Fiona my friend. Hm, that sounds like a threat, but I know I can win her over. As long as I maybe rein in my mouth and general Evie-ness.

"Well, let's spend his money, then!" I exclaim in an especially chipper voice that actually makes Fiona cringe. *Okay, take it down a notch.* "Shall we?"

I go up to the counter and order an iced tea, while Fiona gets an iced caramel macchiato.

"So how's school going?" I ask, but instantly regret it as Fiona recoils.

"It's going. Two weeks left." Fiona's attention goes to a table with three girls, around our age or a couple of years older.

"Oh! What's your type?" I study the curvy dark-skinned girl with the shaved head and floral maxi dress, the light-brown-skinned girl with dyed red hair wearing a halter top with a flowing skirt, and then the pale white girl dressed in all black, complete with black lipstick.

Fiona remains silent.

"You know, I'm an excellent wingwoman," I state with what I hope is a kind smile. "There is a benefit to being friends with someone with a very low threshold for embarrassment. I'll talk to anybody."

Fiona scowls at me for a moment, and I remind myself to take it down another notch. Or fourteen.

Then she tilts her chin to the table. "The bombshell in the halter."

"Oh, nice!" I nod approvingly.

We grab our drinks and I steer us to a table only two away from the group and position us so Fiona has a clear view of them, and they of her.

Fiona plays with her straw, her eyes down. She seems so unsure of herself. It's the opposite of her confident, borderline caustic attitude I've gotten accustomed to.

Not that I haven't also been a bit too judgmental about people, like Poppy.

"So! Do you want me to go up to them and be all, 'Oh hey, I'm American and settle a disagreement with my British friend' and make something up as an excuse to talk to them?" I suggest. The benefit of having my accent in London is that people often will just ask me where I'm from, which is an innocent enough question until I start going on and on *and on* because I'm me.

Fiona actually cracks a smile. "Please do not do any of that. I'm just going to enjoy the view for now."

"Okay, well, whatever you want." I rack my brain for something to talk to her about. I obviously want to ask her a million and one questions about Aiden, but I don't want her to think I'm going to "screw him over." "I'm taking a very long break from dating, myself," I remind her. "It probably doesn't help that I have major daddy issues, so my opinion of the male species has been dwindling for many years."

"That's pretty much my opinion on humanity in general."

I can't help but let out a little laugh. Perhaps Fiona and I have more in common than we realize.

Fiona continues, "Honestly, it's just that my bubble is too small here. I've gone to school with the same people for nearly my entire life. I want a change. I want to meet new people. Shake it up a bit, you know?"

I nod along. "I do. Being here and meeting you all has reminded me of how big the world is and how much more I want to explore."

"For me, it's the whole putting myself out there thing." Fiona leans back in her chair. "That's what I'm scared about the most. Not simply the rejection or being told that someone doesn't like me *in that way*. It's finding that person. Opening up to someone to simply have your heart stomped on. What's the point?"

I like that Fiona and I can bond over this. The uncertainty. How scary it is to make yourself available.

"Yeah, it can be a bit terrifying," I admit. *Although*, if I help Fiona meet that girl, she'd probably love me. And let's face it, if it wasn't for my dad, I'm fairly sure I would have a more positive outlook on love. "But you know, those butterflies were pretty great. And to have someone pick you because you're all they can think about. I know maybe getting rejected or cheated on—Oh my God!" My mind flashes to Sunday.

"What is it?" Fiona asks, her brow furrowed. She's leaning forward in her seat, actually interested in what I'm saying. She hasn't rolled her eyes once.

"It's something Aiden said to me."

"Ah, yes, he can be wise, that one. What'd he say?"

"Well, I disagreed with him at the time, but now I'm . . ." My mind is spinning. "He said we all have to go through things so we can come out stronger on the other side. So I'm thinking that maybe going through all the jerks and cheaters makes finding that one person all the more rewarding. Like the search itself, while scary, can also be exciting."

Wait just one second—am I trying to convince Fiona or myself? Nope, not going there. I am here to encourage Fiona. My new friend.

Fiona looks down at her cup and bites her bright red lip. "Can I tell you something?"

"Of course."

"You have to promise me that you won't tell Dev or Aiden."

"Yes, it'll live in the vault. I don't let secrets slip out," I assure her. Look at us! She's telling me a secret! I'm winning her over!

"It's about Becs." As her name comes out of Fiona's mouth, a tension crosses her face.

"Aiden mentioned you used to be friends."

Fiona lets out a tsk of disgust. "Yeah, since we were little. Being near her—during sleepovers, or when we'd fool around with me mum's makeup—made me realize that I had feelings for her that I hadn't ever had with a boy. She was who I thought of when we used to sing along to Shawn Mendes songs." She narrows her eyes at me. "I'll straight-up murder you if you tell anybody that."

"Um, hello, I'm a proud and true Directioner, but don't worry, my lips are sealed." I even mimic zipping up my lips and give her a wink.

Fiona sinks down in her seat. "I came out to Dev and Aiden, and they were super supportive. Then, one night, I was over at Becs's and we were lying on her bed. She brushed back my hair and told me how pretty I was. She asked me if I wanted to try something and leaned in and kissed me. I hate to admit how much it took my breath away, but it did. I was such a cliché."

Fiona pauses for a moment while I remain uncharacteristically silent. With how things are between Fiona and Becs now, I can only imagine what followed next was not good.

"So I told her." Fiona's voice breaks for a second. "I told her that I was a lesbian and that I liked her . . . and she laughed at me. Laughed right in my face. Told me that she was just fooling around and that it meant nothing." Her voice wobbles at the end.

I reach out and place my hand on Fiona's shoulder. "I'm so sorry. That's horrible."

She looks at me and something in her hardens. "Yeah, so then she went to school and told everybody, so I had no choice but to come out. I haven't talked to her since."

"I'm so sorry," I repeat. "That isn't fair, and it should be up to you when you come out."

Oh God, Dev and his fascination with Becs.

"How could Dev like her after all that?"

"He doesn't know it was Becs who outed me; it was all over school before lunch."

"I'm sure if you explained—"

"No!" Fiona protests. "I'm so horrified that I ever cared about her. All I want is for him to get over her and move on to a new crush. You can't tell him."

"I won't, I promise."

Fiona gives me a small smile. "Thanks, Evie."

"Anytime." I smile back at her.

Oh my goodness. I try to not jump up and do a little dance that I have won Fiona over. She has taken me into her confidence, and I'm not going to get carried away and say we'll have, like, sleepovers and braid each other's hair, but we're getting somewhere.

And I'll take it.

Fiona lets out a long breath. "Plus, I don't think Becs was playing. And since I'm not a selfish scrubber, I'm not going to force her to come out or confront the fact that her hands lingered longer than mine or that she's always very touchy with her girlfriends and hasn't had a boyfriend in ages. But I think what really gets me is that I thought she was my friend."

"Yeah, my best friend stabbed me in the back. In a very different way, but it still hurt. Being betrayed hurts. Putting yourself out there can be disastrous."

Fiona looks over at the table of girls. "I sometimes wonder if it's even worth it. I've seen what it's done to people I care about."

Fiona doesn't need to clarify who she's talking about. Since she doesn't want me bringing up *her* to Aiden, maybe she and I can talk about it. After all, we're friends now.

"Can I ask you a question about Aiden?" I ask.

Fiona nods.

"Okay, but first, know that I didn't open any wounds," I start, so she doesn't get mad at me. Two steps forward and all that. "But Aiden mentioned how hard it is to let go. And I just don't know. He's been so wonderful to me, and I want to do something to help him get over . . ."

I stop talking because the lightness in Fiona's face switches to a whole new level of annoyed and disgusted. "Are you talking about Ruby?"

So her name is Ruby.

"Um, yeah, I guess, I just thought—"

"You think *you* can do something to *get Aiden over Ruby*?" Her voice is raised and has now gotten the attention of everybody in the café, including the girls near us.

I know it's probably something Fiona and Dev have tried, so I don't want Fiona to think I could be a better friend, but I want to do something.

"I only want to help," I defend myself. I'm sure if I had any real friends left, they'd want me to heal as quickly as possible. "I've been through heartbreak recently—"

"Are you being serious right now?" Fiona looks at me with such disgust. "I knew I was right about you. Aiden should've stayed away. You're only trouble."

"Wait, *what*? I'm not—" My head is spinning wondering how quickly things have turned around. "Don't you want Aiden to be happy?"

"*Do I want Aiden to be happy?*" she repeats, her voice rising in pitch and volume. "I knew you were just some self-involved American tourist, using Aiden for entertainment and to think that you, you, can just . . ." Fiona lets out an actual huff. She gets up so quickly from her seat that it falls back, clanging in the café, which is silent save her outburst.

"Fiona, I'm not—"

"Save it. Who do you think you are?"

"I just . . ." Don't even know what to say anymore.

"Stay the hell away from Aiden." With that, Fiona walks out of the café without a glance back at me.

I'm absolutely stunned by her reply.

Who do I think I am? I clearly have no idea.

But I also know that there's absolutely no way I can stay away from Aiden.

16

What did I do? What did I say?

I mindlessly roam the streets of London. The only thing I know is that I messed up everything. I totally pulled an Evie.

How could wanting someone to get past a broken heart be a bad thing?

How could Fiona think I was using Aiden? That the best thing for him is for me to stay away?

I drag my feet down the hallway to Dad's flat. I open the door and freeze when I see him at the kitchen table.

"We need to have a talk," Dad says before I even have a chance to close the front door.

"Well, hello to you, too, Father. *And how was your day, Evie?*" I say in a low voice. "Just fantastic, thank you so much for asking."

He replies by motioning to the chair across from him.

So my day *can* get worse. Awesome.

I begrudgingly sit down and place my cellphone and shopping bag on the table, then fold my arms and wait for whatever it is he has in store for me.

It's far too quiet for a beat. I can't honestly remember the last time he and I were seated face-to-face. I place my hands on the table and try to settle my nerves.

"First, I want to inform you that Poppy and I are no longer seeing each other," he says without an ounce of emotion. This is the first time he's ever told me about a breakup. Usually there's a new model each time I visit.

"Okay," I reply evenly, trying to keep my emotions in check. Besides, it doesn't matter if Dad isn't seeing Poppy anymore. I plan on being friends with her. And after the disaster with Fiona, Poppy may be my only friend left in London. Or anywhere.

"Second, I have heard from the porter that you've been inquiring about babysitting opportunities." He continues his blank stare at me, like I'm a stranger. Honestly, this whole thing feels like a job interview.

"I want to earn some money," I state.

He rubs his temple. "How many times do I have to tell you that you don't need money? I'm more than happy to provide for you."

"I *want* a job."

"And I don't want my daughter working for my neighbors."

Of course, that's what it all boils down to: appearances.

He continues with a slight shake of his head, "You're entirely too stubborn, Evie. Enjoy your summer. I work hard for everything I have. You should benefit from it. I know it's far different from the life you're used to."

Oh no he did not.

"What does that mean?" I ask between clenched teeth, knowing that I'm going to lose the battle to keep my cool.

"Your clothes are old and clearly from some department store." His nose twitches.

"Target," I reply, but with the French accent: *Tar-jay*. "I like my clothes. I like working for money. I like our house. It's not posh, but it's home."

Even though being around Dad could never be considered a vacation by any stretch, coming to visit him does feel like it, in the sense that it's so different from my real life. We aren't poor back home, far from it. We have food on the table. We go out to meals or the movies. We have great Christmases. I splurge occasionally, like on the Homecoming dress I wore the other day. But the way Dad acts, I'm living in squalor.

Dad remains as aloof as ever. "I don't want you babysitting. If you need money, just ask me."

"I *want* to babysit." I feel like a broken record. Then again, Dad doesn't ever care about what *I* want. *He* wants me to be yet another thing he can control: what I do, how I dress, what I eat . . .

He ignores me and instead his attention is focused on the plastic Tesco's bag on the table. He sighs as he takes it and dumps out the contents: a ploughman's sandwich, a bag of sweet Thai chili crisps, and a Crunchie candy bar—otherwise known as my dinner. "Is this what you want to spend your money on? Listen, Evie, I grew up eating this junk food," he says as his cheeks start to redden. "And I've been working off the damage ever since. Sure, I suppose you're okay now"—*gee, thanks*—"but you need to be mindful of your weight. If you don't pay attention, it'll sneak up on you. You need to be careful about your health."

This right here is why it's so hard to try to have a real conversation with him about food.

"Can we please just cut the crap? This isn't about my health, it's about what I look like." I stand up and spin around. Sure, I'm not skinny like Poppy, but I'm rather healthy, despite my love of fried potato products. And yes, I do have a piece of fruit in the morning and usually an apple with my crisps and sandwich for lunch. "You don't need to remind me of the pressures to be thin—I'm a teenage girl, Dad. My mere existence means a lifetime of dealing with unrealistic body expectations. I get it enough from social media; I certainly don't need it from my own father."

Dad leans back in his chair, but I see a slight clench in his jaw. "Don't give me that."

"Give you what? I'm simply stating the truth. And let's continue with the truth theme, shall we?" At this, he shifts uncomfortably. I don't think Dad and I have had an honest conversation since he left. "So what? You're telling me that you'd love me if I was a size zero? You wouldn't have moved thousands of miles away if I was thinner—is that it?"

"Evie," he says in a stern tone. "That's enough. Sit down."

"Oh no, I'm just getting started." I feel it all start to release. Everything I've been pushing down for years is going to come out. I'm done hiding from my father. This is me. I am his daughter.

He's supposed to love all of me, including my curves and big mouth.

That big mouth can keep secrets, but there's one that maybe I should share with Dad. One that will maybe make him finally understand what his leaving did to me.

"Did you know that I didn't eat for three days after you left us? You saw food as the enemy, so I thought you left because Mom and I still ate. I really believed if I didn't need to eat, you'd want to be around me again. That I'd be good enough for you—that you'd come back." My voice cracks at the end.

He looks taken aback for a moment, before he shifts his bored gaze to the table.

"Of course you didn't. Why would you want to know anything about me or the consequences of your actions?"

Tears spring up. It took years of therapy to get my fear of food under control, to be able to start eating normally again. I still check in with Dr. Wallace whenever I feel issues arriving, and no surprise, it's usually after a visit with my dad. I hate that he still has that control over me.

While it took a long time and a lot of work, now I appreciate food, not just as fuel, but because it's delicious.

I like my strong, sturdy legs. They allow me to walk all around London. They carry me through races. Yes, there are days when I see cellulite creeping up on my upper thighs, but cellulite is a fact of life. Needing to eat is a fact of life. It's going to be a lifelong battle, but I'm currently winning it.

And I'm not going to let Dad pull me under with him.

"We know this isn't just about my weight. You want me to be dyed, tanned, and plucked so I can fit in with the perfect little life you've conjured for yourself. How's that life working out for you, Dad?" He remains silent, refusing to look at me. "Yeah, you're successful, but you're also lonely and sad."

He finally glances up at me, and there's a hardness in his expression. "Stop this right now, Evie. I can't talk to you when you're emotional." He swallows like I'm a bad taste in his mouth.

"God forbid you feel anything!" I yell. I want him to scream back. I want him to do something, anything that would prove he still cares about me. That the father that used to be my everything is still there.

He, in turn, remains as calm as ever. "Evie, watch your tone. I'm your father."

"Oh, so *now* you've decided to be a dad to me? You're gone for the important parts of my life, but now you want to be involved, especially when it comes to my diet? God, when was the last time you cared about anyone? When was the last time you bothered to know about anything in my life?" My voice is high; it's near hysterics. And I don't care. Maybe this will wake him up.

He replies calmly, as if we're talking about the weather instead of his neglect. "I asked you about what happened with your boyfriend the other day."

A bitter laugh escapes my throat. "Oh well, then that makes up for you abandoning me when I was little. I am so sorry," I say, dripping with sarcasm.

He finally stands up to face me. "Do you have any idea what it's been like for me with you here? How every time I see you, you have such a look of revulsion. Do you know how it feels to have your own child despise you?"

"I've got a feeling," I throw back at him. I know that look of disappointment from him all too well.

He sighs. "Then why are you still here?"

"Oh, I'm more than happy to go to my room. I'm sorry, the guest room."

"No." He takes a deep breath. "If you're so miserable with me, why are you still in London?"

I freeze. I wasn't expecting this. Is he going to kick me out of his flat? What will I do then?

A smile starts to spread on his face as he sits back down. He knows he's got me. I remember him bragging to me as a kid about how he'd sit calmly across the table during a negotiation. He wouldn't budge until he got everything he wanted. At the time I thought my dad was such a strong, important businessman.

Now I know that he's just a selfish jerk who won't back down until he gets what he wants. It doesn't matter what it is. He wants a win. That's all I am to him: another person to conquer.

I can't believe I thought for even a second that I would someday forgive him.

"Let me repeat myself: why are you still here?"

It's a standoff. If I get any more emotional, he wins. If I leave London, he'll have won. If I stay, he'll win. I don't want him to win. But I also don't care anymore.

"Hell if I know," I spit at him as I exit his flat and slam the door behind me.

I'm angry. I'm hurt. And I have absolutely no idea where to go.

17

If it wasn't painfully obvious, I have no clue what I'm doing.

And of course I left my phone behind in my rush out of the flat. The only items in my possession are my Oyster card and key to Dad's flat. Since there's no way I'm going back there, I do the only thing I can, which is ride the tube.

Even though Chicago has the "L" train, I prefer the London Underground. The trains are bright—white walls, yellow poles, and the seats are carpeted with reds, blues, and yellows. As a kid, I even had a poster of the colorful Underground map on my bedroom wall, along with pictures of Elizabeth Tower, Westminster Abbey, and Buckingham Palace.

I sit down and study the early evening crowd. Tourists with London guidebooks examining the map. Businesspeople carrying work bags. Small children with their parents.

Every person has a story. Every person has a family.

I wonder who else's is as broken as mine.

There are many things I've witnessed on the tube: couples making out, friends fighting, buskers singing, babies sleeping, and a few people crying. I do not want to be added to the latter group. I feel so hopeless. I bite my cheeks in an attempt to stop the tears that are fighting to come out.

The train leaves the station as the overhead speakers announce Gloucester Road as the next stop.

For the first time since Fiona's outburst, I feel a sense of hope. Aiden once mentioned that Gloucester Road is his stop. Maybe it's a sign.

Or maybe it's possible to make today even worse.

Suddenly I'm desperate to see Aiden. I don't care what Fiona thinks, I'm not going to stay away from him. Even though I have no idea what she's said to him or why she got so angry at me. All I do know is that I have to see Aiden.

With a new mission, I get off at the stop with a sense of purpose. The only thing in my way is the teeny, tiny fact that I actually don't know where Aiden lives. Just that this is his stop and he lives across from Cornwall Gardens. Without my phone, I'm stuck studying the map outside the tube station to figure out which direction to go.

As I start walking the few blocks to the garden square, I make a point to look at every person on the street, hoping Aiden's out for a walk. I figure I'm due for some luck.

I turn the corner onto Cornwall Gardens and see dozens upon dozens of white buildings lining the garden for two blocks. They all probably have several flats in each. I'm never going to find Aiden.

This was pointless.

I sit down on a stoop in defeat.

The options I'm faced with are all awful: go back to Dad's flat and deal with his smug face, wait here like a stalker, or—yep, that's it. I don't have any money on me. I don't have my phone. All I have is access to the London Underground system.

Not to mention that I have a bigger question I keep conveniently avoiding: do I stay in London, go to my grandparents', or go home?

I might not even have a choice. Dad could throw me out.

I wrap my arms around my legs and rest my head on my knees.

What a fine mess I've made of things.

"Are you lost, luv?"

I look up to see an elderly woman pushing a metal cart.

She has no idea how lost I really am.

I get up from the stoop and dust off my jeans. "Sort of. Do you by chance know the Hutchisons? I'm looking for Aiden, but can't remember which is his building." It's a long shot, but better than sitting here and fighting back tears.

"They live on the corner over there." She points to a building down the block.

"Oh, thanks!" I give her a warm smile, even though I don't feel like smiling. "Do you need help with your cart?" I offer.

"Thanks, deary, but I can manage just fine. You just put a smile on that boy's face." She pats my hand as she walks away.

As I head toward the white building on the corner, I realize how desperate I've become. I literally have nowhere else to go, so I really hope Fiona didn't tell Aiden some horrible story. I can't have him hate me, too. As I arrive at the front door, I scan the list of apartments. I buzz the ground floor, which says "Hutchison."

I hold my breath as I wait for a voice to come over the intercom. Instead, the front door opens and an older woman answers, "Yes, can I help you?"

Her graying hair is pulled up in a messy ponytail and she's wearing a robe. Even though I've never met her, she has the same bright green eyes as Aiden. It must be his mom.

"Oh yes. Sorry to bother you, ma'am, but I'm wondering if Aiden is home."

Her face softens. "Evie?"

It takes me a minute to realize I'm simply staring back at her in shock. She knows me? "Yes?" I answer like I'm unsure of who I am. Although that's not far from the truth at this current moment in time.

"I've been wanting to meet this American my son's been talking about."

Before I can reply, she's opened the front door wide for me to enter. She walks across the small hallway to the door to flat #1. "Please come in. Aiden's run out for a quick errand, but he'll be back soon."

I walk into Aiden's home. It's full of pictures and comfortable furniture and a disarray of knickknacks. It's the opposite of my dad's place.

"Welcome," she says to me as she gestures for me to sit. "Fancy a cup of tea?"

I nod, knowing I'm being unusually silent. But it's her simple gesture of welcoming me so warmly that's almost done me in. This is a home filled with a family.

I missed this more than I thought possible.

18

Aiden's home is quiet. The only sound is coming from the kitchen, where his mom has put the kettle on.

I study her as she sets out a porcelain tea set. It's after six o'clock in the evening, but she looks like she's just gotten up. She's drawn and tired. I don't know how old she is, but I gather that she's a lot younger than her haggard appearance suggests.

The wall opposite me is filled with pictures in mismatched frames. I get up from the couch and go to the left side, which starts with a much younger version of Mrs. Hutchison in a white wedding dress, holding hands with a tall man with Aiden's smile. As I go through the photos, it's like a timeline of the family.

There's a photo of Aiden's mom holding a newborn, a wide smile on her face. As I go through the photos, I see the same smiling Mrs. Hutchison in the pictures, always laughing and with her bouncing light blond hair and bright red lip. The woman I met just minutes ago is a muted version of the one in the photos in front of me.

As I continue to study the photos—Aiden holding up a tooth with a gap in his teeth, the family trio at the beach, Aiden in his school uniform, him wearing a Santa hat—I see him growing before my eyes. I pause at a photo where he must be six or seven, holding a tiny baby. He's looking down at her as the baby stares up at him in wonder. He's on the couch I was just sitting on.

"Here you go, Evie," Aiden's mom says as she comes into the living room and hands me a mug of tea.

"Thanks so much," I say as I blow on the tea for a moment before taking a sip.

She looks at the photos. "Ah, such fond memories." Her face darkens for a moment, then she gives me a pat on the back. "You've been such a lovely soul to brighten up Aiden's days. We could all use some light," Mrs. Hutchison says softly. Then she perks up. "Biscuits! Let me get you some biscuits! I've got the good kinds with chocolate!"

"That would be great, thanks."

She walks back into the kitchen as I look through the pictures. The baby that Aiden had been holding starts growing up. It's a girl. She's holding on to Aiden as she wobbles on her feet. She has a matching photo of the missing tooth. She's in the group shots.

I thought Aiden said he didn't have any siblings. Or at least I assumed he didn't. Could she be a cousin that he's close to? As I examine her closer, a knot forms in my stomach. She has Aiden's crooked smile and, as she gets older, that same unruly hair.

I stop on the last photo and can hardly breathe. Before I know what's happened, there's a crash as I let go of the mug.

Mrs. Hutchison runs in. "Oh, no worries! Don't move! Let me get a mop."

I can't speak. I can hardly stand. I look at the photo and feel my entire body shaking.

How could I be so naive? I go through everything Aiden has said to me—or hasn't said—about what he'd gone through. His heart was broken. Someone left him.

But as I look at the photo, it all starts collapsing around me. It's of the same little girl, wearing that scarf Aiden wears every day. But it's not around her neck. It's around her head. She's pale and in a hospital bed. There's a sign above her bed with her name spelled out in bright neon colors.

The Ruby whose departure devastated Aiden wasn't some girlfriend.

It was his little sister.

19

Oh my God. Oh my God. Oh my God.

My voice finally decides to work. "I'm so sorry, I'm so sorry," I repeat to Aiden's mom, who is bent down cleaning up the mess I made.

I kneel, my shaking hands fumbling with the broken porcelain. "I can do that. I'm so sorry," I continue.

"'Tis only a mug, luv," she replies as she picks up the shattered remains of the cup I was holding a moment ago.

I'm apologizing for so much more than that.

For not having any clue what was really going on in Aiden's life.

For coming here unannounced and making a mess.

For being so wrapped up in myself that I couldn't see past what I was going through.

The front door opens, and Aiden appears with a canvas shopping bag in his hand. "Mum, I'm—" He stops short when he sees me in his living room. With his mother. In front of pictures of his sister.

"Put the groceries on the counter and then come entertain your lovely friend," his mom says with a bright voice, but the joy doesn't reach her face.

Aiden's cheeks have lost their usual ruddy tone as he walks into the kitchen. He appears a few seconds later, rubbing his head and not making eye contact with me.

"I'm so sorry," I say, since it's all I can think of. "I—" I don't even know what to say except to apologize. I shouldn't be here.

"No worries at all, luv," his mom says. "I'm off to make dinner. Evie, would you like to stay?"

"Oh, I couldn't. I just came here to—" It doesn't really matter why I'm here. Honestly, all of the stuff I was worrying about has suddenly drifted away because this is so much bigger than that.

"We'll be in my room," Aiden announces as he motions his head for me to follow him down the hall.

My eyes can't help but land on every picture along the way that features Ruby. She's everywhere. Aiden opens the door to his bedroom. There's a twin bed with a blue plaid duvet cover, some laundry scattered on the floor, and his guitar lying on his bed. The walls are lined with sheet music and photos, but there are empty pockets where things have been taken down. The only clue of what was there are the blank spaces and remnants of tape.

"How did you—" Aiden starts, but before I can stop myself, I launch myself into Aiden and give him a tight hug.

"I'm so sorry," I say while I fight back tears.

For a moment, we both just stand there. Me with my arms around Aiden. It takes him a second to fold his arms around me.

For a beat, there's this little flutter in my stomach, but I push that down.

Simmer down, Evie, now is not the time.

Although I can't help but realize how right it feels being so close to him.

How just this one moment of being in his arms—albeit one that I sort of forced him into—made me realize how much I don't want to let go of Aiden.

Not just physically, but at all.

I finally break away and try to get myself together. "I didn't know, Aiden. And I'm such a fool and all I can say is that I'm sorry."

I take a step back and Aiden's gaze remains on the floor. He shifts his weight back and forth. The silence is too much. I know I should wait for him to talk, but there's one phrase that keeps circling in my head.

"Why didn't you tell me?" I ask softly.

He finally looks up, and the sadness in his eyes breaks me. "Because I wanted to avoid the look you're giving me right now."

I automatically put my hand up to my face. I have no idea what I look like, but if my face is properly displaying my emotions, I'm confused, sad, and yes, I feel so incredibly sorry for him.

I can't help but think of Josh. If anything ever happened to him . . . I feel an indescribable ache inside my chest. Joshy. My younger sibling. The baby I used to hold in my hands.

I fight back the tears that are starting to come out. This isn't about me or Josh. This is about Aiden.

"Do you know why I went to coffee with you that day at Borough Market?" Aiden asks.

I shake my head.

"I wanted to have a conversation that didn't revolve around something so achingly painful for me. You were just chatting away and looking at me without pity. I could just be a guy having a coffee with a girl. To try and find some normalcy after I had the utter crap kicked out of me. And I hate myself for wanting to get past it, but I know that's what Ruby would want. I've been drowning in misery for so long, it's like you threw me a life raft."

This time I nod because I get it. I've felt like I'm drowning, but my God, the perspective I have now is just . . . too much to think about.

I sit down on his bed. "I'm so sorry."

"Please stop apologizing. I'm so tired of people apologizing."

"Sor—" I stop myself. It's my turn now to look down at the floor.

A miracle has happened: I've finally run out of things to say.

Aiden sits next to me. "I reckon you have some questions."

I'd been asking him questions since we met and not getting any answers. Now I know why. I guess he's ready to finally open up. Well, not like he has a choice, since I barged into his house and burst open the secret he was trying to keep from me so I wouldn't do . . . exactly what I'm doing right at this very moment.

"You don't have to talk about it."

"It was leukemia." His voice breaks at the end, and a little part of me shatters with him.

Oh God. I have no clue what to say to him. Not like there are any words that could erase the pain he's feeling. I reach out and hold his hand. I stare at our entwined fingers and give him a little squeeze.

"You don't have to—" As much as I want Aiden to open up, I don't want to be responsible for the tears he's also fighting back. I glance at the guitar. The worn body shows how much he's played it. If that guitar could talk. "Did you play for her? Ruby?" I force myself to say her name.

He nods. "Yeah." He wipes the sleeve of his shirt on his face and a small smile surfaces. "We used to do concerts—Ruby loved an audience. Anytime someone was over, she would stand in front of the fireplace like it was Royal Albert Hall. I'd play and she'd sing and dance until it was bedtime. We even made up a few tunes. She was particularly proud of 'Father Christmas Is Gonna Bring Me All the Presents.'" He grins for a moment, and then his gaze settles on the small window that looks out to the street.

"I'm sure it's a great song." Then something hits me. "What's the concert thing you do?"

"Oh right. I play at Great Ormond Street Hospital for Children. It's where Ruby was. I'd bring my guitar to sing to her, and then it kind of became a thing. I do it on the weekend. It's become almost a second home to us."

Us. Aiden and his parents. His mother. His poor mother.

"How are your parents handling everything?"

He looks out to the hallway, then his voice drops. "There are some days Mum can't get out of bed. I don't blame her. Dad's the opposite. He's thrown himself into work. I think it's hard for him to walk into this flat without Ruby here."

"And how are you? Truly?"

He sighs. "I'm as good as I can be. I'm lucky I have the release of my music. Ruby and I made a list of all these places we'd go busking together when she got better." Aiden tilts his head back and closes his eyes. "She made me promise that I'd still do it."

The busking now makes sense. He does it for her. But the songs . . .

"I haven't done it," he admits. "Well, the kind of busking we were supposed to do was with fun, upbeat songs. I just can't bring myself to sing these happy songs when I'm so miserable inside. I couldn't find any song that could convey how I was feeling, so I started to write my own. And what I told you about the songs was true—it helps me release the hurt and anger. I was so angry, it just kept bottling up inside. Then I'd go out, get drunk, and get messy. It wasn't healthy."

My mind goes to the wall that he punched. It makes sense now. If something happened to Josh, I'd want to destroy an entire building.

"A few weeks ago," Aiden continues as his gaze is on our hands, "I was walking around with my guitar and just broke it out and started singing. Nobody knew me, so I could just let everything I was feeling come out. I could be anonymous in my pain. And it worked until one day when this chatty American came along."

That's why Dev and Fiona have never heard him play. He didn't want to let anybody in, and then I stumbled into his life. I think back on what Dev said about our meeting—that it was fate. Maybe Aiden came into my life for a reason as well.

"To be honest, I feel like I've let Ruby down. The day you saw me in Battersea, I was supposed to go to Covent Garden and finally do one of our planned concerts, but I couldn't get myself to do it. I kept walking and walking and just ended up there. I don't know, I can't seem to get myself to do our list without her. But I promised Ruby. I promised her a lot, and I've done nothing."

A promise from an older sibling to a younger one means so much. I promised Josh I would take him to the park with a splash pad just to get him to be quiet for two minutes, and it was all he talked about the next day at daycare. And the following two weeks. On our drive over he said to me, "I get to spend all day with you!" I replied, "Joshy, I usually spend the day with you." And his response still warms my heart: "Yeah, but you *want* to do this."

I wasn't forced by Mom or Stuart to look after him. It was just Josh and me, and it meant the world to him when I kept my word. Even though Ruby is gone, the promise still means a lot to her. And Aiden.

I give his hand another squeeze. "You can still do the list. I'll help you with whatever you need. Your one fan wouldn't miss your Covent Garden debut."

"Oh, so *now* you're a fan? See, this is why I didn't want you to know. I finally have a fan, and it's only out of pity." He sinks his head down, but I can see the color coming back to his cheeks.

I playfully nudge him with my shoulder. "I mean, I'm not going to start hanging up posters of you on my bedroom wall, but yes, I am your fan, Aiden Hutchison."

"I knew it!" he says with a shy smile.

"Oh God, don't let it get to your head. My tastes are fickle, and I might be on to the next boy bander in three, two—"

"Okay, okay!" He gives me a smile, and my stomach nearly bottoms out. Because I realize I only want to see him smile. I want to do whatever I can to help him.

"Can I see the list?"

Aiden lets go of my hand as he gets up from the bed. While he walks over to his dresser, which is covered in notebooks and guitar picks, I stare at my hand. It feels cold and empty now. I try to focus on Aiden instead of this—I mean, let's call it what it is—fangirling over him.

Aiden passes me a spiral notebook with a glitter unicorn on the cover. I skim the list, and it's a lot of the main places in London: Covent Garden, Speakers' Corner in Hyde Park, and . . .

"Wembley Stadium?"

"The car park," he states. "Same with Royal Albert Hall—just to play outside. Ruby wanted it before a show so there'd be a bunch of people. The more the merrier for her."

There's another item on the list that stands out. "Liverpool?"

"Yeah, we played a bunch of Beatles songs, and she's always wanted to go."

"Okay, Covent Garden. It's happening. Friday," I say with a nod of my head. "It's what Ruby would've wanted."

Aiden looks doubtful. "Okay, but you'll be there, yeah?"

Like anything could keep me away from Aiden now. "Of course."

"Thanks, Evie."

He sits down at his desk while I try to not get too nosy being in his bedroom. His closet door is slightly ajar, and I see some actual color in his wardrobe instead of the usual combination of black and gray he wears.

Then Aiden shakes his head. "Wait. You're here."

"Ah, yeah."

"How did you get here?"

Oh right, that. "Um, have you talked to Fiona?"

He shakes his head. "She left me a message on my mobile whilst I was running errands for Mum."

"Yeah, we had a bit of a misunderstanding and there was a whole scene." I fill Aiden in on the understatement of the millennium.

He sighs. "Don't take it personally. She's overly protective of me. I told Dev and Fiona I didn't want to talk about Ruby in front of you. I guess I should've clarified that it was because you didn't know. I'll sort her out."

"Thanks." I really want Fiona to like me, because I'm not going anywhere. Well, at least for the summer. Unless Dad does throw me out.

He narrows his eyes. "But that's not it. There's something else, isn't there?"

"Yeah, it's just my dad and I had a bit of a blowup . . ." I think about all that Aiden lost and suddenly it doesn't seem like such a big deal. "You know what, I'll bore you with it another time. Because it's fine. I'm going to be fine."

We both have broken families in a sense. While I'm not sure what's waiting for me when I get back to Dad's flat, he'll at least be there.

No matter how angry I become, I always thought that someday things would get better. Someday Dad would return to the person he once was. Someday we'd be like we used to be.

I now know I can't stop waiting for that someday to arrive, since I don't know how many somedays Dad and I have left.

20

My head is still spinning with everything I uncovered during my visit at Aiden's: not solely his sister, but these feelings that are refusing to back off. Oh yeah, and I also need to figure out what to do about my father.

Here I thought I was running away from drama when I came to London, but there are some things you can't outrun.

I pass on taking the Underground and slowly wander back to the flat on foot, purposely taking random detours on the way. I don't have my phone to occupy me. I don't have music to listen to. All I have are the thoughts that keep swirling around my head.

It's not a great place to be.

Once I get back to Chelsea, I walk along the Thames, trying to avoid the flat a little bit longer. I look out at Battersea Park, where I first saw Aiden. What if he had gone to Covent Garden that day? What if I had walked in a different direction? What if I didn't drop my spoon and never saw Sean's hand on Meredith? What if my father never lost the weight?

There's no point in going down those spirals. I am where I am now, and I have to face this reality.

Even though I don't have a watch, I can tell from the dark sky and empty streets that it must be late. I drag my feet to Dad's building. The evening porter greets me. "Good evening, Miss Taylor."

"Hey, Oliver." I resist the urge to ask whether he's seen Dad. Maybe he stepped out after our fight. But I know there's no avoiding it.

"The O'Shaughnessys on four may be interested in hiring you to look after their wee one this weekend. I gave them your information."

"Great!" I relax slightly. My savings are running on fumes.

Once the lift delivers me to the top floor, I pause at the door to the flat. My hands are shaking as I turn the key and open the door to an empty kitchen and living room.

But something's not right.

I take a deep breath. It smells in here. It smells like fried food.

I ignore the growl of my stomach, since I didn't eat dinner—I felt like I'd already intruded enough on Aiden and his mom. On the marble counter near the refrigerator I find a brown bag with a few empty takeaway containers.

Did Dad have a guest? He'd never eat this stuff.

"Dad?" I call out, albeit a tad quietly, into the flat.

Nothing.

I walk down the long hallway that leads to the master bedroom. I've never really been in his bedroom besides the original quick tour he gave me when I first visited. The door is slightly ajar and the lights are on.

I knock on the door. "Dad? Are you awake?"

After no answer, I hesitantly open the door. He's face down on top of his white duvet cover, softly snoring. He has on workout clothes, but his sneakers are at the foot of his bed. There's a container of food on the bedside table along with a bottle of whiskey.

My stomach completely drops. I've never seen him like this. He looks so vulnerable. New Dad has a hard edge. A rigidness that has come with years of strict discipline.

He couldn't have done all of this because of our fight, could he? No, maybe it's a cheat day. Although I've never known him to take one.

As much as I want to see my father back to normal—to see a glimpse of humanity in him—this wasn't exactly what I had in mind.

I take the food containers and bottle of booze to the kitchen and clean up. I pour a glass of water and find some acetaminophen in the medicine cabinet and place it on the nightstand for when he wakes up.

Before I leave, I turn to study my father. It's gotten harder and harder to look at him over the years. He looks peaceful with his eyes closed. There's a subtle hint of stubble on his jaw. His hair is a bit messy.

Then I notice there's something in his hand. As I walk over to the other side of the bed, I see a few pictures.

Photos of me as a kid. With Dad.

21

I can no longer blame a restless night and late morning on jet lag.

Although I will continue to use that excuse the next time I act up or overshare. Because I'm me, and no matter what else I've learned in the last twenty-four hours, I'll somehow manage to say something I shouldn't.

I tried to rid my body of the unsettled feeling by going for a run along the Thames. The apartment was quiet, with no note from Dad and an empty trash bin. Dad has a maid come twice a week, and since he moved out I've never seen him empty the trash. He got rid of the evidence, but he had to know I was the one to put his food containers in there.

Unless he blacked out and doesn't remember.

Or is in denial that I saw him in that condition.

As much as I want to pretend I didn't see the things I saw, I did. And there's no going back now.

I had thought he'd gotten rid of all those photos from my childhood.

I had thought he didn't care.

After a breakfast of cereal and a banana, I wipe down the counter and sink. Dad always tells me that I don't have to clean up after myself here, but it's a habit. I always leave whenever the maid does show up, since I feel super lazy sitting around while she's cleaning up after us. Back home, Mom has a calendar posted on the refrigerator of everybody's chores for the week. Every once in a while, Stuart and I will try to trade off the bathrooms. The amount of pee in the bathroom I share with Josh is disgusting. That kid has no aim.

I get a text on my phone and my stomach cringes, because I assume it's Dad. Is he going to be mad at me?

DEV: Hey, I hear yesterday was something else. Want to come over to Aiden's after school so he can practice for Covent Garden?

And just like that, my feelings about Aiden and his sister crash around me again.

I would love nothing more than to listen to Aiden sing and hang out with Dev and even Fiona, but I have something else I need to take care of.

I text Dev that I can't make it, but will meet them tomorrow for the big show. Then I open my laptop and wonder if I should wake Mom up so she can help me. What's happening with Dad is beyond me.

Instead I turn to my old friend, Google.

How do you help a loved one with control issues?

As I start reading, it says control issues may be connected to traumatic or abusive life experiences. It also mentions they can be related to a lack of trust and fears of abandonment, which hits a little too close to home.

Not like I can even control my mouth, but as I read further and look at examples of controlling self behaviors, disordered eating and compulsive exercising are the top two listed.

My mind drifts back to my conversation with Poppy. How she also thought Dad has issues with food. Was it the disordered eating or the need for control that came first? I have no idea.

All I do know is that Dad needs help.

I read a list of dos and don'ts on the National Association of Anorexia Nervosa and Associated Disorders website. All of the dos—talk openly and honestly; try to make yourself available; be honest about your own fears, struggles, and frustrations; express your love and support—are things Dad and I haven't done in years. I scroll through more sites that talk about different eating disorders, and my mind drifts back to the secret I shared with Dad.

When he left, I was so upset, I thought the only way to get him back was to shun the one thing he seemed to despise the most: food. I ignored the hunger pangs in my stomach as I was convinced it would bring Dad back to me.

Oh God. I never really thought about what this must've meant for Mom at the time. Her husband had just left her. There was a mortgage she couldn't afford, and her stubborn daughter had to make it even harder for her.

I finally started to eat again because I was hungry and weak. I began to see a therapist who talked about how food nourishes the body and is necessary to function.

But that early brush with disordered eating really made me appreciate food—and very aware of when I start looking at it as an enemy, and yes, when I use it to annoy my father.

Anytime I see a picture of a celebrity online that makes me question every pore and curve on my body, I remind myself that those photos aren't real life. We live in an age where even models get nips and tucks courtesy of Photoshop. I've been guilty of putting the camera above eye level for selfies so it hides my double chin. I've used filters. I guess maybe wanting to control things runs in the family.

The pressures of being a girl.

Looking at all the advice, I keep going back to one of the simplest—in theory: make yourself available.

Maybe it's time Stubborn Evie becomes the bigger person.

I then decide to dial a number I've never called.

"Nigel Taylor's office," a young man's voice answers.

"Yes, hello. This is Evie. I'm—"

"Evie!" The guy's voice brightens. "So lovely to speak with you. Did you enjoy high tea the other day?"

Of course this guy was the one to make the reservation. He was probably also the person to arrange the glass of champagne and payment.

"Yes, thank you."

"Your father is currently in a meeting. Shall I have him ring you back on your mobile?"

"No, it's okay. I'm wondering if he has dinner plans tonight."

I hear the clicking of a keyboard in the background. "He doesn't. I believe he was going to go to the gym, but I can get a booking somewhere for later. I know he'd love to have dinner with you."

I'm not sure about that, but we have to stop avoiding each other. I'm more than aware that taking someone to a restaurant to talk about their control issues, including an eating disorder, probably isn't the best move. One of the don'ts is to try to force someone to eat or stop exercising. But I also read that I can't pretend it will go away. It won't. So I need to make a start, and I want that start to be in public. Just in case.

"Could it be sushi?" I ask. The last meal we had together was during Christmas two years ago. It was at a sushi place, with his girlfriend at the time. He talked about how healthy sushi is if you don't have rice and soy sauce and anything spicy or fried, but still. He enjoyed the meal. His eyes got wide when they put down this plate of raw fish, decorated with microgreens. I liked it because the entrance was hidden away in a mews (basically an alley), so it felt like a secret. It also wasn't super pretentious inside. I had sushi that was served in mini rice cakes that looked like a small taco. "There's a place he really likes nearby, there's a mews."

"Ah yes, Dinings SW3. One of your father's favorites. I can pull some strings and get you in this evening."

"Really?" I find a lump in my throat that his assistant is being so helpful.

"Of course. Let me make some calls, and I'll send a confirmation to your email on file."

"Thanks so much—" I stop because I have no idea what his name is. Or how long he's been working for Dad. This guy who probably has bought all my presents.

"Simon." He fills in for me.

"Thank you, Simon."

"My pleasure. Everything sound good?"

"Yes," I say, even though it sounds absolutely terrifying.

22

My life sometimes feels like extremes.

Work and chores in our modest home in Winnetka versus the posh life when I'm in London.

Wanting to be loved for who I am versus spending an hour primping for my talk with Dad.

I turn into the mews that evening for our dinner. One of my favorite things to do when I'm in London is to explore the tiny streets or mews. I never really know where they'll take me.

This time is no different.

I walk into Dinings SW3 with the same purple dress I wore for high tea. This time I added the Tiffany pendant Dad (or, more likely, Simon) bought me for Christmas last year. I never wear the stuff he gets me, but I found it in my jewelry bag and decided to wear it as a white flag. Albeit one that's made of white gold.

The hostess seats me at a two-person table near the window. I order a sparkling water and calm my nerves. I don't check the time or try to wonder if he's going to even show.

My eyes are glued to the door until Dad walks in. His short hair is slightly damp from the shower he no doubt took after his second workout of the day. He follows the waitress, his face set in a neutral expression.

"Evie," he says with a nod as he sits down. He unbuttons the top button on his gray blazer. He picks up the menu and studies it.

"Thanks for coming," I say with too-forced enthusiasm.

He replies by raising his eyebrow. "Yes, Simon said you made this request, so I thought best to honor it."

I hate how cold and formal he's being. But having this in a public place forces both of us to be on our best behavior.

"How was work?" I ask, trying to get a conversation of any type started.

"It was fine. How was your day?"

"It was good. I went for a run," I state.

This gets his attention. He looks up from the menu. "Really? Where did you go?"

"Along the Thames to Westminster Bridge," I reply proudly. I didn't stop once to catch my breath, although I also didn't push myself. I'm used to shorter distances in track, so I keep a slower, yet steady pace for longer runs.

He puts his menu down. "That's more than three kilometers one way. What was your time? Did you run back?"

"No, I walked to cool down."

"And your time?" he presses as he leans in. I can't remember the last time he was this genuinely interested in me.

"I didn't time myself," I admit.

He picks his menu back up. "You need to keep track so you know what time to beat going forward. I'll get you a tracker so you can see how many calories you burn."

Oh right. This is why I don't talk about running with Dad.

"So everything's going well with work?"

He sets his menu down again with a sigh. "What is it that you want, Evie?"

"I—I—" I stutter before I gain my composure. "I simply want to know how you're doing."

"Whilst that's a lovely gesture, I have to admit it's a bit surprising, as it's a first," he says with bitterness in his voice.

Have to admit: he has me there. I haven't been the greatest daughter, but then again, he kind of started it by abandoning me as a child.

No, I'm going to be positive. *Avoid conflicts and battles of will*, I remind myself from the list of dos and don'ts.

The waiter comes over to go over the specials, and when he asks if we want a few more minutes, Dad says we're ready without even consulting me. He also makes a not-even-subtle look at his Audemars Piguet watch, which probably cost more than our house in Winnetka.

I order the chef's assorted sashimi appetizer and the halibut while Dad rattles off a list of sashimi like a pro and the grilled asparagus "without the sauce and any oils" for his entrée.

Then we're left to look at each other.

"Is there something you want to say to me?" he asks, more as a challenge than an actual invitation.

I can't tell whether this is about what we said to each other yesterday or how I found him last night.

Do not let your fear of upsetting them prevent you from speaking up: communicate.

"Yes, I wanted to talk to you." I take a deep breath. Of everything I thought about saying to him, only one question comes out of my mouth. "Are you happy?"

Dad methodically takes the white cloth napkin from his plate and places it in his lap. "Where is this going?"

"I'm worried about you," I admit.

He replies by taking a careful sip of water.

"Dad, I think you need to see a therapist."

"Is this about last night?"

"Which part?" I ask. "About how we can't be in a room without fighting or how I found you passed out when I got home?"

"Everybody has moments of weakness."

"I think you have control issues, which have manifested into compulsive exercising and an eating disorder," I state right as our appetizers are placed in front of us.

Dad shakes his head and picks up his chopsticks. "I'm eating, see." He carefully places a piece of yellowtail in his mouth. He keeps eye contact with me as he slowly chews.

"You—" I stop myself since "you" statements can sound

accusatory. *"I'm* concerned about your relationship with food and exercising. It doesn't seem very healthy."

He snorts, actually snorts. "This coming from the girl who eats crisps for breakfast." He pauses for a moment to move his food around the plate. "Listen, I understand that a lot of our previous relationship was based around food. I gave you food rewards. It's something I grew up with as well. But planning your life around food isn't healthy." He waves his hand around the restaurant dismissively.

I look at the other diners. There are a few couples getting cozy with glasses of wine. A table of four women laughing next to us. I like meals out, not simply for the food, but because it's time spent with people you want to be with: friends, family. What's better than sharing a delicious meal with the important people in your life? It's something I look forward to, not dread.

"I don't have the time for this," he says as he puts another piece of sashimi in his mouth.

"For this conversation or for me?"

He doesn't reply.

Do express your love and support.

"I miss you, Dad," I say, and my voice cracks at the end. He pauses and looks around the restaurant. Nobody is paying attention to us, but I know he's worried that I'll cause a scene. And he doesn't have a clue about my penchant for dumping beverages on dudes' heads in public.

I don't lose my courage and continue, "I know it's impossible for us to go back to how things used to be, but I used to love spending time with you, and now it's like we can't get past the past. And I want to. I want to be able to sit and laugh with you and talk and not get so defensive."

I can see him softening. "I'd like that, too."

Just that simple admission is almost enough for me.

Almost.

"But more than anything I want you to be happy. Are you happy?"

He sighs, and the tightness in his jaw returns. "Is anybody?"

My heart nearly breaks. What a depressing thing to say. Here he is living the life he's always dreamed of, but it isn't enough for him. Will anything be? That's the real issue. No matter how much he has, it'll never be enough.

"I want my old dad back," I say softly.

I'm not sure whether he heard me until he replies, "You want me to be fat."

"No," I say, a little louder than I intended. A few heads turn, so I place a piece of salmon sashimi in my mouth. When I feel it's safe to go on, I lean in closer to him. "I want the dad who used to smile. The one who I joked around with. Who was excited to spend time with me. Who had fun. I never cared about how much you weighed. Neither did Mom. We were so happy. Or at least I was. What will make you happy?"

I realize there are tears running down my face. I wipe them away with the white napkin, which comes back stained with mascara and foundation. I don't know what my face looks like now, but I don't care. This is about something deeper than the surface.

"Please, Dad," I beg. "Please talk to someone. I'm here to listen, but I think you need to talk to someone who has experience with this."

His face is red. "Do you have any idea how hard I have to work for what I have? How much it's going to take for me to work this off?" He holds up a piece of sea bass with contempt. "But I'm doing this for you. I came here despite the fact that it's going to take me an extra hour at the gym for this meal."

"It's a tiny piece of raw fish!" I spit back at him.

Yep. Heads have definitely turned now.

"Sorry," I reply quietly, while I put a fake smile on my face to placate those concerned about what's happening at our table.

"So you want me to go see a therapist for you."

"No, you need to do it for yourself. But I'll go with you. It's probably something we should've done a long time ago. We've lost too much time already. *We* need to do this. Please."

He remains quiet for a few minutes, so we both eat in silence.

When our appetizer plates are cleared, I give it one more try. "I really care about you, Dad. And I'm worried. Please let me help you."

He looks up at me, and I swear there's a flicker of the old him in his eyes. "You really care this much?"

"Yes, yes I do. You're my father." He doesn't seem convinced. "Don't you care about me?"

His jaw relaxes ever so slightly. "Of course I do."

Our entrées are put in front of us.

It was a really bad idea to do this at a restaurant.

Dad looks down at his food, then back at me.

"Okay."

"Okay?"

"Yes, Evie. We can talk to someone."

I'm so relieved. I resist the urge to stand up and hug him. Any kind of public display of affection is frowned upon from him. Well, the new him. The old one didn't care. So instead I reach across the table and give his hand a slight squeeze.

"Thanks, Dad," I say as I give him a hopeful smile.

He turns his attention back to his food. He examines the asparagus to ensure it hasn't been drenched in anything unseemly and then proceeds to cut it into little pieces.

I want to be hopeful and believe him, but there's another item on the don't list that keeps repeating in my head.

Do not be taken in by lies and excuses.

23

It looks like I've made another friend. Or at least a coconspirator.

I shoot off one more email to Dad's assistant, Simon, before I head off to meet Aiden, Fiona, and Dev for Aiden's busking session.

Poppy gave me some referrals on who Dad should see. She was happy that he was taking it seriously.

So am I, but . . . could it really be this easy? Has my stubbornness all these years blinded me to the fact that he needs help? Is Dad really going to talk to someone simply because I asked?

I'm not entirely convinced, but it's a start.

I weave my way to Covent Garden from the Embankment Underground station. I take note of what's playing on the West End. Maybe Dad and I can go see a play or musical—something that doesn't involve food.

I round the corner that leads to the piazza at Covent Garden, which houses a market filled with stores and restaurants. My heart starts beating faster as I get closer to seeing Aiden again. Those butterflies start to kick in, but I push them down. One male-related issue at a time. I'm getting footing with Dad, the last thing I need to do is mess things up with Aiden by . . .

I don't even know how to finish that thought.

Yes, I have a bit of a crush on Aiden. What's not to like? But that doesn't erase the fact that I'm still bruised from Sean and that I live in another country. It wouldn't do either of us any favors to stir up something that could never be. I mean, not like Aiden sees me as anything but a frantic, yet adorably amusing, American.

Focus on your friendship, I remind myself as I see hundreds of tourists surrounding another busker who has a sound system set up in front of the church across from the market. The crowd is taking pictures of this one singing "Stand by Me" while tapping their phones to give him a tip.

Aiden's is a relatively low-tech affair. I find him waiting with Dev and Fiona at the other side of the market near the Transport Museum.

"Are you ready to acoustic rock?" I say brightly to Aiden, and I resist the urge to give him another hug. Instead, I clap my hands and Aiden replies by looking utterly terrified. "Hey, guys." I can barely look at Fiona, since our last meeting was a disaster and I did the exact opposite of what she told me to do and basically went straight to Aiden.

"Hiya," Dev says as he gives me a hug. "Aiden practiced the setlist for us last night. I personally approved it, so you know it's going to be legendary."

"Can't wait." I finally turn to Fiona. "Hey, Fiona."

She gives me a nod. "Hey."

Silence. Awkwardness.

"All good?" Aiden asks me.

"Yeah." I fiddle with the strap on my purse.

"Things okay with your dad? How was your dinner?"

"Fine," I reply. Right here and now is not about my problems. This is for Aiden. And Ruby. I just want to make Aiden happy, and if that means I need to be on my best behavior and shut up for once, I'll do it. For him.

Aiden grimaces. "See. This is why I didn't want you to know. You're not telling me what's going on because you think it'll, I don't know, burden me or something. You've been here for a minute without a whole monologue. So yeah, you're acting different."

"Oh my God, well *you're* not acting different. Trying to rile me up like always."

"How is asking how you are riling you up? I think it makes me thoughtful, lovely, incredibly good-looking . . ." He wiggles his eyebrows.

I tilt my head at him. "Has that ever worked?" Even though it's so working on me.

"I don't know. Does it?" He goes to put his arm around me, but I duck under it. Mostly because if he holds me, I won't want to let go.

How's that not pining working out for you, Evie?

"Here's a little hint from the opposite sex." I wiggle my eyebrows back at him.

"Oh, she's giving love advice now."

"No, I'm giving you how-to-behave-like-a-normal-person advice."

"So you won't be speaking from experience, then?"

I punch him in the arm. "Hey, I am normal and rational and calm and witty and just an all-around well-balanced and adjusted person."

Said no well-balanced and adjusted person ever.

Aiden just laughs, and I have to admit, it's nice to see him smile, even if it's because I'm being Peak Evie.

"Okay, Evie." Dev throws his arm around me. "We have jobs to do. Clapping, dancing, making fools out of ourselves."

"Oh, well *that* won't be a problem. Don't you start!" I swat Aiden before he can make another comment about my ability to be a bit much in public. Or private. Or anywhere, really.

And let's face it, Aiden's never going to see me in a way other than Inserts Foot Into Mouth Evie.

Maybe if you stopped doing that . . .

"Fine, fine. Just give me a second," Aiden says as he turns his back to us. He starts tuning his guitar.

Which leaves me with Dev . . . and Fiona. I had messaged her an apology yesterday, which she replied to with only one word: OK.

"Look, I'm really sorry, Fiona. I didn't—"

"I know," she replies. "Aiden didn't want us talking about it in front of you, but I assumed you knew. I shouldn't have said the other stuff, I just don't want Aiden to get hurt."

"I don't want that either." I also don't want me to get hurt. Another reason we have to remain friends.

"To be honest, I can't believe you didn't know," Dev says. "You thought his songs were about a girlfriend?"

I look over at Aiden, who is nervously fiddling with his guitar. "Yeah. I had just gotten over a breakup, so I guess I put myself in his shoes. Although he never corrected me, even when I referred to an ex, so . . ."

"I can see why he didn't want you to know. It was bad," Dev says in a whisper. "It was a nightmare anytime we went out. He'd drink, get mad."

"Punch a hole in a wall," I fill in.

"Yeah, that. Aiden is pretty mellow, but he has this side of him that can get really angry, and ever since Ruby got sick, the littlest thing would set him off."

"I once said 'everything happens for a reason' about a bad grade, *as a joke*, and Aiden lost it on me." Fiona makes her voice lower. "'What's the reason Ruby died, then? Make sense of that.'" She shakes her head. "So yeah, he's slowly getting better, but there's a part of him that's changed, probably for good. How could it not?"

We all look over at Aiden, whose lips are moving like he's giving himself a pep talk.

"This is a massive step for him. So we need to be really supportive and dance and do whatever to get him through it," Dev says.

I reply by doing a shimmy and shake of my hips.

"I like your style," Dev says with a wink. "And you know what also will help."

"Don't you dare say it," Fiona warns him, although the corner of her lip tugs slightly.

"There's a party tomorrow night. You in?"

I shake my head. "You never learn, do you, Dev?"

And neither do you, Evie.

Dev grins in response. "Of course not. But this time we're invited. It's a mate from school's birthday. Should be a great time, and my future wife will be there."

Becs. I steal a quick glance at Fiona, who's glaring at the ground.

"Now!" Dev points his fingers at us. "Are we ready to get the party started?"

Aiden faces us and notices all the tourists walking by. "Do you think we can go around one of the corners to a smaller space?"

"Absolutely not." Dev takes Aiden's guitar case and places it in front of him. "The stage is yours." Dev gestures at the sidewalk in front of him.

Aiden looks like he's going to be sick.

A few people passing by pause, as they can sense a show is about to happen.

"Aiden," I say as I approach him. "I've seen you do this a few times. You're great. All you have to do is start playing."

He nods at me. "Okay, but you have to clap and sing along. It's what Ruby used to do."

"Of course."

"And tell me constantly how amazing and brilliant and incredibly good-looking I am."

"I'll do two of the three—your ego can fill in the rest," I tease.

"And how you dream of me nightly."

I grimace in reply.

"And don't make fun of my first song."

"Why would I—"

And then he starts strumming the first few chords of "Wonderwall."

I've only heard Aiden sing incredibly painful and personal songs. But this is the setlist he came up with with Ruby. It's going to be different. Seeing him strum and tap his foot to what has to be the number one busking song makes him seem almost happy.

"It's nearly our turn," Dev says to me.

"Our turn for what?" I ask, but then Aiden gets to the chorus and Dev and Fiona join in loudly.

"Cause maybe, you're gonna be the one that saves me."

I sing along as the three of us move in time to the strumming of Aiden's guitar.

More tourists stop to watch. Smiles start spreading on their faces, and a few join us in singing. Coins and notes are being dropped into his case. Dev wraps his arms around Fiona and me as we continue to sing backup.

When Aiden finishes the song, there are about twenty people around him. They all start clapping. Aiden bows his head and then launches into his next song.

"*Oh, yeah, I'll tell you something,*" he sings as Fiona and Dev start clapping in time to "I Want to Hold Your Hand." I join them.

"Come on everybody!" Dev says to the crowd. People join us in clapping, and more money goes into Aiden's case.

Who knew that Dev could be such a great hype man?

Fiona nudges me to join her in a little dance beside Aiden.

At one point, she even slings her arm around me, a wide smile on her face. We're all smiling and laughing as his set continues, featuring Queen, David Bowie, and Elvis Costello songs.

And you know what, Aiden *is* amazing and brilliant . . . and incredibly good-looking.

What? I've got eyes.

After half an hour, Aiden finishes with an American—Stevie Wonder's "Superstition."

The three of us join the nearly fifty people in the crowd cheering Aiden on after he finishes. He takes a step back, almost like he couldn't believe he did it. He looks around Covent Garden, and for a second, his eyes flash upward. He gives a little nod to the sky.

"She's so happy," I say to him. I barely know anything about Ruby—and, to be honest, Aiden—but there's a feeling in my gut that I'm right. This was for her. And also for him.

"Yeah, mate. That was amazing." Dev grabs Aiden in a hug and then tousles his hair.

Aiden smiles, but it doesn't reach his eyes.

This is only one step for him. It's going to take a long time for him to fully recover.

When I first met Aiden, only early last week, we were both so broken.

And now, our mending process has begun.

24

"I think emergency means something different in the States."

"Get back here," I hiss at Aiden as I stay crouched behind a corner.

Okay, there's a slight chance I may be overreacting. *Slight*.

It's the following Tuesday afternoon and I'm having a full-blown Evie attack.

"Evie, you've been on high alert for, like, two hours." Aiden comes around to the courtyard nestled in between office buildings where I've been hiding. He doesn't even attempt to conceal the amusement on his face. "Okay, I need us to go over this one more time. You texted Dev it was an emergency and you needed me—let me state for the record that you said *I need Aiden*, we'll get back to that in a minute—solely because you had pizza with your dad."

"I know, right?" Even I still can't believe what happened today.

Dad was true to his word. I met him at his fancy office, we went to a therapy appointment where I waited outside, and then we went out for pizza. I saw my dad eat carbs. And dairy.

What is actually going on?

So yes, I asked Aiden to come meet me outside my dad's office building. And yes, it's a nice excuse to hang out with him. I need—and yes, I'll use the word *need* in regards to Aiden—backup. Although so far it's been a lot of standing (for him) and ducking (for me).

"Okay. Let me be blunt: why are we stalking your father?"

"I keep telling you, we're not stalking!" I say entirely too loudly—surprise, surprise—causing the customers exiting a nearby coffee shop to look at me with concern. Like I'm a stalker.

Which I'm definitely not.

Even though I do plan on following my father. Secretly.

"Okay," I say softer, trying to compose myself. "I realize eating pizza for lunch may seem like something normal for most people, but for my dad and me it's not."

Aiden tilts his head. "Just admit the truth, Evie. You missed me and were looking for any excuse to hang out." *I plead the fifth.* "I mean, you couldn't take your eyes off me at Arvin's party on Saturday."

"I did not!" I protest, even though yes, I maybe also glanced a time or two in Aiden's direction. After all, that's what friends do. Look at each other 'n' stuff.

I'd also like to state for the record that I was able to go to a party with Aiden, Dev, and Fiona and *not* cause a scene, thank you very much.

"I know you weren't looking at me!" Aiden glowers. "You were too busy focusing on Dev and Becs."

"Becs really doesn't seem to know he exists. Poor Dev."

"Poor Dev?" Aiden scoffs. "Poor me! You were ignoring me—"

"I wasn't—"

"*Ignoring me*, whilst I had to sit in a corner all by myself." Aiden pouts, and I have to say, it's a pretty good look on him.

"You were not—"

"*And then*, you just assume I'm at your beck and call, so I come running—*running!*—from school to rescue you."

"I don't need rescuing."

You so do.

"*And*," Aiden continues in an exasperated manner, which oddly reminds me of how I get and it *is* rather adorable, "I assumed it was an actual emergency so I didn't change." He gestures at his school uniform: gray blazer, black pants, white button-down shirt, and a blue-and-black-striped tie. Ruby's scarf is tied to his backpack. "I know, I know, it must be what it's like for Lois Lane to see Superman as Clark Kent."

"Oh my God, did you seriously just say that?" I shake my head. *Boys.*

Although it was this particular boy I first thought of after parting ways with Dad. I was too excited/hopeful/freaked out/anxious to simply hang out at the flat alone.

I continue, "Do you really want to start something with me when I've got *this*?"

I hold up my half-finished iced latte.

Aiden cowers. "Please, please show me some mercy, Queen Evie."

"Oh, Queen Evie, I like it. Yes, yes, that does sound rather nice." Aiden looks up and gives me a smile. "All hail the queen."

"You may bow," I say with a nod of my head.

"I should've known better than to give you any ideas." But he does oblige me with a deep bow.

Have to admit, it feels good.

"Okay, stop trying to distract me. Your dad is doing everything you asked him to do. He's going to therapy. You aren't fighting. Why the secrecy?"

I'm almost embarrassed to admit it, but here I am hiding in a courtyard waiting for my dad to leave work. So it's probably not possible for me to make a bigger fool out of myself. "There's just this feeling I have. That today was too good to be true. I just want to make sure my dad wasn't lying to me about having a meeting later."

Basically, I want to catch my dad in the truth.

"Okay." Aiden nods slowly, then glances around the corner. "What does he look like again?"

"Be careful, he may see you!"

Aiden slowly turns back to me, that amused smile once again on his face. "Wait. How does your dad know what I look like? Do you show him pictures of me when you go on and on *and on* about me?"

"I don't have any pictures of you." Which is technically true. However, I have maybe once or twice—who's counting, really?—found pictures of Aiden on Fiona's and Dev's profiles, as Aiden, annoyingly, doesn't have social media.

But I'll never admit to it.

"So you *do* talk about me."

"Oh my God." I hang my head. "Just look out for this guy." I pull up the picture of my father on his company's website. He's got on a suit, no smile, and it screams professional and zero personality.

"Okay." Aiden's gaze is at the glass-and-steel building across the street. "But aren't you going to Devon tomorrow with him? That's good, right?"

"And that's another thing! He offered it at lunch. Out of nowhere. *Let's go to Devon.* Like that's something we do." Dad was just sitting there, eating a slice of pizza and pretending like this is just any other day for us, but it wasn't. Let me tell you something, I know weird—*I am weird*—it was even weirder than me! *Can you imagine?* "He even said it would be good for us! Which, um, obviously. *And*, he's even taking a few days off work, which he never does, but he says he has a development project that will be approved soon and then he'll be rammed at work and the fact that I even know that is bizarre. I just can't believe we're going to Devon and it was his idea. We haven't been to see his family together in years."

"What an absolute monster."

"Aiden!" I punch him in the arm.

Okay, technically, yes, these are all good and wonderful things.

But I'm worried about how much it all means to me. Dad and I would always go to Devon when we came to England. The last time we there together was five years ago. My dad's younger brother is the spitting image of Past Dad, including being absolutely hilarious. Uncle Gabriel had insisted he and Dad take a picture side by side. Him holding a "before" sign, while Dad held an "after" sign. Dad grimaced throughout. Then he decided to preach to Gabe about complex carbs. Gabe kept saying "fascinating, go on" while opening bottle after bottle of beer.

Dad left the next morning.

I plan on calling Gabe when I get back to the flat to tell him to be on his best behavior. No teasing Dad about anything he eats, drinks, or does. This needs to be a new start for all of us, and I can't have him messing everything up by being . . . well, by being Uncle Gabe.

Aiden turns around for a moment to face me. "I know your dad has to earn your trust, but trust needs to go both ways, Evie. I guess you need to trust that he's trying."

"I know, you're—" Then I catch sight of Dad across the street. "There he is!"

I push my back against the wall and keep my eyes on Dad as he strides along the sidewalk. A leather messenger bag is slung over his shoulder, his attention focused on his phone.

"We need to see where he goes." Then I turn Aiden around and hide behind him as I push him forward.

"So that's a no on trust, then," Aiden replies with a laugh.

I ignore the questioning looks from people passing us as I guide Aiden by the shoulders—I practically have my face jammed up against his arm so I can see. I can't help but notice that he smells really nice.

What? I have a nose.

Dad finally looks up from his phone as a black car pulls up alongside him. Dad gets inside and the car pulls away. I feel helpless—and like a complete fool—watching it go down the street.

Yeah, that went well.

"We should go after it!" I reply, trying to flag down a taxi.

"Evie," Aiden says softly. "You know I love it when you're . . . *you*, but you've got to believe there is good in your life. You need to trust your dad. You don't want to waste any time with him assuming the worst."

There's that sadness that flashes across Aiden's face.

"You're right."

His face lights up again. "Oh, I don't think I caught that, could you perhaps repeat it?" He puts a hand up to his ear.

"Aiden, I . . ." I look at this boy in front of me. Who had his heart torn apart and he's here with me. He's trying to move on. Why can't I? "I want you to know that I really appreciate you being here and, well, if you ever want to talk about, you know . . ."

"I know." He gives me that crooked smile. "But I'd much rather focus on all your problems."

"Hey!" Not that I don't have enough of those to keep us occupied for hours and hours. "I just want you to know that I'm here for you."

"Thanks, but I just want to be a bloke with a girl hanging out after school. You know, basic rom-com stuff. Boy meets girl. Girl stalks father."

I roll my eyes at him, although he has a point.

"Okay, I'm relieving you from your post. We need to get you back home so you can do homework."

"You have no idea how lucky you are to get the entire summer off."

"Oh, I know." It's the first time in a while that I *am* feeling rather lucky. *Which probably means the apocalypse will be starting up in three, two . . .*

Aiden and I walk for a few minutes in silence. He keeps darting looks at me. "Ah, is there something else going on? I feel like there's something else going on."

I debate how much to tell him. I don't want to keep burdening him with my problems.

"See!" Aiden points his finger accusingly at me. "More proof that you are different. There hasn't been a single soliloquy since, *you know.* You're being so normal."

"No, I'm not! I'm stalking my father, for God's sake!"

This causes Aiden to actually bend over in laughter. I nudge him with my elbow.

It's better to be a bit unpredictable and fiery than boring. At least that's what I keep telling myself. "Now who's causing a scene?"

He straightens up and slings his arm around me in such a casual way, but it causes my breath to catch. "Come on, Evie, spill it."

"Okay, well, you did ask." I pull up an email from Meredith on my phone.

"I certainly did. And please feel free to add as many random asides as you'd like. The more, the—Ow!" Aiden winces as my previous playful nudge turns into a full jab into his ribs. "Point taken."

Aiden takes my phone, then moves to the side to not block the sidewalk.

So I guess I have to email you since you've blocked me everywhere else. I mean, really? I understand you're upset. You have every right, but you can't just up and leave and refuse to talk to me. Or is this your way of saying that our years of friendship meant nothing to you? Yeah, that stings. You can't ignore me forever. Just talk to me. Tell me what I can do.

"You didn't block Meredith's email?" Aiden asks.

"I honestly didn't think about it. We don't email. We text. We DM, we don't email."

"Can you stop making it seem like email is such an old-fashioned concept? *We* email." He waves his finger between us.

"Yes, because of your phone. Are you one of those quirky-emo guys who needs to seem more interesting because you don't have a smartphone? And when can I expect your pretentious art house film about a manic pixie dream girl?"

"You got the manic part right." He tilts his head at me as he bats his eyelashes.

"Honestly, you're the worst."

Yeah, keep telling yourself that, Evie.

Aiden sighs. "Okay, so yes, I used to have an iPhone. Of course I did. But the thing is . . . Ruby used mine all the time to play games and watch videos. So when she . . . I was so upset and angry at the world, I . . . sort of . . . threw it into the Thames." Aiden clears his throat.

"Oh God, I'm so—I, um . . ." I don't even know what to say. He doesn't want to hear *sorry*.

"Does this mean you'll stop teasing me about it?"

"Of course." I curse myself for having to make it such a big deal.

"See!" He points at me accusingly. "You are treating me different now. You love teasing me!"

"Well, it's not that hard to do!" I fire back.

"Come on." He flings his shoulder around me again, and I try to not think about how much I like the feeling of it.

"So . . ." he presses. "What are you going to do about the carrier pigeon, I mean, the *electronic mail*?" He scrunches up his nose in exaggeration.

"Honestly?"

"No, please lie."

I grimace. "I kind of don't want to deal with it. We'll eventually have to talk. Our school isn't that big. But for now, I feel like I already have my hands full with drama. Meredith is the one who lied to me; she can sit and stew for a bit longer."

"*Or* you can just move here and never return to the States."

I laugh. "Yeah, I don't have a family back home or anything."

He throws up his hands. "Hey, can't blame a guy for trying."

Uh, is he joking? He's joking, right? Why would I—Why would he even—

"Are you guys just going to be studying until the Pride parade on Saturday?" I blurt out to get the topic off of . . . whatever that was. And maybe I don't want to even think about what it means when I get on that plane back home, leaving Aiden behind.

"Unfortunately. We're doing a study group on Friday."

"No parties? Or Becs stalking?"

"Okay, so *fortunately* we'll be studying on Friday." He looks down at the sidewalk. "And because of the parade, I'm doing my hospital gig on Sunday. You know, if you wanted to come."

"I'd really like that." While I'm always up for watching Aiden perform, this will give me just a little glimpse into that part of his life. "When are you going to start busking again?" He hadn't mentioned anything to me—you know, his one fan—since Covent Garden.

He shrugs. "I haven't been in the mood to do the kind of busking I did when you first saw me. Even though it was difficult, Covent Garden reminded me how much fun I used to have playing. It was a nice memory to have come back. When I played at Great Ormond's the next day, I didn't have to force myself to perform the upbeat songs. I was enjoying myself again. I may even add some more songs to my setlist. Ones where I don't go on and on about heartbreak."

"Yes, that probably would be best for the children."

He laughs, and the corners of his green eyes crinkle.

When I think about it, Aiden seems to be a bit more at ease recently. Maybe it's because he's no longer hiding something from me. Maybe it's because performing those songs has put him in a better mood. The weight of losing a sister is always going to be there. I can't imagine that it's ever going to be easy, but he's moving forward.

Step by step.

His phone beeps. "Ah, it's my mum. Do you want to come over for dinner?"

"I'd love to, but I need to pack and get everything ready for our trip." We reach the corner where we have to head in different directions. "But thanks for meeting me and putting up with my Evie-ness."

"It's one of my favorite things." He nudges me before shifting uncomfortably. "So, um, have fun in Devon."

"Thanks, and good luck studying. I'll see you Saturday."

He nods.

I'm about to turn away to head to the Underground station, but Aiden has this uncertain look on his face. "Is everything—"

Before I can finish, he pulls me into a tight embrace and then kisses me on the forehead. "See you soon." Once he lets go, he turns around quickly to walk toward his bus.

I touch my forehead where his lips just were. I'm surprised it's cool to the touch, since it feels like it's on fire.

So that just happened.

25

I'm going to say something I never thought in a million years I'd admit to: Dad was correct.

I know, right?

Will miracles never cease!

But going to Devon is just what we needed.

First, my grandparents' two-story stone cottage is out of a fairy tale. Their nearest neighbors are sheep. I'm not joking. It's quiet and green—rolling meadows as far as the eye can see. The front and backyard are decorated with flower bushes my gran expertly maintains. And it's only a two-hour train ride from London. And then a thirty-minute drive on narrow, twisty roads to the tiny village of Bridford, and *then* an extra fifteen minutes to get to the cottage my father grew up in. And my father and I did it together with zero drama.

Let me repeat: zero drama. With my father and me. In a semi-confined space. In fact, we spent most of it in comfortable silence. He worked away on his laptop while I tried to read a book.

I say *tried* because, well, it was sort of hard to read a romance and not get distracted by the forehead kiss from Aiden. No surprise, I keep overanalyzing it. I'm sure it was nothing to Aiden. Just a little peck. It can't be anything more. As I've made clear, I've got enough drama as is.

And yet . . .

"Enjoy the silence whilst we can," Dad says to me now as we arrive to his parents' house. Because while yes, it's a peaceful and quiet landscape, I didn't get my big mouth from my mom's side.

The front door opens. "The prodigal son has returned!"

And there we have it. *Two seconds.* Uncle Gabe was able to behave for all of two seconds. To be fair to him, that might be a record.

Dad grimaces as Gabe approaches him. Whenever I see Gabe, I think about how Dad used to be. Gabe has longer, curlier hair than my dad, but they used to look so similar, people assumed they were twins. Now Gabe is a fuller version of my dad—not solely in body, but in spirit: louder, more fun.

Gabe picks Dad up in the driveway. "Look at you!"

"Hey, Gabe, still as . . . Gabe as ever," Dad says with a shake of his head as Gabe sets him down.

"And look at this wee one." Gabe then proceeds to pick me up. But unlike Dad, I laugh as he twirls me around.

"Stop that!" Gran scolds her younger son. "Let me give my granddaughter a proper welcome."

Gran places her hands on each side of my face as she smiles at me. Her face also reminds me of the father from my past: full, with dimples when she smiles. The three of us share the same button nose; it's the only thing on Dad's new gaunt face that's remained.

"'Ello, Evie." Grandpa approaches me next and gives me a big hug. I feel his bushy white beard brush against my cheek.

Next, they turn to Dad, who has been studying them with raised eyebrows the entire time.

"Mum, Dad." Dad gives each of them a stiff hug as Gran wraps her arm around him and leads him inside.

Gabe takes the luggage from the back of the taxi. Dad insisted we take a car from the train station instead of having anybody pick us up. It stormed earlier, and he claimed he didn't want anybody driving on slick roads. That was his thinly veiled excuse. First, anybody who lives in England is a pro when it comes to driving in the rain. Second, it was obvious he needed some more time before having to come face-to-face with his family. Leave it to Uncle Gabe to prove Dad's point.

"What did I tell you?" I slug Gabe in the arm.

"Ouch!" He rubs his arm with a pout. "I'm happy to see me big brother, is all. And I'm using *big* in the term that he is older than me. We both know that I exceed him in looks, personality, and belly." He rubs his protruding stomach proudly.

"Don't forget mouth," I add.

Gabe replies by giving me a hearty laugh. "Ah, luv, I'll behave. However, if I behave too much, he'll suspect something. Yer dad's smart."

Uncle Gabe has got me there.

We walk into the house and Gran gives me another hug. "I'm so delighted to see you, Evie. We're going to get spoiled having you in England for the entire summer. What a treat!"

Gran and Grandpa used to come visit us once a year back in the States, even though Gran hates flying. It's the only reason I don't pressure them to come visit since Dad moved back.

"Shall we?" Grandpa gestures down at the kitchen table.

The large wooden table has a roasted chicken, vegetables, and a big salad on it. There are wineglasses filled with water and a bottle of red in the center. Glasses of beer are already at Gabe's and Grandpa's places.

"We have wine, unless you fancy a pint?" Grandpa asks Dad.

"A lager would be great, thanks."

I nearly have to pick up Grandpa's jaw from the floor. I don't remember the last time I saw my dad drink a beer. So many "empty calories."

"Please sit," Grandpa says as he pours Dad a beer while the rest of us sit down. He hands Dad his beer before taking his place at the end, opposite Gran. "Ah, just like old times. My two boys here."

I feel a slight twinge of pride that we are finally all here together. I smile at Dad, and he gives me a smile back, albeit a strained one.

"Go ahead, don't be shy," Gran says as she passes me the salad bowl. "You must be hungry after your travels."

I mean, when aren't I hungry? Although I did bring snacks for the train: bottled water, baby carrots, and almonds. Not a bag of crisps in sight. It's like I'm a whole new person.

The table is silent as I dish out some salad and hand the bowl to Dad. Every eye is on him as he scoops the lettuce, cucumbers, and tomatoes on his plate. He then takes a slice of chicken breast and veggies.

We are so not being subtle as we watch him eat. Gran purposely made a healthy dinner to appease Dad, but usually he would take one spoonful of salad and pick at it all night.

So yeah, I'm not being overly dramatic at how unusual it is to see him eat. Even his family is stunned. My question is: if, as he stated to me the other day, he really does eat and treat himself, then why is it such a shock for his flesh and blood to see him enjoying a meal?

"How's your summer been, Evie?" Grandpa asks, slicing through the silence.

"Good."

"Yes, Evie has made some friends," Dad states. "She's even been babysitting for some of my neighbors."

"I have!" I reply a little too enthusiastically.

Take it down a few thousand notches, Evie.

I may be a little desperate for this to go well. All I want is for us all to move forward.

"It seems like you're settling into London life quite well," Gran says with a smile.

"Yes."

More silence. The only sound is of the utensils hitting the plates.

Dad looks up at his younger brother. "You're being unusually quiet, Gabe."

Gabe shoots me an "I told you so" glance. I return it with a warning look.

"I'm simply savoring this lovely meal with me family. What's so unusual 'bout that?" Gabe raises his eyebrow.

Dad smirks. "I wasn't aware you could go more than a minute without talking."

There's some light chuckling. Uncle Gabe throws down his napkin and points at me. "Evie told me I had to behave!"

"Uncle Gabe!" I scold him. *Seriously.*

Dad shakes his head. "Oh Evie."

"I just thought . . ." I didn't want to tell Dad the real reason I needed Gabe to not tease him. Although it's pretty obvious.

Dad stands up from the table.

Great. I've ruined everything. Dad's going to leave. He couldn't be in his childhood home for ten minutes.

Dad reaches into his back pocket.

"Here we go," Uncle Gabe says as he folds his arms.

Dad opens up his wallet and pulls out two crisp hundred-pound notes. He throws them on the table.

"This!" Dad says as he points at the money. "Is how you get Gabe to shut it." He turns to his brother. "That is all yours if you keep your trap closed until the end of the meal. And by end of the meal, I'm referring to when all the plates are cleared and dishes washed."

"Looks like Gabe will be doing the washing up tonight," Grandpa says with a laugh. "Probably before we can even finish eating."

Dad extends his hand to Gabe, who reluctantly shakes it.

"Now!" Dad claps his hands together excitedly. He has a mischievous twinkle in his eye. "Evie, have I ever told you about how I was a superior athlete to your uncle?"

Uncle Gabe grips his fork so tightly I'm expecting it to break in two.

"Weren't you also more popular with the ladies?" Grandpa adds.

"Oh, you two," Gran says with a shake of her head. "Poor Gabriel."

Gabe points at his mother and nods. His face is red. It's possible he may explode.

"Your uncle looks up to me in so many ways," Dad says, drawing out every word to torture Gabe. "I believe he's used the word *idol* more than once to describe his admiration of me."

To this Gabe throws his head down on the table. It lands with a thud, and we all start laughing.

"See, Evie." Dad holds up his glass of beer in a cheers. "This is way more fun."

Everybody at the table is smiling—well, except for Uncle Gabe, whose head is down. Here I am, with my dad and his family, having a great meal.

It's way better than anything I could've expected.

♪♪

I wake up the next morning still grinning.

The house is quiet as I go downstairs and see my grandparents at the kitchen table. "Good morning, luv. Would you like a cuppa?" Gran asks.

"Yes, please."

"Your father is already up and went for a run. Let's hope he comes back," Grandpa states with a laugh.

"Gerald!" Gran scolds him. "Now Evie, we made sure to get crumpets for you. Would you like one?"

"Oh God yes!"

They both laugh at my love for crumpets. A crumpet is basically a superior version of what Americans call an English muffin. It's plump. It's buttery. I swear angels bake them. Buttery angels.

Gran heats the crumpet on their always-on AGA cooker, while I grab a yogurt out of the refrigerator.

"Last night was good," I state. I already filled them in on Dad seeing a therapist and our conversations when I called them about our visit. "Is it wrong that I have my hopes up that the old Dad will return?"

Gran and Grandpa exchange a look.

Gran hands me a mug of tea and pulls a chair next to me. "Not at all. We simply want your father to be happy." She pauses for a moment before stealing a glance at Grandpa. He gives her a nod. "I don't think we realized how hard things were for your father growing up. He was always a bigger boy. He got teased a lot. He was more sensitive and never took it as well as Gabe, who'd give as good as he got. No, your father was always searching for a way to escape. First, it was uni in Scotland. Then, he studied abroad in

America before settling there." Gran looks sad, her voice now a mere whisper. "I guess there are some things you can never run away from. I worry about him. So please believe me when I say that I hope he sees this through and does the work."

The elation I had felt disappears. When I was younger, Dad always asked me about how my classmates treated me. I got bullied—what kid hasn't? I was made fun of for my looks by boys, because *boys*, and teased for simply existing because kids can be cruel. While the taunting stung, it didn't have lasting effects. Besides, I think I've proven that I can handle a bully quite well.

Grandpa puts his hand on top of mine. "Just be careful, honey. Your father is a very charming man. One of the reasons he's been so successful is that he knows how to tell people what they want to hear."

"What does that mean?" I ask. It comes out harsher than I want it to.

Gran sighs lightly. "It just means that you should be cautious about what your father tells you. He's lied a lot to us over the years about things he's done. He even told us that it was your mother who left him."

"He *what*?" I practically shout. It makes me so angry that Dad would blame Mom. But I guess he realized admitting the truth to his parents—*Oh hey Mum and Dad, I abandoned my wife and daughter*—would have made him come across as a selfish jerk. Because he was.

"Your dad was probably embarrassed he covered it up." Gran gives me a kind smile. "Evie, your father loves you, so much. But luv, please remember *he's* the parent. You are not responsible for him."

"So, what? That's it. I shouldn't try to help him." My voice cracks.

It's not like my dad hasn't lied to or disappointed me. But I want to help him, and as hard as it is, I have faith. The last few days have given me a slight peek into how things used to be with us. It's made me miss what we used to have even more.

"We will never give up on him," Grandpa says with a squeeze of my hand. "He's family. You don't give up on family."

I nod, even though I almost did give up on him. In a way, he had given up on me, too. But here we are now. It's somewhere I didn't think we'd ever get to. It's made me even more determined to dig in and keep going.

I won't give up on my dad.

♪♪

Here we go again.

"Let me make one thing clear," Uncle Gabe declares as we approach the local pub after dinner. "There is no amount of money that will keep me quiet tonight."

Dad raises his eyebrow. "Should I take that as a challenge?"

We approach a blue door with purple flowers framing it. Gabe holds it open. "Get yer scrawny arse in here and buy me a pint o' lager, brother."

Dad walks into the pub shaking his head while I glare at Uncle Gabe. Who, in return, pokes me in my side until I let out a laugh.

"You're incorrigible," I say as I sit down at a table in the corner.

"Why, thank you." He gives me a little bow.

"That's not a compliment."

"Hiya, Cassandra!" Uncle Gabe calls out to the woman pouring a pint for Dad. "That's me older brother, remember him?"

The woman looks back up at Dad. Her eyes become wide as she stutters. "Oh—it—it—"

"Watch the precious lager!" Gabe says loudly as the pint she's pouring nearly overflows.

"Sorry!" she calls out. She puts her hand to her mouth in embarrassment. Then she looks at my dad again. "Nigel?"

Dad takes a deep breath. "Hello, Cassandra. Good to see you."

"Why—I didn't recognize you!" she begins. "You look—"

"Yes, it's been a while," Dad replies coolly. He turns to me. "You want a cider, Evie?"

I nod.

Dad furrows his eyebrows at me. "You okay? You keep rubbing your forehead."

It's at that moment that I realize my fingertips are touching the same spot Aiden kissed two days ago.

"Um, yeah. Fine. Ah, think I'm getting a zit," I babble in my Classy Evie way.

"Then you shouldn't touch it," Dad replies before turning back to the bar to get our drinks.

Okay, so here's the thing: I have been thinking about Aiden, quite a bit. I haven't seen him in a couple of days, and I can't text him because of his phone and he's busy with school. Whenever I'd read a Jane Austen or Regency novel, there's all this distance and time between the two potential lovers, and it seems so romantic. Writing letters. Waiting for that person. Pining. Well, let me tell you, it's not. It's torturous. And it just sucks.

But if being only a few hours away from Aiden is this bad now, what's going to happen when I finally get home to the US?

That right there is why I've got to push these feelings back. Besides, Aiden doesn't see me that way. I'm amusing to him. I make him laugh. He doesn't see me in that special chosen way. Although he did kiss me. On the forehead.

No. I can't keep repeating my mistakes.

And yet . . .

Dad returns to the table with our drinks.

"How long since you've been at this pub, brother?" Gabe asks. "I can't believe you agreed to come."

I not-so-subtly kick Gabe under the table, although I need this distraction. Our family has come to this pub since I could remember, but Dad hasn't joined us in years. When I was little, I'd sit with a coloring book while Dad and Gabe would regale anybody within earshot of stories about their childhood.

The music on the speaker near us switches to an acoustic song. It reminds me of Aiden.

So much for a distraction.

"Oh, I know that look," Uncle Gabe says as he nudges my shoulder. "I've made more than a few lasses have that look back in the day."

"Huh?" I try to play dumb.

"What's the bloke's name?"

"I thought you two broke up." Dad crinkles his forehead.

"We did," I reply.

"But there's someone new? Huh? Huuuuh?" Gabe keeps jostling me. You'd think he was the kid here. He takes another sip of lager, the foam giving him a tiny mustache. "Take it from me: men are not to be trusted. I'm speaking from experience. I mean, look at the lot you're hanging out with!" His laugh blasts through the room of people trying to enjoy a nice, quiet meal on a Thursday evening.

I raise my eyebrow at Gabe. "Oh, I know all about the wicked ways of your kind. I know not to get involved." Even though I clearly don't.

"That's a load of crap," Gabe says with a raise of his glass.

"Evie?" Dad prods.

"What? There's nothing to tell. I'm just friends with Aiden and Dev."

"I think I need to meet these alleged friends. Be a concerned dad and all."

"Oh, so *now* you're going to be a concerned dad" slips out. It's just a knee-jerk response when it comes to him. *Emphasis on* jerk. "I didn't mean—" I try to explain myself, even though up until a few days ago, Dad didn't really care that much about what was going on in my life.

No, that's not fair. You're both guilty of being stubborn.

"I don't believe it!" A tall guy with a balding head and ruddy cheeks approaches us. "Nigel Taylor!" The guy clamps his hand on Dad's shoulder, and Dad tenses up even further.

"Hey, Jay," Gabe says without his usual vigor. "You alright?"

This Jay guy ignores Gabe and continues to focus on an increasingly agitated Dad. "Jesus, I haven't seen this bloke in years. Look at you! I almost didn't recognize you without all that blubber around yer gut." He then pokes my dad in the stomach.

Dad pushes his arm away.

"Oi, Cassie, I owe you a tenner, it *is* Blubber Taylor in the flesh. Well, with less flesh." He then laughs. *Because this is funny?*

Gabe stands up and puts his arm around this jerk. "How 'bout I buy you a pint at the bar? Give Nigel some time with his daughter."

The guy glances at me. "You're Nigel's daughter? Guess he did have to lose some weight to get some lass to drop her knickers for him."

My dad has shrunk in his seat. All the color has drained from his face.

The old schoolyard reply of "sticks and stones will break my bones but names will never hurt me" is utter crap. Words can hurt. They can leave scars that never heal.

A rage starts to boil inside me. All I wanted was to pop by the pub for a pint with my dad and uncle. Then this guy has to come over and ruin everything.

No wonder Dad doesn't like coming back here.

I push my cider far away from me. Just in case.

Don't do it. Don't cause a scene. Don't make this worse for Dad.

"Better watch how much you drink, sweetheart," the guy says to me. "Don't want to balloon up. It runs in the family." He then puffs out his cheeks.

Oh, screw this guy. Have at him, Evie.

I stand up. "Does this make you feel good?"

"Evie," Dad says quietly, but I ignore him.

"Come on, Jay," Gabe tries to pull him away, but he keeps laughing.

"No, answer my question," I demand loudly. "Do you feel proud of yourself for putting down someone's appearance? Do you feel like a big, strong man now? Well, do you?"

The Jay guy blinks in response while Gabe chuckles, which only encourages me, to be honest.

"Do you have kids?" I don't even wait for a response. "How would you feel knowing that some heartless goon was torturing them every day? Although they're probably the bullies. *That* runs in families. I believe you owe my father an apology."

The guy holds his hands up. "Relax, sweetheart. We're just having some fun." He then grabs my dad by the shoulder.

"Does it look like anybody is having fun?"

He looks around. "Well not now, but we have a loud American

to blame for that, don't we?" He laughs, but nobody joins him.

"Get out!" I point at the door. I don't know who I am to think I can kick this guy out. *When has logic and reason stopped you before?*

"Jay, it's best you leave," Cassandra says from behind the bar. "I can call Cath to come get you."

Jay backs away with a laugh. "Go on then, you sad sacks. Enjoy yer evening."

He pushes the front door open and slams it shut. All eyes in the bar are on me.

"Um . . ."

Uncle Gabe claps his hands together. "We can always count on this one for some lively entertainment. Ah, Americans. Next round is on my brother—that would be my incredibly successful and wealthy brother, so you lot go for the good stuff!"

That prompts a round of cheers from the patrons, and everybody gets back to their own conversations.

I plop down on my chair, ashamed. "Dad, I'm so sorry."

Here we are trying to have a nice evening and I had to ruin it. I had to make a scene. And I wonder why people want to replace me?

Dad's gaze is down at the table. I might be imagining things—or maybe it's wishful thinking—but it looks like Dad is fighting back a smile. He finally looks up at me. He gives a small shake of his head as he lets out a chuckle. "Oh, Evie, your mother has raised you well."

I . . . wasn't expecting that. First, he never really mentions

Mom; he certainly doesn't acknowledge that she's basically raised me on her own. But also, he seems proud. Of me. *Because* of my big mouth.

I can feel myself melting more around my dad. Knowing that maybe this time things will be different.

"Mother?" Uncle Gabe says with a scoff. "That outburst right there was pure Taylor."

26

London Evie is becoming many things: closer with her father, a maker of new friends, an expert on various baked goods, and also super mature and, like, her emotional growth is astonishing, if I do say so myself.

Case in point: I've been able to stop from swooning over Aiden since I arrived back in London. Things are going well with my dad, so there's no need to stir up drama with a boy . . . who will eventually get tired of my Evieness. A boy I'm going to leave behind at the end of the summer. I'm focused on being just friends with Aiden, and it's going really well. Okay, so it's only been two days, but still. Go me. Yesterday, we went to London's Pride parade and cheered and danced along with Dev and Fiona as friends. No forehead pecks. Just a hug. See, friends.

And today, well, you'd have to be a complete sociopath to find a children's hospital a romantic setting.

"Hey!" I greet him at the entrance of the Great Ormond Street Hospital for Children. The reception area is bright, with colorful couches and a giant green-and-orange circle on the floor.

"Hey! I just have one thing to do first," Aiden says as he approaches a donation jar. He reaches into his guitar case and takes out the plastic bag where he puts the money he's earned from busking.

Of course that's what he does with the busking money.

"So, I . . . uh," I begin. I'm not sure how he's going to take this. There's earning money and then there's the privilege of having a wealthy father. But at the end of the day, it's about what that money can do. I reach into my back pocket and hand him an envelope. "I wanted to do this for you and Ruby."

Aiden's brow is furrowed as he opens up the envelope and sees the check my father wrote out to the hospital. "Oh wow."

"It's a donation made in Ruby's name, I hope that's okay."

"Blimey." He nods vigorously, shocked by the donation. "Yeah, of course. Wait, you asked your dad for money?"

"I thought maybe he could use his money for good. I'd rather it go here than to me so I can buy something frivolous."

When I got back from the parade yesterday, Dad was in the living room watching the news. I just blurted it out: "Could I have some money?" He was surprised and pleased. "Of course. I'll go get my wallet." I was expecting him to ask me what it's for, but the only question he had was how much I needed. I explained to him about coming to the hospital and how I wanted to do something. Technically, he was the one doing the giving—all I had to do was ask.

I only asked for a hundred pounds, but he wrote a check for a thousand without thinking of it.

All I had to do was ask him to see a therapist and he did it.

There's the pride of the parade yesterday, and then there's the stubborn pride I've been guilty of the last few years. I've missed out on so much with my father because of it.

"I can't believe you did that for me. And Ruby." Aiden's cheeks get flushed. "Thank you. And thank your dad."

Aiden is smiling as we go over to the check-in counter. The receptionist warmly greets Aiden by name. We sign in and are given name tags with a cute cartoon dog on them. Aiden leads me down a hallway that has windows looking out into a courtyard.

"Oh my God!" I exclaim as I see a huge pirate ship marooned in the middle of the corridor and a giant squid and . . . "Is that Ariel?"

Aiden nods. "Yeah, Disney did this whole courtyard for the kids. There's Mickey, Minnie." He starts pointing out all the different characters featured in this really cool space. "Ruby loved sitting over there; she felt like a mermaid." Aiden looks out at this giant seashell that also serves as a chair.

"Oh, wow. I believe it."

"Shall we?" He gestures for me to follow him as we twist our way through the first floor to the bright activities center. There's a little stage off to the side and dozens of kids are there, waiting for him.

"Hi, everybody!" Aiden greets them with the biggest smile I've ever seen. "How are we today? Kylie, I see you have a new friend. What's his name?"

This tiny girl in the front, connected to an oxygen tank, has a stuffed turtle in her arms. "This is . . . Aiden," she says with a giggle. The others join her.

"Oh, I like that name. Aiden seems very intelligent and kind," the human Aiden replies with a pleased nod.

I hang back, but one of the volunteers gestures for me to sit in an empty chair next to a young boy who has a baseball cap on to cover his bald head.

"Everybody, I want you to meet my friend Evie," Aiden says as he points to me.

The kids all say hello, and I put my best smile on my face as I wave.

"She's pretty," someone says.

"Is she your girlfriend?" another asks to even more snickers, while I actually hold my breath.

Calm yourself, Evie. You are not *a sociopath.*

Aiden wags his finger playfully. "Ah, you lot are too much. Did you know that Evie came all the way from America to be here?"

There were some impressed woos.

"Say something in your funny accent, Evie!" Aiden smiles at me.

I stand up awkwardly. What the hell am I supposed to say?

Maybe don't use the word hell?

I'm looking out at all these hopeful faces, but these kids are really sick. Ruby was here only a few months ago, and now she's . . . I keep thinking about Josh's sweet face. How I hardly see it when we FaceTime since he's always playing out of the shot.

Oh my God. I feel tears prickle behind my eyes.

Get yourself together.

Josh loves it when I'm stupid and silly. Not something I really have to work hard at, so I guess I'll just . . .

"Good day, mates!" I say loudly in what I think is an Australian accent before I switch back to my normal one. "Ha! That's not how I talk. Nope, this is how Americans talk. I do have a funny accent, don't I?"

I get a bunch of yeses and laughter. I then do the fishy face Josh loves, where I suck in the edges of my lips so the middle pops out like a fish. That gets another round of laughter.

"Well, Aiden has told me so much about you, and I just had to come and meet you all. Thanks for having me." I sit down, since I feel that my job as opener went as well as I could expect.

"Okay!" Aiden sits down and puts his guitar in his lap. "Are you ready for some music?" He gets a round of applause. "This is a new song I've learned just for Evie, and I hope you guys like it."

He learned a new song for me? He starts strumming the guitar, and I don't recognize the music. Did he write something for me? I hate how much I want that to be the case. To be the girl he sings about. But without all the heartbreak. I want a sappy love song.

Aiden starts signing, *"We go together like rama lama lama . . ."*

Of course he did.

It's "We Go Together," the closing song from *Grease*.

I am never going to live that down.

While I really want to give Aiden the you-are-in-so-much-trouble-and-I-don't-find-you-remotely-amusing glare right now, I can't help but clap and smile along as the kids crack up over the "boogedy boogedy" lyrics. It really is a funny song. And I guess it's more suited for this occasion than, say, the one song that starts with "Summer lovin' . . ." Just an example that popped into my head.

Ahem.

Aiden moves on from the lovely reminder of my school outburst to more non-traumatic songs: "Wheels on the Bus," "London Bridge Is Falling Down," and a few more popular upbeat songs like "We Don't Talk about Bruno" and "Happy."

I assumed today would be really sad, but it isn't. Aiden has brought a bright spot to their days, and mine, too.

I start to think about what else I can do to bring joy to Aiden. As a friend, obviously. Maybe something special to celebrate when he's done with school. Something he and I can do together. Just the two of us. *As friends.*

When Aiden's done, he talks to each of the kids, so I start introducing myself. Luckily, because of Josh, I'm an expert at talking to kids about all the very important things in life, like favorite colors and animals.

"Purple is my favorite color, too!" I say to Rey, a seven-year-old who has a French bulldog named Sophie. I point to my purple shirt. "You clearly have excellent taste."

"Hiya, Rey!" Aiden comes over and gives her an elbow bump. We take a picture with Rey and then make our way toward the exit.

Once we get outside, Aiden takes a deep breath. It's not until now that I see the weight of what he's been through.

Yeah, I need to do something fun for him.

As friends.

Keep telling yourself that, Evie.

"That was a really special and wonderful thing that you did in there," I say as I resist giving him a hug. "I'm sure it's hard on you."

He looks down the street. "It is, but it also helps. It has gotten easier. It was fun having you here today." He perks up. "Hey, what did you think of your song?"

"You just couldn't resist." I bump my hip against his as we begin to walk.

"I think I'm going to have to add it to my setlist."

"Of course you are." I dramatically roll my eyes. "Do you want to go get a coffee or a bite to eat?" Because that is stuff friends do.

"I'd love to, but I need to run an errand and then . . ."

"Exams," I finish for him. I try to not show my disappointment as we get to the Russell Square Underground station.

"I have to go down the block for my mum." Aiden puts his hands in his pocket.

"Oh." I was expecting us to ride the tube. To have a few more minutes together. "Okay, then."

He looks down at me and my hands start to shake. Okay, here's the thing. I don't want to be just friends with Aiden. I don't want another forehead peck from him. No. I want a full kiss. One that will cause me to lose my breath. For my knees to buckle. For me to forget that the United States of America even exists.

I know I shouldn't feel this way around someone who I'll eventually have to say goodbye to. I know I should protect my heart. I know all of this.

And yet . . .

"Bye," I say softly to Aiden as I turn around to the train station and force myself to keep walking. To not glance back at him. To not jump into his arms.

Let's be honest, shall we? Who here is shocked that I am, in fact, a sociopath?

Because I've learned nothing.

And I have to face the truth.

I'm in love with Aiden.

27

What is one to do when they realize they can't outrun their emotions? Apparently, for me, it's to physically torture myself.

"Move it NOW!" Poppy yells at those of us at her eleven a.m. class on Tuesday.

Yep. Moving my legs and going nowhere is a pretty apt metaphor for me.

"Turn up the resistance!" Poppy instructs in her friendly but firm teacher's voice. I turn the dial on the bike and my legs ache in protest. It also doesn't help that I went for a long run yesterday. Anything to try to distance myself from thinking of Aiden.

It hasn't been working.

Luckily, Poppy asked me if I was free for lunch. Unluckily, it was after her spin class.

I get a glance of my drenched body and red cheeks in the mirror. Poppy, on the other hand, looks dewy. So do most of the women here. Women who I made sure not to judge, even if I got some side glances at my ripped Old Navy T-shirt. My empathy shouldn't be restricted to those less fortunate. Not everybody with money is soulless.

"Last song!" Poppy announces, and I couldn't be happier. In four minutes this will be over, we can stretch, shower, and then eat. I feel a rush of happiness until Poppy makes us do intervals until the bitter end. And I do mean bitter. So very bitter.

"You were brilliant!" Poppy declares after I shower. We walk out of the studio, and she links her arm with mine. "It's easier the second time, yeah?"

I laugh, but feel a cramp in my stomach. "You do this every day?"

"Well, not every day. It's good to have a rest day."

"How about a rest decade?" I reply, to a giggle from Poppy.

"It's gorgeous out. Let's dine alfresco, and I know exactly where we should go." Poppy puts on her oversized sunglasses. She has on tight jeans, a navy sheer flowing top that falls off one shoulder, and a tank top underneath. While I am pure Evie: jeans, flip-flops, and a T-shirt. And yes, I'm still sweating despite the shower.

We walk to Bluebird, where Poppy guides us to their outside terrace and we're seated under an awning, surrounded by smartly dressed young people. There's a row of hedges that block the sidewalk, but we can see the old redbrick buildings across the street. It's these peeks at history that make me love exploring Chelsea. The other day I stumbled on the former house of *Mary Poppins* author P. L. Travers. Houses with famous former occupants are denoted with a blue plaque, so I always stop to see who used to live there.

"I have a modeling gig later tonight, so I'm eating light—they always have loads of free food backstage," Poppy says as she studies the menu.

I like how she drops "modeling gig" as if that was normal. It's like me saying, "Oh tonight? Nothing much, I'm just doing a wee bit of babysitting."

"Modeling?" I inquire.

"Yes. There's a launch party for a new athletic-wear line, so a bunch of the instructors are going to model. I'm sure I can get you in, if you want to come."

"I'm cool, thanks." I doubt I'll be able to walk tonight, let alone want to be around a bunch of super-fit people.

I look at the menu. Poppy's having the yellowfin tuna tartare and endive salad. I wonder if I should do the same.

"What is it?" Poppy asks.

I wasn't aware I made a noise. "I realized that since Dad and I had our talk and he's been seeing a therapist, I've been making better food choices." I haven't even brought a bag of crisps into the flat. I don't know whether it's because I don't want to trigger Dad or I want to impress him.

"That's not a bad thing," Poppy states. "As long as you're doing it for yourself and don't feel pressured."

I nod as I study the menu. Because I was in such a rush to get to London, I didn't get a chance to talk to *my* therapist, Dr. Wallace, before I left. Usually, I check in before and after seeing Dad. I know she'd remind me that while healthy eating is good, if I let my dad influence me to start being fussy over my food, it's almost like I'm going back to that little girl who thought her dad would love her only if she didn't eat. Our relationship should be about more than food.

"I think I'll get the cheeseburger," I say, almost as a dare to myself.

"Oh, it's delicious." Poppy nods in approval. "So . . ." She raises her eyebrow. "What's going on with the dreamy busker you're always hanging out with?"

I nearly drop my water glass.

Poppy laughs in delight. "Well, that answers that. I knew you fancied Aiden by how much you talk about him."

"I don't—" I start, but then I realize I need to stop lying. "Well, um, yeah, I kind of . . ." Think about him all the time. And want to be more than friends. Although, those confessions get caught in my throat.

Poppy starts cooing anyway.

"Shh!" I swat at her. "It's not like that. For him. I think. I don't know."

Poppy moves her sunglasses up on her forehead to look me in the eyes. "Evie, you must know if Aiden fancies you."

"I honestly don't have much experience."

"Don't give me that. You're a gorgeous girl, you've had to have loads of boys ask you out."

That's the thing: they haven't. Or maybe I was too closed off before to pay attention. I've never been the kind of girl that guys look at that way. When I've been out with Lindsay, she's always having guys and girls come up to her. I've been in the background. It was a place I felt comfortable being.

But now that I've had the butterflies and long, lingering kisses—it's hard to not think about wanting them again.

"This may surprise you, Poppy, but I'm not someone who understands subtlety. So I have no idea if Aiden likes me in that way. I think he finds me amusing. I mean, because I am, obvs, but he did kiss me—"

"HE KISSED YOU!" Poppy squeals in delight.

"On the forehead!" I whisper, sinking in my seat. "Like I do with Josh when he's being cute. Like a puppy."

"Come on, Evie, I think Aiden does fancy you. Besides, what's not to like?" Poppy gives me a wink. "And more importantly, you like him." She puckers her perfect pout into a kiss.

How could I not like Aiden? He's sweet, funny, and cute. I like being around him, even when he's teasing me. Things always flow in this natural way between us. I look forward to seeing him. *But* . . .

And that one word is always the crux of most problems.

"I do, a lot. *But* he lives here; I live in the US. And that's just to start. We both have these issues. The thought of opening myself up again to just—" I clear my throat.

This really is what it comes down to: am I willing to take a chance when I'm most likely going to have my heart broken all over again?

"And let's not forget everything I told you about what Aiden's gone through," I add, because I would never want to hurt him.

Poppy gives me an encouraging smile. "It sounds like what Aiden needs is a lovely American to cheer him up with a big ol' snog."

"Poppy!" I shake my head, but the thought of kissing Aiden literally makes my heart ache. *This is so not going to end well.* "But I can't. We both have so much baggage."

Poppy throws her head back. "Oh my God, Evie, who doesn't? Everybody is carrying something with them from a past relationship. I guess it depends on if you're willing to check it at the gate before you decide to board."

"Oh wow, nice airport metaphor." We both laugh.

"Thank you! I really should make T-shirts or greeting cards."

"Self-help book," I offer.

Poppy looks down at the burger and fries that have been placed in front of me. "I think I'm going to self-help myself to one of your chips."

I push the plate toward her. "Well, I'm jumping way ahead of myself. I don't even know if he likes me, and even if he did, there's no point in going there."

Poppy shakes her head in disappointment. "Oh, Evie, your father has done a proper job of messing you up."

"And Sean," I add.

When I have to really think about it, I've never had a guy that hasn't screwed me over in a way. I guess Stuart, Mom's husband, has been a good guy. I also made sure to tell him at their rehearsal dinner, "If you ever hurt my mom, I will hunt you down and destroy you." I was twelve.

Twelve.

"I just don't know. I don't want to ruin anything," I admit.

Poppy leans in. "How do you feel when you think of kissing him?"

There's a flip in the pit of my stomach.

Poppy smiles. "You don't even need to say a single word—I can tell by looking at you."

I instinctually touch my face. It's warm.

"Seems to me like you have a crush!" Poppy declares before she pops another fry in her mouth.

Yeah, but I'm worried it'll end up crushing me.

28

After my lunch with Poppy, I'm reminded how good it is to have a girl friend to talk to. Someone to confide in. Especially about a very cute boy.

I know what putting up emotional barriers can cost. I don't want to be someone who pushes people away. I've let my dad back in, and it's going well. Maybe if I let go of some of the animosity I have about home, I will be ready to fully open my heart to Aiden.

Of everything that went down back before I left, I'm most ashamed of how I simply cut off Lindsay. Even Theo. I wouldn't listen to them. I hold my phone in my hand. Maybe it's time I put that behind me. Maybe it's time I forgive.

Before I can give myself the millionth reason not to do it, I unblock Lindsay's number and hit video chat.

While I listen to the ring, I wonder if maybe they all decided to give me a taste of my own medicine and block me, too. I haven't been a great friend the last couple of weeks. I wouldn't even give them a chance to explain before I fled the states.

The phone illuminates with Lindsay's face. Her dark eyes are wide. "Evie? Oh my God, I'm so happy to see you!"

"Eves?" I see Theo's toned, brown arm in the shot before he pulls the phone away from Lindsay. His face fills up the screen. "Hello, stranger. I just . . ." He rubs his head.

"Oh, hey, Theo," I say, surprised he's hanging out with Lindsay. Then my stomach plunges as I wonder if Sean and Meredith are also with them. The whole gang back together and all that.

"I know," Lindsay says, probably sensing the question on my lips. "I have to deal with this dude since one of my best friends left the country while the other is dead to me."

"Same," Theo says as he gives me a cautious smile. "We're so sorry, Eves."

"I know." I can see the anguish on their faces. That's the benefit of having close friends: so much can be said without uttering a single word. "And I'm sorry for leaving and refusing to listen to you."

"We didn't know for sure, really," Lindsay states as she twists a strand of her hair around her finger. "That's the only reason we went to talk to them after school. To figure out what the hell was going on. And we haven't spoken to them since. We're on your side."

"There doesn't have to be sides," I comment, even though I'm secretly glad they've chosen me.

They both look shocked. "Um, yes, there does," Lindsay says. "What they did to you was wrong. They spent weeks lying to us as well. But most of all, Theo and I are so sorry you had to go through this."

"Thanks." I feel a pull on my chin.

"But no matter where you are, you're not alone."

"Yeah, we've got you, Eves," Theo says.

I start nodding. There has been a part of me that thought that maybe I overreacted. Maybe I was in the wrong. While it's nice to have Poppy and Aiden tell me that I have a right to be hurt and angry, it's different when it's coming from two people who were there.

Two people who I also hurt.

"Oh, Evie," Lindsay says as she puts her head on Theo's shoulder. "It's not the same without you. Can you please come home? I'll buy you all the frozen mochas, and Theo will promise not to say anything stupid for a whole day."

"I agree to no such thing!" Theo protests.

I open my mouth to reply but realize I don't know what to say. I'm grateful to see that there's a very important part of my life back home that's still intact. "While that's all tempting, I just . . . I'm not sure when I'm coming back."

Lindsay and Theo exchange a look. They've heard enough horror stories about my dad to wonder why I wouldn't be on the first flight to Chicago.

"London has been surprisingly good. I'm working on a few things with my dad. I've made some friends." I'm about to tell them about Aiden, but I stop myself. Talking to Lindsay and Theo reminds me that I have a whole other life I'm going home to.

"I'm so glad it's going well," Lindsay says with a small smile.

She tilts her head as if she's studying me to find the hidden meaning behind my desire to stay a little bit longer. "Are you sure everything's okay? You have every right to be mad at us still—"

"I forgive you guys, I do." I instantly feel a heaviness lift off my heart. "I think it's going to take longer to do the same with Meredith and Sean, but I'll get there. They've been a huge part of my life. It would be weird to shut them off completely, but that's going to take more time."

As I say those words, I realize how true they are. Meredith and Sean have betrayed me, lied to me, and hurt me. We'll never get back to the place we once were, but I don't want to have to cower from them in the hallways at school and feel uncomfortable if we're in the same class. They were the ones who did this, after all, not me. I shouldn't have to be the one to hide.

"Take all the time you need," Theo says. "Although not too much. Because we miss you. I haven't had to move an umbrella fourteen times a day since you left."

I narrow my eyes at Theo, who laughs in response. Theo's a lifeguard at a swanky community pool and sneaks us in. While the others soak up the sun, I huddle under the umbrella. I got my fair skin from my British side. Dad gets his currently glowing complexion from a bottle.

"And I haven't had to put on sunglasses without your pasty white skin blinding me," Theo says with a wink.

"See, you have to come back to save me from his horrible attempts at humor." Lindsay gestures her head at Theo.

"Yeah, nobody realized how bad *my* jokes were until *you* left."

"Hey!" My jokes aren't that bad—granted I get most of them from Josh. "Oh, do you want to hear the latest from Josh? Are you ready?"

Both Theo and Lindsay smile back at me.

"Why was Tigger's head in the toilet?" I pause for them to ask why. "He was looking for Pooh!" Then I giggle, mostly remembering how hysterical Josh was when he told me.

"Better yet, stay in London," Theo says dryly as Lindsay hits him.

We're on the phone for nearly an hour, and when we hang up, it takes me a second to remember that I'm not in my bedroom. Talking to them was my first twinge of wanting to go back home. But being here is not about my friends or Sean and Meredith. This is about me. Maybe I left because of them, but once I arrived, I knew I had things I needed to work on.

Namely, what I want out of life. The people I want to be in it. What I should let go of, and, maybe more important, who to let in.

29

I've never been happier for other people to be done with school. Especially when one is a boy I'm utterly helpless over.

"Here you go." Aiden hands me a pint as I try to not slobber all over him. We're at a pub to have a celebratory drink before heading to the end-of-term party nearby. I can't believe Aiden and Fiona were able to walk up to the bar and order us drinks without being carded. Aiden slides next to me, and I try to keep my breath steady having him so close. He's even wearing a blue top and—

"Oh my God, Aiden," I say as I take him in. All of him. And notice something is missing.

"Are you just now realizing how devilishly handsome I am?" he says with a wink.

Please, I knew that the second I laid eyes on him.

"Um . . ." I feel a bit panicked and don't want to cause him any stress now that exams are over, but . . . "Where's Ruby's scarf?"

He's not wearing it. He always wears it. Always.

"Oh, I took it off."

"Can you believe it?" Fiona says. "That thing was starting to *smell*."

Aiden laughs. "Yeah, I'm going to wear it when I busk, but it doesn't really matter what I wear. Ruby will always be here." He taps his chest.

I don't know whether I should be happy or sad. It was a crutch for him, but also a comfort. It's amazing that Aiden was able to move past it. And it's true, it doesn't mean he doesn't still love Ruby.

Aiden smiles at me, and I need to look away or I'm going to launch myself onto him. I've promised myself that I need to behave tonight. Maybe be the kind of person who isn't too much, but just enough for a certain someone. I'm going to Goldilocks myself to be juuuuuust right.

"Okay!" Dev raises his half-pint. "In the words of Evie: to independence!"

"To independence!" Fiona, Aiden, and I clink our glasses with his.

I'm trying to focus on Dev sitting across from me, but my entire body is buzzing from having Aiden nearby. I scoot a couple of inches closer to Fiona.

Yeah, that'll stop you from yearning.

"Okay, Evie, now that we're done with exams, I need to ask you for a favor," Dev says as he wiggles his eyebrows playfully.

"Here it comes," Fiona says with a snarl.

Dev continues undeterred, "I need your help talking to Becs. I figure if I dangle an American in front of her, she might want to have a conversation."

Fiona holds on to her pint a little tighter. Her jaw tenses.

"Dangle?" I ask, trying to lighten the mood. "As in you're setting a trap and using me as bait?"

Dev shakes his head. "No! Please don't think that I'm trying to use you."

"Dev, it's okay, really." I pause, thinking about what could potentially happen if I get into a conversation with Becs. Actually . . . "I'll do it."

I keep my eyes glued on Dev's happy face. I don't want to glance at Fiona, because I'm fairly positive she's probably glaring at me.

"Grand." Dev looks so happy, I feel bad that he's probably going to have his heart broken tonight.

"I think we're all forgetting something," Aiden says.

I take a deep breath as I turn to face Aiden. When his green eyes meet mine, I nearly drop my pint glass.

Get yourself together, girl.

"What do we have to think about now that term is over?" Dev says as he takes a sip of his beer, while I take a large gulp of mine.

"Um, Evie is giving me a surprise in two days!" Aiden reaches over and pokes me in the ribs, causing my traitorous heart to flutter.

But what did I seriously expect? I've only spent the last couple of days planning a special day for Aiden. Because I can't stop thinking about him.

I also haven't seen my dad all week, which is weird even when he is busy, but I used this surprise as an excuse to call his office to talk to him. Even though it was Simon who helped make the arrangements.

And not to brag, but it's so good. And what's even better is how much not knowing what we're doing is messing with Aiden.

"Come on!" he begs. "Give me a hint!"

"I told you all you need to know," I say with a wiggle of my eyebrows.

"Ah, *meet me at ten in the morning on Saturday at Euston station with your guitar* just makes me more confused."

"Mission accomplished." I give him a flirty wink.

"It is an excellent plan," Dev says with a mischievous grin, even though I didn't tell him anything. But it seems I'm not the only one who loves getting Aiden flustered.

"I can't believe you told Dev and not me!" Fiona protests.

"Or *me!*" Aiden says as he throws up his hands. "*I'm* the one who's going to be surprised by a . . . holiday? Yes, you're taking me on some weekend holiday trip. So do I or do I not need to bring an extra pair of pants?"

I open my mouth to tell him he doesn't have to, but close it. Giving him any hints would ruin the fun. And it's nice to rile him up for a change. "Dev, feel free to tell Fiona."

"Yes!" Fiona leans in as Dev whispers in her ear. She pulls away and looks at Aiden with such glee. I can only assume Dev just told her to mess with Aiden. "It's a brilliant idea, Evie."

"Come on!" Aiden protests. "Just give me one teeny, tiny hint."

I shrug my shoulders, which causes him to tickle me even more. Which, to be honest, I'm not mad about.

I realize this is a dangerous game I'm playing, but if I only have a few more weeks with Aiden, I want to make them as special as possible. Spend as much time with him as I can.

"Stop it!" I protest, even though I'm loving how close together we are.

Fiona puts her hand out to prevent me from practically sitting in her lap. "Leave me out of your demented version of foreplay."

Aiden stops touching me. He even scoots back a couple of inches. Huh. So I guess it *isn't* flirting, if Fiona's insinuation causes him to freeze.

Yeah, okay, it isn't what I was hoping for, but I guess this proves that Aiden doesn't see me that way. I try to not take the rejection personally, even though it is personal. But this is for the best. Yes.

Keep telling yourself that.

Dev downs the last of his half-pint and stands up. "Let's go make some memories."

"If you keep drinking like that, you won't remember anything," Fiona fires back.

We walk out of the pub, but Fiona stops me with her hand. "What are you playing at by agreeing to talk to Becs?" She looks hurt.

"Fiona, have you ever known me to have a conversation with any of your classmates that has ended up being a *good* thing?" This causes Fiona to raise an eyebrow. "As much as I don't want Dev to get hurt, perhaps it's time for him to see the real Becs, courtesy of one mouthy American."

A look of actual glee crosses Fiona's face before she releases her hand from the door. I know I promised to behave, to not be too Evie, but I'll just do this one thing and then I'll be on my best behavior. I swear.

Besides, this gives me something to do at the party instead of follow Aiden around like a lovesick puppy. I have some self-respect.

Not a ton, but still.

♪♪

As soon as we walk into their friend's flat, I know tonight is going to be a notch up from the other parties. The ground floor is packed with people. Music is blasting in the living room, and there are bodies pressed together dancing. There's one table of beer and another of hard alcohol. I see only one bag of crisps in the middle of all the booze.

"End of term!" someone screams, to the cheers of others.

I missed the end-of-year party back home. While my fellow classmates celebrated the start of summer, I sat at home and cried under my blanket. At one point, Josh brought me some ice cream. I was so touched, I didn't mention the big hole in the scoop or the chocolate on his chin.

"Cider?" Aiden calls out over the music. He leans into me. "But remember to behave, as we have an adventure coming up . . . on a boat?" He fishes for another clue.

"Cider, please," I reply with a shake of my head. Like I was going to fall for that.

Fiona's gaze settles on the dance floor, where Becs is pressed between two of her girl friends. She has on a halter top that shows off her toned stomach when she moves back and forth. Becs isn't even being subtle—she's now backing up into some random guy, but her eyes are on Fiona.

Although I'm the only one who really seems to notice it. And Fiona, who has now maneuvered herself further into the throng of partygoers.

A song comes on that I recognize from some movie. It's mostly in German, I think? It's ninety-nine-something balloons. The beginning is just a voice, but as the beat kicks in, Dev moves a bit, so I take his hand and lead him to the dance floor near Becs. It's better for us to just get this over with. Dev and I are forced to be a little closer than two platonic friends should probably be, but we just go with it. We sway together to the beat. Dev puts his hand on my hip as he glances at Becs to see if that's gotten her attention.

It doesn't.

I take Dev's hand and then spin myself around him, to clear some space and draw attention to us. This may come as a surprise, but I do not relish having a room focused on me. But I do it for Dev. As the beat increases, we move a little faster. I shimmy around Dev, who jumps in place. The beat drops back and I put my arms around Dev as we rock back and forth.

A few more people join us, and we all jump around as the music picks up even more. It's freeing to jump around and dance with strangers. Then the song slows down again and Dev takes my hand and spins me around.

When he dips me at one point, I see Becs noticing us. Most are... until the song ends. There are some cheers until another eighties song comes on. This one I know: "Push It" by Salt-N-Pepa. Dev goes to another level as the "*Ooh, baby, baby*" chorus starts. He's moving like he's studied a video or something, and it's amazing.

Most of the dance floor has made room to cheer on Dev. I move to the side and join them.

I swear, I feel like I'm in a movie right now, one where the nerd's hot dance moves get him the girl. Not that I want him to get Becs. But she's clapping and cheering along with the rest of us. There's even a "Dev" chant that has started.

I catch Aiden's eye across the room. He looks pretty shocked—and amused—by what's happening.

Dev is sliding side to side to the beat. He seems to be in another world. Then he gives me a wink, and he slides over toward Becs. He definitely has her—and most of the party's—attention now. He looks her directly in the eye and points to her. He starts motioning his finger for Becs to join him.

This is it. This is the moment he's waited for. All his classmates are cheering his name, he's got the girl of his dreams in his sights.

There's a part of me that wants things to go Dev's way, as I would never want anybody to be crushed, but then I think of Fiona. There's probably no winning in this scenario.

"Shall we?" Dev says to Becs as he reaches out his hand to her.

Becs cringes as she takes a disgusted step backward. "You've *got* to be joking." And then because that's not bad enough, she bleats out

"Ewwwwwww!" before she whips her glossy hair and stomps away.

Dev stops dancing and looks absolutely gutted.

Poor Dev.

And it didn't take me making a scene with my loud mouth.

I grab some random person to join me in the now-vacant middle so people aren't staring at a dejected Dev.

Once the dance floor is back to being packed, I move over to Dev. I link my arm through his and lead him to Aiden and Fiona, who are leaning against a wall.

"Told you she wasn't worth it," Fiona states.

"You've been holding out on me, Dev," Aiden says as he jostles him. "I didn't know you had those moves. Guess I have even more songs to add to my act."

Dev tries to smile, but I can tell he's defeated. "Maybe I shouldn't have invaded her space."

"Dev, we're at a party," I say right as my back is elbowed by a guy trying to carry four bottles of beer. "Personal space isn't really a thing. Plus, you were killing it."

Fiona laughs. "You really were."

"Hiya, Dev." A girl with light-brown skin and a head full of curls approaches him. "You have some pretty wicked moves."

"Oh hey, Neena," Dev says shyly.

"Are you going to get back out there?" She glances at the dance floor.

Some other song has come on that everybody seems to know, but I don't.

"I'm not sure," Dev says with a frown.

"Too bad. Well, if you do . . ." Neena gives him a shy smile.

Maybe Dev will get the girl after all. And I don't know this one, but she has to be better than Becs.

Dev yelps as Fiona jabs him sharply in the ribs. "Oh," he says, and his eyes get wide as he realizes Neena is asking him to dance. "Oh! Yeah! Wicked!"

Neena laughs as she takes him by the hand, and they disappear among the crowd.

"Dare I dream?" Fiona says. "Neena is cool. And sweet. Here's hoping Dev can take a hint."

Aiden crosses his fingers. "Yes. And speaking of hints, so Saturday . . ." He looks at me with hope in his eyes.

Hope that I'm going to crush. "Well, I need to get a cider." I turn my back on Aiden and try to push my way toward the table of drinks.

"Sorry," I say to someone I bump into.

It's Becs. "Do I know you?"

I shake my head. "I don't think so."

"Oh, you're American!" She gets excited. I guess Dev knew her enough to realize that this would be of interest to her. "Where do you live?"

"In the States?"

"Yes!" She gives a little shake.

"Near Chicago."

"Oh, Chicago! The Cubs! Navy Pier! The Willis Tower! The

Magnificent Mile!" She starts saying random Chicago places. "I just love the States. Life there must be so exciting."

"Um." I don't really know what to say. "It's okay."

"Where are you staying here?"

"My dad lives in the Chelsea Barracks."

Becs's jaw is practically on the floor. I'm always embarrassed that Dad lives in such a fancy development. "That's so posh. We have to be friends!"

She takes my hand before I can respond and drags me to a corner that isn't packed. She pulls out her phone. "Selfie!" she says, and I don't even have time to protest as she snaps a picture. "We have to follow each other! Give me your handle and I'll tag you."

"Oh, I'm taking a break from social media."

"What?" Becs looks like I just sprouted two heads. "Why would you do that? Anyways, I have loads of followers, so you can get more exposure."

"I don't really—" I start to explain, but then I see Fiona approaching us with Aiden behind her.

"We're going to go," Fiona states.

Becs looks between Fiona and me. "Are you friends with *her*?"

"Yes, we are," I state proudly.

Becs laughs. "Oh darling," she says as I realize at no point has she asked me my name or told me hers. It's possible she assumed I already knew. "You can do so much better. Unless you're also"—she leans in and says in a fake whisper—"a lez."

That familiar boil starts to rise in my gut. I open my mouth, but

Fiona places her hand on my forearm. She smiles sweetly at me. "Don't worry about it, Evie."

I take a deep breath and nod.

Fiona then turns to Becs. "Because I so have this."

Becs is typing on her phone. "I'm sorry, are you talking to me?"

Fiona laughs in reply. "It's a shame to waste the breath and brain cells, but yeah, I am."

Becs stops typing and looks at Fiona with a smirk. "Do you really want to start this with me of all people?"

"What exactly do I have to lose if we start talking about the truth?" Fiona says loudly. A few conversations around us stop. Becs looks panicked for a second, before she flips her hair. Fiona continues, "You and I both know that I'm aware of things that could bring down your disgustingly fake image."

"And I see you're still an angry lesbian," Becs says with a bored look to her fingernails, although I can sense the panic in her eyes.

"You were my friend and I trusted you," Fiona says loudly, wanting people to hear it. "I was bullied and shamed because of you. You made me come out before I was ready. You treated me like garbage, yet you suffered zero consequences. How is that fair?"

Becs looks around and sees the curious people nearby. "I don't know what you're talking about."

If Becs wants to be an actress, she needs some lessons. No one is buying it.

"I'm not going to do what you did to me," Fiona says. "But at least I have the courage to live my life as me. Like me or loathe me, this is who I am." Fiona gestures at herself. "And you lost the privilege of being my friend. So move aside, because I'm not going to waste another moment of my life on you."

Fiona brushes past Becs, and Aiden is quickly on her heels. I see Becs rolling her eyes and calling Fiona a drama queen before I follow them out.

"I'm so proud of you," Aiden says as he hugs Fiona outside the building. "I didn't know any of that, and you can tell me as much or as little when you're ready."

Fiona nods. "That felt good." She looks at me. "I mean, I did learn from the best."

I actually feel a swell of pride. My big mouth did something good for a change. "Oh Fiona, you were amazing in there."

"Yeah, and without the sacrifice of any innocent beverages," Aiden says as he winks at me.

"Night's still young," I counter. I give Fiona a hesitant pat on the back. "You doing okay?"

"Yeah. I had all these things I've wanted to say to her, but I kept bottling it up. It just made me so angry every time I saw her. I'm glad I said something instead of just avoiding her. Maybe she'll be the one avoiding me for a change."

"What's going on?" Dev walks out of the flat. "I saw you all leaving."

"I needed some air," Fiona says.

"Oh, okay." Dev's brow is wet with sweat. "So, um, Neena is pretty brilliant, yeah?"

Fiona lets out a laugh into the humid evening. "Here we go again. But she is great, Dev."

"Is it okay if I go back in?" Dev points to the door.

"Go be a dancing machine!" Fiona motions to Dev.

He quickly turns around and goes inside.

Fiona looks up at the sky with a smile. "It's funny, because I've been so worked up about Becs, now I have this weight off my shoulders. It's like it was this hurdle that I'm past. And you know what, I'm not ready to leave the party." Fiona practically runs back into the flat.

Leaving Aiden and me alone on the sidewalk.

"So . . ." Aiden begins. "Should I wear a tie or a swimsuit on Saturday?"

He's looking at me with so much joy and anticipation. I think of Dev, who got rejected but is taking another chance with Neena. Of Fiona going back into the party, not caring that Becs is there.

I know where I want to be, and it's right here.

With Aiden.

"Evie?" he leans in. "Are you o—"

Before he gets another word out, before I can convince myself of the millions of reasons not to, I grab Aiden by the shoulders and pull him in for a kiss.

The second our lips touch, it feels like I've been struck by a million bolts of lightning. I don't know what I thought a kiss was before, but this is something else. It's both sweet and intense. It's almost too much.

I pull away for a second and touch my lips, wondering if this is even real.

Aiden's eyes are wide. His hair is tousled, from me. I did that.

"Um, Evie, I don't know if you meant—" Aiden starts, but I don't want to talk about this. I don't want to do anything but feel Aiden's lips back on mine.

"Stop talking," I say as I take him back into my arms.

"That's pretty ironic coming from—" Aiden starts, but I kiss him again.

I don't know how long we're out there, in each other's arms, but all I know is it feels right.

It's not until a group exits the party and starts shouting at us that we pull away.

I should be embarrassed by my abruptness, but why start showing any self-awareness now?

"For the record," Aiden says, a bit out of breath. "If that's my surprise, it's even better than I could have imagined."

I realize I'm smiling so widely, my cheeks hurt. Aiden feels the same way. Or at least doesn't mind snogging me. "Oh, that was nothing," I say, even though it was everything.

"Yeah?" His face is bright red. "But, um, can we still do that on Saturday? In addition to . . . rock climbing?"

"I've got three words for you." I lean toward him and feel sparks all around us, as I whisper in his ear, "Just you wait."

Because we're just getting started.

30

Things are good.

Scratch that. Things are great. Brilliant. Amazing. Perfect. Who knew opening yourself up to someone again could be a wonderful thing?

Like, legitimately everybody but you.

Aiden and I are spending all day tomorrow together. We've been sending each other yearning missives via email, and I imagine him writing like Mr. Darcy, using a quill even though he has a laptop. So yeah, boy stuff—amazing.

I'm talking to Lindsay and Theo again. Friend stuff—amazing.

The only not-super-amazing-but-not-that-bad-and-who-am-I-to-be-so-selfish thing is my dad. I just haven't seen him that much. While I used to consider that a good thing, I want us to keep building our relationship back up. Make myself available to him.

So I decide to surprise my dad after his therapist appointment. It's his third with Dr. Basini. I want to show him how much it means to me that he's doing this for him. For us. So I'm going to be there for my dad.

"I'm just waiting for her two o'clock to finish up," I say to the receptionist who gives me a polite nod.

My plan is to ride back with Dad to his office. See how he's doing. See if we can get a show on the West End on his calendar. Maybe plan some type of holiday in August. I'm also going to be better about accepting things from my dad. I'm going to ask him either for a UK cellphone or for him to pay to put my phone on international roaming. And yes, that also means I can text with Aiden. Win-win all around.

The door to Dr. Basini's office opens. Instead of my father, an older woman steps out.

"I'm sorry," I say to the receptionist. "Did Nigel Taylor reschedule his two o'clock? I know he was just here on Tuesday as well."

"What's the name again?" she says as she begins to type in her computer.

I feel silly. I should've checked with dad's assistant, Simon. It would make sense that Dad might have to reschedule his appointment since work has been busy.

"And you are?" she fishes.

"I'm his daughter." I'm sure there might be some issues with privacy at a psychiatrist's office.

"And you're saying he has a regular appointment on Fridays?"

"And Tuesdays." I feel a lump in my throat. "He just started last week though. And he couldn't make last Friday because we were in Devon, but he said he went this past Tuesday and then today. So it's his first Friday appointment. Maybe I have the time wrong?"

"Is there a problem?" Dr. Basini approaches us.

"Yes, sorry. I just thought my dad was here, Nigel Taylor."

Dr. Basini walks around the desk and looks at the computer. She glances up at me with worry on her face. "Did your father tell you that he was going to be here?"

"Yes, I was going to surprise him."

"Please come into my office," Dr. Basini says. "You're his daughter?"

I nod meekly. "Evie."

"Yes, I remember we met briefly last week," she says warmly as she gestures at her couch.

I hesitantly sit down, unsure of what's going on.

Dr. Basini sits at her desk and folds her hands. "I'm not allowed to discuss what transpires during my sessions."

"I didn't come here to snoop." I thought, at best, Dad and I might be able to get some pizza afterward.

"Your father has only been here once," Dr. Basini states.

"He said he was here on Tuesday."

"He wasn't," Dr. Basini says with a concerned frown. "I'm looking at my notes, and I can say that your father was worried about you, so please know that he cares."

While that's nice to hear, I'm still so confused. "Did he talk about his control issues? His problems with food?"

Dr. Basini remains silent but looks genuinely perplexed. Her brows are furrowed as she looks between her notes and me. I know she can't divulge what he said.

"I want to make sure I understand this correctly: my father came here once, talked for an hour, and didn't mention his controlling tendencies, his obsession with food and exercise and how it ripped my family apart, how he abandoned my mother and me. Nope. Nothing."

Dr. Basini returns a blank stare. She doesn't need to say anything. That's enough of an answer.

"Thank you for your time," I say in a daze as I slowly walk out of her office.

"Is there something we can do to help you? Would you like some tea?" she offers.

I glance at the phone on the receptionist's desk. "Can I make a phone call?"

"Of course." The receptionist moves the phone over to me.

With shaking hands, I dial Dad's office number. I remind myself to keep calm as I wait for Simon to pick up.

"Nigel Taylor's office."

"Simon, it's Evie!" I say cheerily.

"Hi, Evie, you alright?"

"Yes! You know, I just realized that Dad probably isn't back from his appointment with Dr. Basini."

There's a slight pause, which I probably wouldn't have read into before. I know better now. "No, he isn't."

"Wow, this is his second appointment this week. I'm so proud of him going."

"Yes, he's committed to it!"

God dammit, Simon! We thought we could trust you!

"Well, I'll talk to him when he gets home tonight. Does he have any evening meetings?"

I hear Simon clicking away at his keyboard. "He's doesn't. He's signed up for a seven o'clock spin class and then a session with his trainer."

Typical Friday night.

"Okay, thanks." I hang up and can't look at the receptionist or Dr. Basini. I'm barely able to croak out a thank-you before I head outside and start to aimlessly wander.

I think back to the meals. He ate when we were in Devon. He ate pizza in front of me. But then how much did he work out after? What about the many other meals since then? Is that why he hasn't been around as much? Was it really work, or did he think he could eat two slices of pizza and I would believe all was right with the world?

Well, you did believe that.

Okay, I knew that this was going to take a long time, but I also know that he needs to get help if he's going to get better.

I don't know why I'm so surprised, that he only told me what I wanted to hear. Dad's lied to me many times before. He's lied to his parents, too. They even warned me.

Why did I think this would be different?

Because *I* asked him? Because it was something *I* wanted?

Yeah, well. We now know how much I mean to him.

Nothing.

31

I've spent the last two hours in the flat, staring at the front door, waiting for Dad to come home.

Every sound has made me jumpy. My stomach is in knots. My mind is in an even worse disposition.

I'm tired of the lies.

There's a rustling near the door and I sit up straight. Dad comes in, freshly washed from the gym. "Oh, hello, Evie!"

"Hi, Dad!" I say brightly, reeling him into a false sense of security. "How was your day?"

"Busy," he replies as he pulls out a bottle of water from his bag. "Sorry I haven't been around as much—this new deal has us rammed at work. How have you been?"

"Good!" I smile at him—it hurts my face and my mouth. "Oh hey, today was your appointment with Dr. Basini, right?"

"That's right." He doesn't even hesitate. It's that easy for him to lie right to my face. Then again, he's had enough practice.

"How's that going? It's your . . . third appointment?"

"Yes. I might start going just once a week, but I'm committed to it." It's the same line Simon recited back to me. He sits down at the table next to me. I put my hands in my lap so he can't see that they're shaking. "She's really made me think a lot about my life."

"That's great," I say and realize there's a tremble in my voice.

"Evie?" Dad leans in and that's when I feel it.

There are tears streaming down my face.

"Are you okay?"

I shake my head. "Why are you lying to me?"

He looks genuinely surprised. "I'm not lying to you."

"You didn't see Dr. Basini today."

"Of course I did," he says with a tsk.

"YOU DIDN'T. I WAS THERE! I KNOW YOU HAVEN'T BEEN TO HER SINCE THAT FIRST DAY!" I yell. It feels good to get it out.

Dad rubs a nonexistent stain on the kitchen table. "So you're checking up on me. You don't trust me."

I laugh resentfully. "Do *not* try to turn this around on me. Of course I don't trust you. And you just proved why I shouldn't!"

Dad sighs. "Oh, Evie, I didn't want to lie to you, but there isn't a problem."

"There isn't a problem?" I get up and start opening his empty kitchen cabinets. "You don't have food here. You only keep green juice. Do you realize if there's a zombie apocalypse that you'd be dead in less than a day? You don't have any nonperishables!"

Just a small suggestion: perhaps you shouldn't have started off your argument with talk about zombies.

"Nonperishable foods can be highly processed," Dad states with a blank look on his face.

"You're obsessed with food and your weight and calories and working out."

"Those are all healthy things, Evie. I'm fit for my age."

"When was the last time you were at a doctor?" I ask. He opens his mouth, and I cut him off. "You know what, I know it's going to be a lie. You're too skinny. Your face is gaunt."

"You saw me eat. I had pizza for you. I drank a pint for you."

"And then you went running for hours the next day," I remind him.

"It's healthy to work off what you ate."

"But you're not healthy. You're obsessed. It's not about the calories. It's all about control for you!"

Dad pinches the bridge of his nose. "Do you know how hard it was for me to get in this shape? And if I slip, even a little, it comes back on. Every year, I have to work harder as I get older. Yes, that involves having a great deal of control—I have to be careful of what I put into my body—and I won't apologize for it. It's a lot of hard work and it's exhausting, but I will not, *will not*, go back to how I was."

"You mean happy and with a family?" I throw in his face.

He doesn't react. "I don't understand why my family is so obsessed with wanting me to become a slob."

"That's not what we want. We want you to be happy. We want you to laugh again. We want you to not have to be so fixated on every single calorie. You shouldn't be miserable when you're forced to sit down with people for a meal."

"Evie," he says with an even tone, but it's strained. "Do not tell me how I feel."

"You need to let go. No way is all this stress good for your heart, no matter how much you run or don't eat fat. By the way, there's good kinds of fat."

"I will not be lectured about food by someone who eats crisps," he says with such disgust. He gets up. "Having control is a good thing, Evie. Maybe you should practice more of it, especially when it comes to your emotions."

"You're my dad," I say in near hysterics, just to prove his point. "I care about you. I just want you to be happy."

"But I'm not happy," he states. "And eating carbs isn't going to fix it."

It's such a sad and defeated thing to say.

"So then why don't you get help?"

"It's late. I have to get up early for—" He doesn't finish, as I know it's for some ungodly early workout class. "Maybe we should look at a good time for you to go back."

"To Devon?"

"No, to Chicago."

And with that, he goes to his bedroom and slams the door.

32

As much as it would have pained me, I should've canceled on Aiden.

But unlike my father, I don't back out on commitments.

So here I am at Euston station on Saturday morning after not getting any sleep. Every breath hurts. Every blink of the eye is an effort. I thought I could trust my dad. I had opened myself back up to him, and he just slammed the door right in my face—literally and figuratively. It's also fitting that when I open myself up to Aiden, I have to be the one to shut it down.

Why? Oh, well, maybe because my father is forcing me out of the country. I know I have a flair for the dramatic, but it's true. Dad bought me a train ticket to go to my grandparents' tomorrow. I get a week with them before he's having a car pick me up and take me directly to the airport for a flight back to Chicago. Do not pass London and do not collect any of the life I was trying to piece back together. This is what I get for breaking down the wall between us. He wants to get rid of me. It's the same thing that happened with Sean. I took a chance on someone only to have a dagger shoved into my heart.

Because I'm too much. My wants. My feelings. And above all, my mouth.

I'm not ready to say goodbye to London just yet.

Or Aiden.

But I don't have a choice.

Aiden and I took a giant step forward at the party, and now I have to be the one to step thousands of miles back.

Today is going to be so hard. I got a glimpse of what it's like to be with Aiden, and I have to end it before we truly began.

I try to plaster a smile on my face as I arrive at the departures board. I stand on my tiptoes to see if I can find Aiden among the crowd, when there's a tap on my shoulder.

"I thought it would be best for me to come to you," Aiden says with such a hopeful smile, I don't know how I'm going to possibly get through today without losing it. He leans in to kiss me and I step away. "What's wrong?"

"Nothing!" I reply quickly. "I'm just, ah, not into public displays of affection."

"That's not how you were the other night." He raises his eyebrows, and it's then I notice he's wearing a green tee that matches his eyes. It looks so good on him. He looks so good. His lips look so good. Those lips that are curling into a smile.

I want to kiss those lips. To hold his hand. To be with him. But I can't. Dad has made that impossible.

Let's face it, my big mouth made it impossible.

Whatever look I'm giving Aiden causes him to pull away.

"Okay, I can be a gentleman. But are you sure you're okay?"

"You know, it would be super great if you could stop trying to always assume there is something wrong with me."

"In fairness to me, there usually is."

I open my mouth to respond, then close it because he's right.

When I got ready this morning, I knew the last thing I wanted to do was ruin today by burdening Aiden. It's probably our last time hanging out, which causes my throat to constrict. Today isn't about me. This is for Aiden and Ruby, so I'm going to bury it down and deal with it . . . tomorrow. Or never. *Never* sounds pretty fantastic right now.

"I'm sorry, are you speechless?" He playfully jabs me. "Which would be unfortunate since I'm here and I've got my guitar." He points to his guitar strapped to his back. "How much do I have to beg—"

"We're going to Liverpool!" I blurt, needing to get the attention off me. "Is that okay?"

Maybe Aiden wanted to check this off his busking-for-Ruby list with his family or Fiona and Dev, and I'm sort of forcing his hand right now.

Aiden takes in the train station and looks up at the board and sees Liverpool Lime Street station. "Are you serious?"

"If you want to do it another day or with someone else, I'm sure I can exchange the tickets," I start to explain, but Aiden cuts me off.

"This is amazing, Evie. Thank you!" He grabs me in a tight hug, and I find myself melting into him.

There we are, in the middle of a busy train station, but in a way it feels like we're the only two people here. If only we could stay frozen like this, where I don't have to face the reality of having to say goodbye to him in a few short hours.

An announcement comes on, alerting us to board on track fourteen. I hand Aiden his ticket and we get in the line. Sorry, *queue*. Brits *queue* up.

Once we get settled on the train, I take out a notebook and get to business. "So! I thought we might want to go over your setlist. I figure you'd want to go somewhere associated with the Beatles, since that's the reason for Liverpool. I did all this research, and first of all, did you know that Liverpool was the most bombed area in the UK outside London during World War Two? They have a huge port where ships—"

"Evie, are you sure everything's okay?" Aiden asks as he reaches for my hand, but I pull it away to flip through the notebook.

"Of course, I'm just excited," I lie.

"Okay, if you say so," he replies, but I can tell he doesn't believe me. "Not that I haven't missed your soliloquies."

"A soliloquy is when someone talks about their feelings aloud. Oddly enough, I'm not doing that." And I have zero intention of getting emotional today. "I am simply stating some facts about Liverpool. *Anyway*, there are a few places we could go: Mathew Street, where the Cavern Club is—that's the place the Beatles played a lot."

"Oh, is it?" Aiden says with a wink.

"Um, there's also Penny Lane, the train station, their childhood homes . . ." I start flipping through all the notes I made, along with printouts of maps.

Aiden takes my notebook. "You did all this research?"

"I wasn't sure how much you had figured out about your trip."

Aiden nods along as he looks at my messy handwriting. "Ruby and I talked about doing it near the Cavern. It seems appropriate. We never came up with a setlist because Ruby loved all the Beatles songs, especially the early stuff." He pauses for a moment. "I really can't believe you did this for me, Evie."

"Calm down that ego of yours—this is for Ruby." Even though all of this is for Aiden.

"Of course." Aiden moves so he's facing me. He let me have the window seat so I'd be able to see more of England. "But remember you did admit that you're my fan."

"Only fan," I remind him.

"So that makes you my number one fan." He leans forward, his eyes on my lips.

I shift to look out the window. "Yes, but you should know by now that I have horrible taste."

He laughs.

"I think that 'Baby Shark' is the greatest song of all time."

"Pure poetry, that one," he says as he nods.

"Yeah, and my favorite singer is that one guy on *American Idol* who was really tone-deaf."

"I've never seen it, but I can only imagine. But just know that show was first in the UK. Most of the best things are from here: the Beatles, James Bond, One D, *me* . . ." He then takes his hand and tucks a strand of my hair behind my ear.

My breath gets caught in my throat. Aiden really is the best. But I can't go there. So I'm going to do what I do best: deflect.

"Yeah, but my dad also comes from here, so . . ."

Aiden takes my hand and puts it in his, and this time I can't resist. "I'm sure it sometimes feels impossible with your dad. I'm proud of you for saying something to him and trying to help. And also for helping me. I don't know if I'll ever be able to properly tell you how much I needed you to come along when you did."

I'm staring at our entwined hands. I can feel my palm start to get sweaty. But I also don't want to let go.

But I have to. I'm leaving for Devon tomorrow. I don't know when or even if I'm coming back to London. I turn eighteen in a few months, and I won't be required by the divorce settlement to visit Dad, and he won't be obligated to pay for my plane ticket.

As much as it pains me, I have to let go of Aiden. But I'm going to give him this last day. I'll tell him tonight on the way home. Well, the way back to London. I don't have a home here.

"Can we not talk about my father for the rest of today?" I ask.

Aiden studies me, and it takes everything I have to not look away. "If that's what you want."

"It's what I want," I state firmly. "So!" I say, a lot louder than I intended, causing a few heads to turn. "We should discuss songs."

I take my hand from his and put down the tray table to write in my notebook, but also to get my act together.

My heart literally aches. I want this so much. It feels right. But I can't have it.

As the last twenty-four hours have proven, sometimes it's best to protect your heart.

♪♪

Once we arrive in Liverpool, I assume we'll be greeted by statues of the Beatles and the sound of their music playing. But nope. Just another thing I'm wrong about.

"Hold on," I say as I pull out an actual paper map to figure out where to go. It's nice to have a sense of purpose. A task. It prevents me from thinking about later. For now, we've got to get Aiden to a busking gig.

"You're such a tourist," Aiden teases. He covers his eyes with his hand as if he's embarrassed to be seen with me. I start spinning in a circle, trying to get my bearings. I probably should be slightly humiliated, but that bar for me now is incredibly high.

I point across the street. "I think we walk over there and should hit a pedestrian mall, which will, I think, lead us to the Cavern. I hope."

"She says with confidence. But I'm up for an adventure." Aiden starts walking to where I pointed.

We walk a few blocks and hit an area closed to traffic with stores. A lot of the same places we have in the US—H&M,

Starbucks, McDonald's—and then I see my savior: a map and arrows.

"Ah, we're almost there," I say with delight as I see a sign saying we're only a couple minutes' walk to Mathew Street. "Do you want to warm up here?" There are a lot of people walking around—we even passed a busker who was playing "Wonderwall," because of course he was.

"No, it's okay. I'm just a little nervous. Playing the Beatles in Liverpool, near the Cavern. No pressure or anything."

"It's for Ruby," I say to encourage him.

"It's for Ruby," he echoes, which seems to be the only convincing he needs. "Okay, let's go."

We turn and walk a block and then stop. Mathew Street is more like an alley. There aren't any cars, just flocks of tourists walking down the gray brick road. As we walk into the street, we hear another busker. This guy is older and playing a Beatles song I don't know. I assume it's the Beatles because . . . Liverpool. And it's not "Wonderwall." He's standing next to a statue of John Lennon, which is leaning against the wall.

"Picture!" I say to Aiden. I make him stand next to John and take a photo. I want to remember every detail of today.

"Get in here," Aiden says as he takes my phone. "We have to get one of those self-taking pictures the kids love so much. That's what it's called, right?"

Aiden puts his arm around my waist and brings his chin to my shoulder as we try to fit John in. Aiden and I are cheek to cheek, and I can't help but see mine are becoming increasingly flushed.

I quickly snap the photo and Aiden examines it. "Can you send this to me?"

"Sure. I'll put it in an electronic mail attachment for you, because that's something my mom does, Grandpa."

We arrive at the Cavern Club, which has a line of tourists standing near a red neon sign. People are taking pictures, and music spills out from inside.

"We should go in when you're finished. Maybe find somewhere for lunch?" The train had a food and drinks cart come through, so we got a couple of sandwiches, but we'll want a proper meal before we take the seven o'clock evening train back to London.

And say goodbye.

"Sounds perfect," Aiden replies as he gets his guitar out.

"Play 'Blackbird'!" someone in the line shouts, to the cheers of others.

"I'll be happy to take requests," Aiden replies. He turns his back on them while he tunes his guitar.

"Anything you need me to do?" I ask.

Aiden faces me with a shy smile. "Just enjoy the show."

That's all I want to do today. Enjoy every minute with Aiden. Even though my heart feels constricted. It's going to be so painful to say goodbye.

Which is exactly why you shouldn't have gotten involved in the first place. Yet here we are. Again.

There's a lump in my throat as Aiden strums the guitar starting with "I Want to Hold Your Hand." A few people in line at the Cavern start singing along. People stop to dance, throw some money in Aiden's guitar case, and take pictures.

Hearing Aiden sing brings me so much joy. His voice is so much clearer and brighter than when I first heard him sing. I forget my feelings for a moment and sing and dance along. I start taking pictures and videos to share with Fiona and Dev when we get back. And let's be honest, probably watch on repeat while ugly sobbing on the plane to Chicago.

There's a round of applause as he finishes. He takes a bow and then says, "This next one is a request from the line over there." There's some cheering as he starts playing "Blackbird."

"Miss!" someone in the Cavern Club line calls out. He's waving a five-pound note. "Can you give this to him as a thanks?" I run over and take the money. They start shouting other song requests.

And Aiden starts playing them. "I Saw Her Standing There," "Penny Lane," "We Can Work It Out," "Get Back," "Hello, Goodbye." The songs and requests keep coming. Aiden's case fills with notes and coins.

"Thank you," Aiden says after another round of applause. "I'm going to do a song for a very special girl in my life."

I feel my chin tug. He's going to talk about Ruby. She must be so happy he's doing this.

I'm wondering what song it's going to be: "Yesterday"? "Let It Be"?

I'm anticipating a slow song, so I'm surprised when it starts with the guitar doing some broken chords and then picks up the tempo. It takes me a moment to place it: "I've Just Seen a Face." It's not the most popular Beatles song, but the crowd is enjoying it.

However, it seems like a weird song to dedicate to Ruby. The lyrics start about not forgetting a girl he's just met. The part that really gets me is when he talks about how he might've looked away if it was another day and he dreams of her.

He isn't talking about . . .

I look up at Aiden, and we lock eyes as he gets to the chorus.

"Falling, yes I'm falling . . ."

I know this is clichéd, but OH MY GOD.

I'm frozen. I'm shocked. I'm absolutely loving every second of this song even though I absolutely shouldn't. I was jealous of this fictional girlfriend I thought Aiden was singing about when we first met, but now—now he's singing about falling in love.

With me.

He's chosen me.

But we can't.

I feel a sting behind my eyes and am grateful when an older guy with a bushy ginger beard and Beatles T-shirt comes over to me. "Come here, luv, let's have a dance."

It's probably a good thing since I don't know what to do or say. So I dance. I focus on this moment. This feeling of joy and excitement. I want to hold on to it for a moment longer. Before I have to face the truth.

When Aiden finishes, I clap along with the rest of the group.

"I think that's my last song," Aiden says as he rubs the back of his head. He glances at me.

The crowd begs for a couple more. Aiden looks at me and I can only nod. I want him to keep playing. Once he stops, I'm going to have to tell him. Tell him that I'm leaving. That we . . . That we can't . . .

Aiden starts strumming. The sound of people singing along with Aiden is drowned out by a voice getting louder in my head.

I hate agreeing with Dad, but he had a point. I should've been safer with my feelings. I shouldn't have let my emotions take over. This is going to hurt so much. Especially since I feel more for Aiden then I ever did with Sean. Sean is *meh* in comparison. While Aiden is everything.

"Evie," Aiden says to me, and I jump.

"Sorry, I was in my head." It's the worst place to be sometimes.

"Thank you for today." He keeps his gaze on me. He puts his hands around my waist.

The noise and people of Mathew Street melt away. Aiden leans in and I find myself both breathless and utterly terrified as his lips inch closer to mine. I want to kiss him again. To feel that electricity once more. For only a moment. But I know if he starts, I'm not going to be able to stop. As much as it physically pains me, I need to stop making this worse. For us both.

I take a step back. "I'm real sorry, Aiden."

The devastated look on Aiden's face is exactly why I shouldn't have taken him to Liverpool.

"It's not you," I begin. "I like you. A lot. Maybe too much," I finally admit aloud.

"And I like you, Evie. Entirely too much," Aiden states. "How is that a bad thing?"

"We can't." I fight the tears that want to creep up. "I can't be hurt again. Not by you."

"I won't hurt you," he states, and by the look on his face I want to believe it.

"That's what they all say," I reply as I swallow the hurt. "But the thing is, you're just starting to get to know me. You'll get sick of me. How I don't know how to behave like a normal person. My big mouth. My erratic emotions. I'm just too much."

"Impossible. I can't get enough of you."

"Aiden, you just . . . It doesn't matter, I'm lea—"

"Evie," he interrupts me as he takes my hand. "I wake up every day thinking about you. When I'm going to see you again, what utterly ridiculous thing is going to come out of your mouth, how your face scrunches up in this gorgeous way when you're overthinking things—like you're doing right now. I always asked about what was going on in your life because I want to know every single thing about you. I've already missed out on so much, and I don't want to waste another moment without telling you exactly how I feel. You're the most—"

"Stop," I beg him. "Please don't."

I can't have him be kind. I can't have him say all the things I want him to.

I can't do this.

I just can't.

"I know how much your father—"

"Stop, Aiden, please." My voice breaks. My entire heart shatters with it. "It doesn't matter."

"What doesn't matter? *My* feelings?" Aiden's face starts to harden. "What was the other night, then? What about this? You can't just kiss someone and take them on a trip and then . . ." His hands ball up into fists. He throws his guitar down with a thud. "Was this all some sort of game to you? Or are you so incredibly self-involved you don't realize what your actions—*your actions, Evie, not your dad's*—can do to people? Or maybe that's what you and your dad have in common."

I actually recoil from his vitriol. But I can't say that I blame him for his anger.

I'm angry, too.

Aiden's breathing becomes harder. "So that's it, huh? I was just some joke to you? Some experiment? Because I'm really having a hard time understanding how you could be all over me one minute and shutting me down the next, how you could do such a wonderful thing as taking me here, but then push me away. So explain it to me, Evie. You owe me at least that."

I do owe him an explanation. I owe him so much more.

"I . . ." I don't know what to say. At the end of the day, we can't be together. Maybe it's better for Aiden to think I'm a horrible person.

And the thing is, maybe I am. If I hadn't pushed Dad to do what *I* wanted, maybe Aiden and I would've had some more time. I can never control myself, and look what it's cost me.

"Really? *This* is when you choose to say nothing?" Aiden is looking at me with so much hurt. "Seriously? Okay, wow. Well, congrats, Evie. You got me. I'm such a fool."

With that, Aiden picks up his guitar and walks away. He gets applause from the Cavern crowd as he passes by, but he ignores it.

It's easy to blame other people, but when it comes down to it, this is all on me.

I ruin everything.

I don't know how long I stand there reeling from Aiden's words. How much I hurt him. I convince myself that by the time we take the train home tonight, I'll have figured out what to say to him. I'll right this wrong. I have a few hours until our train home. By the time I arrive at our assigned seats, I'll know what to say to Aiden. I'll have some sort of plan.

I don't.

It doesn't even matter.

Aiden never shows.

33

Here I thought my summer couldn't get worse.

Dad lied to me. He wants me out of the country and out of his life.

I hurt Aiden. I hurt myself.

At least I get to say goodbye to my grandparents.

I dig my toes into the green grass of my grandparents' backyard the next afternoon.

"I brought you some tea, luv." Gran walks over to the wooden swing I've been camped out on since I arrived a couple of hours ago. She hands me a blue-and-white ceramic mug.

"Thanks, Gran."

"I'm so glad you're here." She sits next to me, and I rest my forehead on her shoulder as we lightly swing back and forth.

"Me, too."

Gran picks up the book I'd borrowed from the den, which is filled floor to ceiling with books.

She laughs lightly. "A biography on Henry the Eighth? I think your uncle got this in school when he went through his Tudor phase."

I had another book to read but couldn't get past the first few pages. I wasn't in the mood to read some sappy love story where a couple meets cute and then everything works out. I guess that's why they call it fiction.

Instead, I made the healthy decision to read about the king who chopped off the heads of his wives. Plural. And it's nonfiction. The true story about what really happens when you fall in love.

"Are you up for a family dinner tonight? Thought I'd cook up some pasta. Have your uncle over."

"Sounds good," I reply, even though I don't think anything will make me feel good again.

"Do you want to talk about it?" she asks as she brushes my messy hair back from my face.

My chin starts to twitch and I fight back tears.

"There, there," Gran says as she puts her arm around me. "Let it all out."

And I do. It's as sad and pathetic as possible. See, *this* is exactly why I shouldn't have trusted Dad and put myself out there with anybody, especially a sweet boy.

That thought makes me cry even harder.

If I thought it wasn't possible to feel worse, I know I've caused Aiden similar pain. Aiden, who has dealt with the loss of his sister. Aiden, who was willing to put himself out there to the one person he shouldn't. And look where it got him.

Gran rocks me back and forth. "Does this have to do with your father?"

I nod. Even though he is just one piece of my misery puzzle.

"Oh, luv. I'm so sorry."

We rarely talk about Dad when I come to visit, as he's an unpleasant topic for us all. We have a better time without him. We'll have family dinners, cream tea, desserts, and laugh while we enjoy life instead of trying to control every moment.

When it comes down to it, who really needs him?

Not us.

And certainly not me.

♪♪

For the past few days I've done nothing but read, go for walks, and hang out with my extended family. But in my head, there's a ticking of a clock counting down to my flight back to Chicago in two days.

"Gorgeous," Gran says as we take in the vast green view from the waterfall at Canonteign Falls. We followed a dirt trail and nearly a hundred Victorian steps to get to the top.

I get out my phone to take a picture and even a selfie of me and Gran. I've been using my phone mostly to listen to music. I haven't connected it to Wi-Fi since I arrived. It's been easier to block everything out.

We look out at the view before Gran puts her arm around my waist. "Have I ever told you how much I adore your mother? She's such a lovely woman. I'm glad you have her."

Is she telling me this because she realizes I no longer have my father?

"Your mum gave my son love and confidence when he needed it. And whilst I don't agree with how he's handled himself, I'm grateful to her for giving me the best gift possible: you."

She lifts my chin up so she can look in my eyes, then wraps her arms around me and holds on.

I think about my mother. She loved my dad for who he was, not what he looked like. Dad would probably never have given her a second glance had New Dad attended Northwestern. What a complete hypocrite.

It's hard to compare my parents side by side.

My mom gave so much of herself to him and got her heart handed back to her. She had a child to raise by herself. Yet she somehow moved on with her life. She survived. Not only that, she made her life bigger and better. She has a great husband, two wonderful children (if I do say so myself), loads of friends, and a full life. At times maybe it's too full, but it's hers. And I know she loves it. Even when she's tired and Josh is having some kind of meltdown, I see the look of contentment on her face when she takes in her family.

Then there's Dad: a self-involved jerk who doesn't have anybody close to him. All he has is his fancy possessions. His posh apartment. *Things.*

Which life do I really want?

The thing is, I already know that answer. I want a big life. How could I not? I've certainly got a big personality. I want to open myself up to people. I want love. And it was within my grasp, and

I was too scared to do something about it. Why? Because I was hurt before. Who hasn't been?

I think about Sean and I feel . . . empty. I already moved on because someone better came into my life. Someone who is worth it all.

Yes, I made a mess out of things because of my actions, but I'm also the one that needs to fix things.

I need to get Aiden back.

I need to get my father to let me in . . . and not kick me out of his house.

"Gran?" I say as I start to form a plan. "Would it be okay if I went back to London?"

"For your father?" she asks, confusion lining her face.

"Yes, but also for me."

34

Later that evening, I make my way into Dad's flat. I hold the key in my hand, wondering if he changed the locks. There's a relief when I hear the click as I turn the key.

I used to dread coming to see my dad—I'd hope that he wouldn't be home. Now I want to see him. Need to see him.

My pulse quickens as the door swings open. I freeze upon seeing my dad at the kitchen counter, reading something on his phone. He looks up and his face hardens.

"Hi, Dad," I start cautiously.

"What are you doing here, Evie?" he asks, entirely too calmly. "I wasn't expecting to see you before your flight. You're supposed to be in Devon."

There are a lot of things I'm supposed to do. While nothing has changed for him, everything has for me.

I gesture to the kitchen table for us to sit down, but he remains standing at the counter.

"That's the thing. I'm not flying back," I state with a quiver in my voice. "I'm not giving up on you."

He sighs. "This is silly." He moves to go to his bedroom, but I stand in his way.

"Do you have any idea how much I ache for my father to be back in my life?" I don't even fight back the tears. I let them flow, as I've become an expert at crying lately. "I miss you, Dad. I want you to be happy. I want you to be healthy. I want us to have a good relationship. That shouldn't be so hard."

"I'm not the one making things difficult," he says defensively.

"Okay, fine, it's me," I say, even though it's an *us* problem. "But *we* need to do something. We need to see a therapist *together*. We have so much to figure out, and it's not all about food or exercising. It's about trust. It's about love. I love you, and I need you to stop trying to live this tidy, controlled life and let some mess in, especially when that mess is your daughter."

He looks past me, and I don't know what he's thinking.

"Dad, I'm asking you to try to fix this void between us. If you refuse, well, I can't force you to want me in your life. I can't force you to love me."

"Of course I love you, Evie." I see an emotion—anguish—cross his face. "I've always loved you."

"Then come with me to therapy. Let's talk it out instead of burying it. Because if you don't . . ." I don't know how to finish that thought. Because if he doesn't agree to therapy, it's not like I want him completely out of my life. I don't want to give up on my dad, but we can't stay like this. I also can't give him an ultimatum, because that would be the ultimate control move. "Dad, I'm always going to be here for you. You're my father. But I can't keep doing this. It's too painful for me. To come here and feel like a stranger. Like an inconvenience. So I'm asking you to do something to help me. Help *us*. Because I love you and I want you to be a part of my life. Will you do this, for me?"

I can feel my heart pulsating. It takes everything I have to not fill the silence that stretches between us.

This is the moment I find out whether my father truly does love me. Whether he's willing to fight for us.

And if he doesn't, it'll sting like hell. But then I'll go home and be with a mother who does.

He nods. "I'll make arrangements straightaway, then." He purses his lips together, like he's fighting something back. Anger? A tear?

"Arrangements for a car to take me to the airport or for a therapist?"

My father opens his mouth, and I see wetness around his eyes. A crack in his façade. The first sign of Real Dad in a long time. "To see Dr. Basini. Together."

Then without another word, Dad comes over and gives me a hug. A real hug. Not a formal one.

"Thank you," I whisper to him. "Thank you, Dad."

I have no idea if this will be the time Dad will do what he says. If this is another lie. If he'll get better. But he's willing to go to therapy with me.

It's a start. And perhaps a new beginning. For us both.

35

The next morning, I'm on my laptop replying to Dad's message about our upcoming therapy appointment.

It's a start.

As for Aiden, well, I sent him an email to ask him to meet me and never heard back. It wouldn't surprise me if Aiden has given me a taste of my own medicine and blocked me.

Can't say that I'd blame him.

Maybe I should respect his wishes and leave him alone. Maybe I've already damaged him too much.

A knock at the door startles me. You can't get into the building without passing security, and it's not the cleaning lady's day.

I look down at my sweats, and the fact that I'm not wearing a bra. I shuffle over to the door and look out the peephole. I don't believe what I'm seeing so I look again.

I would've been less surprised if the duo was Elsa from *Frozen* and the clown from *It*.

"We know you're there, open up!" a voice comes from the other side of the door.

I attempt to calm down the flyaway hairs on my head before opening the door to Poppy and Fiona.

Again, that's Poppy *and* Fiona.

"We brought treats!" Poppy states in a singsong voice as she places a bag on the counter and starts pulling out baked goods.

"You've looked . . . better," Fiona says as she takes in my appearance.

I try to find my voice. "How did—Where did—You two know each other?"

Fiona gives me an *are you kidding me* look. "No, but there aren't many spin instructors in London with the name Poppy," Fiona states.

I keep looking between the two of them. Poppy, the human Barbie doll, and Fiona, Barbie's punk rock younger sister.

"You found Poppy? Why?" I ask. "Don't you . . . hate me?"

Fiona cocks her eyebrow at me. "Evie, I'm not going to be someone who fawns over someone and be all . . ." She gestures at Poppy, who has her arm wrapped around me. "But if you need me to admit it, yes, I am your friend. And Aiden is one of my best mates. He won't talk about what happened. Instead, he got drunk and started singing the most depressing songs. Before getting into a fight with a tree. *A tree.* It was pretty sad and pathetic. So it's clear you both need help, and I was trying to reach you, but your phone was off and I knew I had to come to you. Since the Chelsea Barracks is massive, there's no way they'd let someone like me just waltz in. Plus, this one was able to sweet-talk the doorman to let us up."

"I've always liked Oliver." Poppy puts her chin on my shoulder.

"Wait . . . you're my friend?"

Fiona rolls her eyes. "Out of everything I said, that's what you're hung up on?"

I mean, I do have a lot to be confused about.

Poppy points at the couch in the living room. "Now sit. And spill."

I do what she says and sit down as they flank me on either side, although I don't even know where to start.

"I'm really sick of crying," I admit. Sitting there, with the two of them, I realize how utterly exhausted I am by everything. Feeling, truly feeling, for someone takes a lot out of you.

"Oh, Evie." Poppy gives me a hug. "It's okay."

I sit there for a few minutes and just take in everything that's happened. "Should I start with my dad?" I figure that will be easier, since at least something is happening.

And I'm not the jerk in that scenario.

So I tell them everything. About how he lied to me. How it began to crack me in two. How I'm trying to see if there's anything worth saving.

"You're a good daughter," Poppy states. "And I'll help you with whatever you need. I know loads of nutritionists who can help him with his diet to make it more balanced. For him to see that food isn't the enemy. Whatever you need, I've got you."

I can only nod.

"God, Evie," Fiona says as she takes my hand. "I didn't know. I came here wanting to talk about Aiden."

As soon as Fiona says his name, I let out a wail.

Guess you're not done crying.

"Oi, calm down, mate," Fiona says as she looks to Poppy for help.

"It's okay, Evie. Let it out," Poppy says as she rubs my back. "Take deep breaths."

"I know he hates me, I don't blame him," I say in between sobs. "My life is such a mess right now."

"Yeah, it's not great," Fiona states dryly.

"Fiona!" Poppy scolds her and playfully hits her arm. "That's not helpful."

"It's the truth."

I can't help but laugh, because it's so true. But I've also stopped running away, so I guess it's time for me to face the thing that might be scariest of all.

Love.

"Can I just say that I told you he liked you?" Poppy says with a smile on her face. "And why wouldn't he?"

I look at her and then point at my tear-stained face, my unwashed hair, my rumpled state. "I can come up with some reasons."

Fiona snorts. "We never said Aiden had great taste."

"Fiona!" Poppy calls out.

Fiona sits closer to me. "Look, Evie, do you remember that conversation we had at the coffee shop?"

"Which part?" A lot was said that day, including me putting my foot in my very big mouth.

Fiona looks thoughtful. "You mentioned how Aiden said that we all have to go through things so we can come out stronger on the other side. Then you talked about how all the drama in finding that person makes it even more rewarding." Fiona folds her arms. "You had a point."

"How dare you throw my words back at me!" I try to lighten the mood. But it's true. Going through everything with Sean made me realize how special Aiden is. How his lips turn up a certain way when he's going to tease me. How his hair never goes in the same direction. How he sings with so much emotion. How he listens, really listens, to me. His big heart.

"Basically, you have to make a decision," Fiona tells me. "Do you want to be with Aiden?"

"It's not that—"

"Stop making everything so complicated, Evie." Fiona lets out an annoyed breath. "It's a yes-or-no question."

"Of course I do," I admit. "But it's not that simple."

"Oh, for God's sake."

"Fiona, I'm eventually going back to the States."

"That's just an excuse," Fiona replies.

"It's true!" I can't help the fact that I'm an American and need to go back to America.

An American with dual British citizenship . . .

"Why are you making that decision for Aiden?" Fiona replies. "Besides, Aiden would be annoyingly perfect for pining. He'll probably write you actual letters."

"Oh, I love that, bless him," Poppy coos. "You need to let go, Evie, and take a chance on Aiden. It'll be worth it, no matter what happens."

"I know that! I do! I'm all for opening my heart and taking a chance with Aiden."

"Huzzah!" Poppy claps excitedly.

"But there's one small problem: Aiden has blocked me." I know the amount of hurt it takes to shut someone off. I also know it took me weeks to get ready to talk to Lindsay and Theo again. But I don't have weeks. I don't want to waste another minute. "Aiden doesn't want to hear from me."

Fiona smiles. "Well, luckily for you, you know two of his best mates, and we've got a plan. Aiden's back to busking with those incredibly depressing songs and not telling us where he's going. So Dev is going to stalk his flat tomorrow and follow him. He's beyond excited about it. He keeps referring to himself as James Bond—he's even bringing his new girlfriend along and everything. Who knew Dev would be more insufferable once he actually got a girlfriend? Anyways, turn on your mobile so Dev can let you know where he is."

"But what if Aiden won't hear me out?"

Fiona actually scoffs. "Mate, we both know you're ace at forcing people to listen to you. Preferably don't pull an Evie and throw a beverage in his face."

"That was two times!" I mean, *really*.

"What's that?" Poppy asks.

"I'll tell you later," Fiona says to Poppy before turning back to me. "Listen, Evie, we'll get you to Aiden, the rest is up to you."

36

The rest is up to me.

Waiting for Dev's text the next day is torturous. Deciding what to say and do when I see Aiden is worse.

Having Poppy and Fiona show up reminded me that I don't have to suffer alone. I have people to lean on when things get rough.

I actually yelp when my phone buzzes.

DEV: He's on the move. Agent Double-O Dev is on the case.

I pace the flat and feel like I'm jumping out of my skin. I make sure I have everything I'll need once I know where he is. I just hope I can get there before Aiden finishes up.

DEV: He's not going to the tube. Think he's going toward Hyde Park.

I can't take it anymore and run out of the flat and get on the Tube so I'll be close by. The London Underground isn't completely underground, so I'll be able to get service. Oh yeah, I finally took my father up on his offer to pay for international roaming. No more shutting myself off, no more blocking. No more excuses. No more making myself unavailable to others.

As the train approaches the South Kensington stop, another text comes through.

DEV: He's near the Albert Memorial. Hurry up. These songs are depressing.

I run up the stairs and weave between the people heading toward the Victoria and Albert Museum and Natural History Museum. I don't stop my stride as I see the green of Hyde Park up ahead.

The Royal Albert Hall, in all its red-and-yellow-brick glory, is up to my left, but Aiden is across the street.

"Psst!" I turn as I see Dev and Neena hiding in a doorway. "Go get him!" Dev gives me a thumbs-up as I run across the street and see Aiden off to the side of the massive gothic memorial for Queen Victoria's husband. He's near a tree, away from people. But the anguish in his voice is clear.

I fumble with my phone in my bag and attach a portable speaker to it.

Aiden's eyes are closed as he's wailing, *"How could you tear my heart in two?"*

I stop dead in my tracks, realizing *I'm* responsible for this song.

I really hope this works.

Aiden finishes up, and I stand in front of him. My heart is racing as I wait for him to open his eyes.

Once he does and sees me, he blinks for a few seconds. His face is pinched. I can't tell if he's angry or hurt. All I do know is that it's a look I don't want to ever see on his face again.

"Hi." I cautiously take a step closer to him. "I'm so, so sorry,

Aiden. I shouldn't have turned away from you in Liverpool. There are a lot of things I shouldn't have done, but a lot more that I should have. There is so much about my future and the next few weeks that have me absolutely terrified. I came here to London to run away from things, and I never imagined I would find someone like you. I want to tell you everything, but I'm not like you—I can't just write all of my emotions down into a coherent thought, let alone a song. So I thought I would, well, I would do what you do."

My hand is shaking as I FaceTime Lindsay. She gives me a nod as she turns toward Theo, who has his guitar in hand. He starts strumming.

As soon as Aiden hears the song, the corner of his lips begins to twitch.

Because today is going to be the day I'm taking a chance on love. As I start singing, my voice is shaky and definitely out of tune. But I don't stop. With every word, I can feel the wall that I had built slowly break down brick by brick. I don't know how I get through the first two verses, but once I get to the chorus, I can feel the tears streaming down my face.

"Because maybe, you're gonna be the one that saves me . . ."

Aiden takes a step forward and I stop singing. I don't know if he's going to walk away or kiss me.

"Is my voice really that bad?" I say to lighten the tension as I wipe the tears from my face.

"Did we stop?" I hear Theo's voice over the speaker.

"Oh, sorry, guys. Um, yeah, I think we might be done?"

Theo gives me a thumbs-up as Lindsay mouths "He's cute!"

"Ah, thanks, I'll talk to you later." I hang up. "So um, yeah."

"Your phone works?" Aiden says as he looks down at me.

"Some things are worth an extra fee."

Aiden's gaze settles on me, and I shift. He has this way of really looking at me. It makes me feel seen. I want him to see me.

"Listen, Evie," Aiden begins as he fiddles with his belt loop, the scarf no longer there for comfort. "You came bursting into my life and rattled me, but in the best possible sense. I can't make you any promises about how things will end, but I will do my best to make sure I never see you cry again, at least because of anything that I've done. I never want to make you distrust the male species—as questionable as some of us may be. All I know is that I want to spend as much time as possible with you. Every part of you. The part who can turn an observation into a twelve-hour monologue. The part whose face lights up with a delicious meal. The part that trusts me and opens up to me. The part that makes me feel a little less alone."

I take another step closer to him. He does the same.

He continues, "And when you think about it, Chicago isn't that far away. I mean, you come here often, probably more now that you're working on things with your dad, and how long of a flight is it anyway? And there's so many movies I can watch during the flight and—"

I can't take it anymore. "Just shut up and kiss me already!"

He throws his head back and laughs. "Thought I'd give you a taste of your own medicine."

He moves his guitar so it's on his back as he takes three purposeful steps toward me. He wraps one hand around my waist, the other around my neck, and kisses me. It's even better than I remember, which is saying a lot. I press him closer to me as I run my fingers through his hair, savoring every part of this moment.

After a beat, Aiden pulls away. "Bloody hell, is that cheering?"

We look across the street to see Dev and Neena jumping up and down and screaming.

"So much for secret agents," I mutter under my breath.

"What?" Aiden asks.

I wave Dev and Neena away. They cheer once more before they leave, hand in hand.

"Now, where were we?" he says as he pulls me in even closer.

As I kiss him, I feel a lightness I haven't felt in months.

There's so much I don't know, but I do know that right here, right now will be worth whatever may come: good or bad.

We part and he kisses my forehead lightly.

"I can't believe I almost messed this up."

"Me, too," he says as he wraps his arms around me tighter. "I'll do whatever I can to prove that I'm worth the risk."

"You already have," I admit as I rest my head comfortably on his chest.

I'm not sure how long the two of us stay in each other's arms—all I do know is that I'm in no rush to leave.

"Ah, Evie," Aiden says as he motions at a tour group coming toward the memorial.

"I guess we should go," I say as I take his hand.

"Where to?" he asks.

I shrug my shoulders. "It doesn't really matter as long as we're together."

We begin to walk aimlessly, hand in hand.

"If I may give a wee bit of a critique of your performance," Aiden says as he gives my hand a squeeze.

"Oh my God. I tried to make a grand romantic gesture with very limited talent."

"I thought the performance was brilliant. It's just that . . . you're the one who saved me. I was drowning, Evie, and you gave me a reason to smile. You made me feel happiness again."

I stop walking and take his face in my hands. "And you made me believe that not all men are steaming piles of garbage."

"Why, Evie, you romantic, you." He smiles at me, and my heart simply melts.

"I'm kidding—well, I'm not really kidding. Because the male species overall has proven to be quite inferior in most areas, except in jerk-like behavior. There you lot are superior. It's not really fair to make one person—as amazing and thoughtful as you are—be responsible for making up for centuries of questionable male actions. But I guess you could change my mind. Only time will tell. I'll just be sure to always have a beverage around me just in case—"

"Just shut up and kiss me already!" Aiden says with a laugh.

I don't need to be told twice.

ACKNOWLEDGMENTS

Let me be real for a moment: writing acknowledgments is hard. And with this book it's nearly impossible, since I started writing it back in 2018. Yep. There are many reasons it's taken so long: Other deadlines! A global pandemic! Being told my YA career was over! (Clearly that person will *not* be thanked.) So I know I'll fail miserably to remember every person who has helped me along the way. Instead, I'm going to focus on those who are responsible for this version being out in the world.

First to Maya—oh, Maya! My amazing, wonderful editor, Maya Marlette. I can't count the number of times I would go back and reread your enthusiastic notes when I was stuck or that dreaded imposter syndrome kicked in. Thank you for being you. I'm your number one fan. *(She says in a totally not creepy way.)*

This book would not be out in the world if it wasn't for my superagent, Kate Testerman. Thank you for taking me on and lifting me up. I'm so excited to see where we'll go together next.

To quote Sir LL Cool James, *Don't call it a comeback, I've been here for years*. My publishing career started at Scholastic, as did my writing career. It feels good to be back home writing swoony stories again.

Thank you to David Levithan, Aleah Gornbein, Lizette Serrano, Maisha Johnson, Janell Harris, Stephanie Yang, Erin Slonaker, Jessica Rozler, Vanessa Christensen, and Nicole Ortiz. Cheers to Julia Sanderson at Scholastic UK for your thoughtful read through.

I turned into the heart-eyes emoji when I saw Leni Kauffman's cover art for the first time. Thank you for making me swoon over my own characters . . . and that gorgeous girl, the Elizabeth Tower.

As I mentioned in my author's note, I tried my best to handle the sensitive nature of disordered eating and control issues. I'm very grateful to have had the input from Karlee McGlone, a licensed marriage and family therapist at the UC San Diego Eating Disorders Center.

They say write what you know. Well, I am someone who has a tendency to go on tangents and talk a lot just like Evie, but I like to think I'm just as delightful! Thank you to my author friends for putting up with me and being so incredibly supportive as I navigated an international move and return to YA. Big hugs to Robin Benway, Holly Black, Sarah Rees Brennan, Jen Calonita, Cassandra Clare, Dhonielle Clayton, Donna Freitas, Sarah Mlynowski, Marie Rutkoski, Tiffany Schmidt, Jennifer E. Smith, and Amy Spalding.

Writing a book like this reminds me how fortunate I was to be born into my family. Thank you to my dad, mom, Eileen, Meg, and WJ for always being there for the baby in the family, especially when she decides to move to the city of her dreams.

Finally, I'm always amazed anytime someone has picked up one of my books. Thank *you* for taking a chance on this love story and me.

ABOUT THE AUTHOR

Photo by Amelia Walker

Elizabeth Eulberg can be a lot, but like in a totally delightful way. She's the internationally bestselling author of dozens of books for young readers, including *The Lonely Hearts Club* and *Better Off Friends*. She plays several instruments, and although she doesn't busk, she can rock out a decent rendition of "Wonderwall." While she was born in Wisconsin and then lived in New York, Elizabeth now calls London home. When she's not writing, you can find Elizabeth taking really long walks in which she'll turn down any mews she sees—as well as selflessly sample all of the British baked goods. It would be rude not to.